Sh... ...**ng**
the... ...**m.**
'H... ...**ch**
an intimate manner?'

'I think it only fitting, since we're engaged.'

There it was again, his knowing smile, the one he found so infuriating. What was it about this man who annoyed her with such charm?

'Yes, engaged, and not even that, yet you already act like a husband.'

'I hadn't undermined your authority some servant would have pummelled you.'

'I do not wish to discuss it.' She continued towards the house, too worked up by the fight, the wound and the Captain to stand still.

'Julia, please stop.'

The tender request held more power than any of his commands, bringing her to a halt. He walked around to stand in front of her but she refused to meet his face. She kept her head down, studying his boots.

'Whatever you think of my interfering, I only want to help, and whether our engagement is real or fake doesn't matter. I had no desire to see you hurt.'

'Perhaps we shouldn't play this game.'

He took her hand. 'I very much enjoy this game, my little Artemis.'

AUTHOR NOTE

ENGAGEMENT OF CONVENIENCE was fun to write, but at times it proved a challenge. When I was three-quarters of the way through my first draft Julia and James stopped talking to me and everything stalled. I waited patiently for them to tell me where they wanted to go, and when they remained stubbornly silent I threatened to burn Knollwood to the ground if Julia didn't start talking to me again. Thanks to a little inspiration from a history-themed daily desk calendar, and some research, I didn't have to resort to such drastic measures.

Research was key to crafting this story, and I studied subjects ranging from Thomas Jefferson's agricultural innovations to *HMS Pickle*'s return from the Battle of Trafalgar. I enjoyed weaving real events from the period into the lives of my fictional characters and using it all to help Julia and James reach their happy ending.

Now that their story is in print I'm enjoying something of my own happy ending, all the while heading back into my non-fiction history books to find more inspiration for my next novel. I hope you enjoy ENGAGEMENT OF CONVENIENCE. Please visit my website www.georgie-lee.com to learn more about me and my other historical works.

ENGAGEMENT OF CONVENIENCE

Georgie Lee

First published in Great Britain 2013
by Mills & Boon, an imprint of Harlequin (UK) Limited.
Harlequin (UK) Limited, Eton House, 18-24 Paradise Road,
Richmond, Surrey TW9 1SR

© Georgie Reinstein 2013

ISBN: 978 0 263 89855 2

A dedicated history and film buff, **Georgie Lee** loves combining her passion for Hollywood, history and storytelling through romantic fiction. She began writing professionally at a small TV station in San Diego, before moving to Hollywood to work in the interesting but strange world of the entertainment industry. During her years in La-La Land she never lost her love for romance novels and decided to try writing one herself. To her surprise, a new career was born. When not crafting tales of love and happily-ever-after, Georgie enjoys reading non-fiction history and watching any movie with a costume and an accent. Please visit www.georgie-lee.com to learn more about Georgie and her books. She also loves to hear from readers, and you can e-mail her at georgie.lee@yahoo.com

This is Georgie Lee's fabulous debut novel
for Mills & Boon® Historical Romance!

Enjoy the witty, playful attraction
between Julia and Captain Covington.
There will be more historical novels by Georgie Lee,
coming soon…

A very special thank you to Natashya Wilson for
seeing the potential in this story and for all her help.
Thanks also to my editor, Linda Fildew,
my agent, Ethan Ellenberg, and my friend Kristi
for sharing her knowledge of horses.

Also, thanks to my dear husband, Matt,
who always believes in me, even if he wouldn't have
believed it if someone told him years ago
he'd someday be married to a romance writer.

Chapter One

❧❧❧

October 31, 1805

Julia heard the shot from the top of the hill. It split the early morning still, sending a shock through her body and silencing the birds in the surrounding trees. Pulling hard on Manfred's reins, she brought the large black horse to a halt and examined the woods below the riding path for signs of the shooter. Brilliant shades of orange, red and yellow dominated the trees and a gentle breeze sent many of the leaves cascading to the ground. A flock of birds rose from the forest, indicating the shot's origin, but she saw nothing of the gunman. Uncle George often hunted here, but he was not expected back from London until later today.

How dare they, she fumed, nudging Manfred

down the sloping hill and into the thick cluster of trees growing along the small valley floor. Only a guest of their neighbours, the Wilkinses, possessed the audacity to hunt uninvited on Knollwood land.

Low branches tugged at her hair, freeing it from the loose bun fastened at the nape of her neck. Pushing it back out of her face, she knew her sister-in-law Emily would object to such a display, but Julia didn't care. She wasn't about to allow the Wilkinses' good-for-nothing friends to poach in her woods.

As she urged Manfred deeper into the thicket, it didn't occur to her to fetch the gamekeeper until the horse stepped into a small clearing as the culprit let off another shot in the opposite direction. Julia flinched at the thunderous noise, but Manfred, true to his warhorse breeding, stood rock still. Only his twitching ears acknowledged the explosion.

'What do you think you are doing?' Julia demanded.

The stranger whirled to face her and she drew in a sharp breath. Here was no fat wastrel, but the most handsome rogue she'd ever seen. The low sunlight cutting through the trees highlighted the deep-red tones in his dark hair and sharpened the bones of his cheeks. The shadow of a beard marked the square line of his jaw, emphasising his straight nose and strong chin. Her pulse raced with an emotion far different from fear. She could not name it, but it emanated from deep within her body.

'I'm hunting,' he answered plainly. Leaning his gun against a tree, he straightened into a stance reminiscent of the one her brother Paul assumed when a superior officer commanded him to relax.

'You are poaching in my woods. Now remove yourself at once before I call the gamekeeper. He's only a short distance away,' Julia lied, hoping he believed it. The knowing smile tugging at the corner of his lips told her otherwise.

'I'd like to see your gamekeeper try to remove me.'

Julia scrutinised him, hard pressed to imagine any of the servants, except perhaps the blacksmith, taking on such a sturdy man. He was tall and slender but solid, his wide shoulders and strong chest radiating a strength his loose-fitting hunting clothes could not hide. Following the line of his long arms to his hands, she imagined them around her waist, lifting her down from Manfred and pressing her against his body. She bit her bottom lip in anticipation of him claiming her mouth, the warmth of it driving away the morning chill.

Swallowing hard, the danger of the situation rushed back to her at the sight of the hunting knife dangling from his belt and she mustered her anger to counter the scandalous thoughts. His gun might be empty, but there was no way to know his skill with the blade. 'I demand you leave, at once.'

'I must say, I've never been addressed in this fashion before.' His blue eyes dipped down the length of her, then rose to her face. 'Especially not by such an attractive young lady.'

Julia grasped her riding crop tighter, ready to whip him if he threatened her, but he still did not approach. 'If I were trespassing on your land, I'd have the decency to be humble, but since you are trespassing on my land I may address you as I please.'

'You would have to travel a great distance to trespass on my land.' He laughed, much to Julia's chagrin.

'Then be off,' she ordered, 'for the sooner you leave, the sooner you may reach your land.' With all the grace of an accomplished horsewoman, she pulled Manfred around and cantered away.

James watched the woman disappear through the trees. Her horse, if one could call such a beast a horse, kicking up the soft earth, leaving behind clouds of dust to dance in the dappled sunlight. Nothing came to mind except pure awe, like the first time he'd been at sea with no sight of land.

Neither the dark maidens of the islands hardened by tavern life, nor the plantation owners' daughters with their languid speech, ever struck him as this woman had. No, she seemed too much of the world, yet strangely innocent of it. What would he give to slip her from her horse, lay her on the damp leaves and make her more knowledgeable?

His body stiffened at the delightful fantasy before the shifting sun piercing the trees nearly blinded him. Judging by its height, he knew it was time to go. Grabbing the haversack from the ground with his left hand, he felt pain tear through his shoulder and the bag fell from his weakened hand, landing on the ground with a thud.

'Hell.' He snatched it up with his right hand and flung it over his shoulder. The gun's recoil had irritated his wound more than he'd realised. Despite the stinging ache, he didn't intend to give up hunting. He'd already lost too much to sacrifice more.

Picking up the gun, he hurried through the woods along a small footpath leading up to the top of the hill. Climbing out of the shallow valley, the pain and all the emotions it brought with it taunted his every step.

Damn it, damn it all, James thought bitterly, striding off down the opposite side of the hill and up the next steeper one, scattering a small group of sheep grazing in the wet grass.

Up ahead, Creedon Abbey rose before him, its grey stone, small windows and numerous turrets and chimneys betraying its roots in the Middle Ages. James's old friend Captain George Russell had done well for himself, investing some of the fortune he'd gained in the Navy in this small estate. Only the broken and charred roof timbers and smoke-blackened stone ruined the idyllic scene. George had failed to extinguish an oil lamp one night two weeks ago and the resulting fire had gutted a large portion of the house. Scores of workmen now bustled about the front drive, unloading large blocks of stone from carts or carrying wood inside to begin the first day of repairs.

James shook his head at the damage, not sure whether to feel sorry for his friend or to laugh. Thirty years in the navy, fifteen as a captain and George had never once lost a ship. Within four years of resigning his commission, he'd nearly burned his house to the ground. For all George's bragging about how much he'd learned from his niece about running an estate, he'd failed to master the simple skill of not setting it on fire.

James's amusement faded as he walked. He'd seriously considered investing his money in an estate like this, but now he wasn't so sure. Whatever he decided to do, he needed to do it soon. With his wound sufficiently recovered, it was time to settle on something meaningful to occupy his days, instead of frittering them away.

He moved faster up the footpath following the drive, eager for activity, anything to shift the restless agitation dogging him this morning.

'What's the hurry?' a familiar voice called out from behind him. 'Run across a ghost in the woods?'

James turned to see George leading Percy, his large, cream-coloured stallion, up the drive. In his friend's wide, carefree smile, James caught traces of the bold captain he'd first met in the colonies ten years ago. At fifty, the lines of George's face were deeper now, while the quiet life of a country gentleman had lightened his once sun darkened skin and thickened his waist.

'I might have.' James fell in step with his friend. 'Describe your niece again.'

'Why?'

'Because I'm curious.'

George shrugged. 'Just what you'd expect from a girl of one and twenty. Clever, well formed, somewhat eccentric. Takes after me in that regard. Why?'

'I met her in the woods.' James remembered the striking young lady with her auburn hair falling in delicate waves about her face, her creamy skin flushed with excitement and a few headier emotions.

'Really?' A noticeable gleam danced in George's eyes. 'And?'

'Eccentric, well formed. Though from all your descriptions, I'd taken her for more of a dour governess and less of an Artemis.'

'When I described her she was still a girl.'

'She's no girl now.' James wondered if such a woman had ever truly been a girl or if she'd simply sprung from the foam of the sea.

'I'm glad to see you find her so interesting. Staying at Knollwood will give you a chance to get better acquainted. Who knows what you might discover?'

James shifted the haversack on his back, resisting the urge to run his fingers over the jagged scar on his left shoulder. 'Must we go to Knollwood?'

'Yes, it's all been arranged. Besides, by the end of the day it'll be more like a shipyard here than a house and, with the weather turning, you don't want the rain leaking on your head.'

'It wouldn't be the first time. I've lost track of the number of storms I've slept through at sea.'

'And my guess is you won't miss it. We wouldn't have stayed here last night if we hadn't dallied so long at Admiral Stuart's dinner, but I hated to disturb everyone at Knollwood so late at night.'

James laughed. 'I wasn't the one who insisted on opening another bottle of port.'

'It doesn't matter who caused the delay. I'll be happy to sleep in a comfortable room that doesn't smell like a cooking fire. And here I'd thought those bedrooms had escaped damage.'

'You've gone soft.'

George shrugged. 'You will, too, in time.'

James didn't respond, this revelation not improving his mood. He'd already lost too much since resigning his commission to contemplate losing something as simple as his hardiness. 'Why didn't you tell me before we left London that the house wasn't fit to live in?'

'I think I greatly underestimated the damage.' They stopped as two men carrying a large plank walked past them. 'Besides, the ladies are quite excited at the prospect of meeting a new gentleman.'

'You know I came here to escape such affairs.'

'Does any man ever truly escape them?'

'You seem to have avoided it.'

'And you wish to follow my lead?'

James scrutinised his old friend, suspecting more to all this than the extensive fire damage simply slipping his mind. 'What are you about, George?'

'Nothing.' George held up his hands innocently but only succeeded in looking guiltier. 'I want you to enjoy yourself while you're here. Now hurry and change. We're expected at Knollwood.'

George pulled Percy off to the stables and James headed around to the back of the house, his footsteps heavier than before. Reaching under the loose jacket, his fingers traced the raised scar on his left shoulder through the thin fabric of his hunting shirt. Unconsciously, he flexed his left hand, feeling the weakness and cursing it. He stomped on a large clump of mud, mashing it into the earth. This was exactly what he didn't want, the whole reason he'd allowed George to convince him to come to the country.

He cursed his luck and George's carelessness. If his friend had extinguished the lamp instead of leaving it to overheat, James could have spent the next two weeks here, not forced into Artemis's cave waiting to be ripped apart by her wild beasts. He'd experienced enough clawing and tearing in the ballrooms of London. He had no stomach for it here in the country. Give him a French fleet any day; it was preferable to a matron with a marriageable daughter.

A flash of movement on the opposite hill made him stop at the rear door. He watched the young woman ride at a full gallop over the green downs, the horse moving like a shadow, her amber hair a streak of sunlight through the dark clouds. The memory of the little Artemis astride the black beast, face flushed with anger, pert breasts rising and falling with each excited breath, filled his mind. His loins stirred with desire before he checked himself. It was one thing to idle away hours with the willing widowed sister of a provincial governor; it was quite another to dally with the niece of his best friend.

Besides, no spirited creature wants a broken man. He pushed away from the wall, angrily slapping the door jamb. The rough stone stung his palm, reminding him that any interest in Miss Howard could only be to learn from her estate management skills which, according to George, were considerable. If James decided to follow his friend into the life of a country gentleman, he'd need to know more about it than what little he'd learn from books.

Manfred reached the crest of the hill, breathing hard, his dark coat glistening with sweat. Julia eased him into a slow walk and they ambled down the bridle path tracing the top. A thin mist crept through the crevices of the valley while sheep grazed quietly in the green meadows. The three estates situated on the three high hills overlooking the rolling valley came into view.

Creedon Abbey, the smallest, stood on the hill closest to Knollwood. Though some five miles off, the tips of the turrets were just visible above the surrounding trees. All the land here had once belonged to the old monastery before the Reformation and some debt-ridden descendant saw it sold off to create Knollwood and Cable Grange. There was little difference between Creedon land and Knollwood land, but drastic changes marked the boundary between Knollwood's lush, well-tended meadows and Cable Grange's weed-choked fields. Cable Grange stood on the third-highest hill in the area. Farther away than Creedon, she could just see it sitting on its hilltop perch, the distance obscuring its neglected state. Being so close to Knollwood, she knew Cable Grange could be one of the finest houses in the county.

If only it were mine. She didn't know who to curse more, her brother Charles for inheriting Knollwood or Mr Wilkins for ruining Cable Grange.

Adjusting her leg against the pommel, she wished she'd chosen her standard saddle instead of the side-saddle. It was still early and the rest of the house had yet to rise, making it unlikely Emily would catch her riding astride. Soothed by Manfred's gentle gait, she settled into the seat, her mind wandering back to the woods and the handsome stranger.

He called me attractive, she mulled, remembering the heady way his blue eyes raked her body, their heat warming her skin. Four years ago, standing against the wall during London balls, she'd seen gentlemen examine other young ladies with similar hot eyes, nudging each other knowingly. For all her London finery, not one gentleman had cast a single amorous glance in her direction. How strange to garner a lustful stare while dressed in her old riding habit.

If only he weren't one of the Wilkinses' good-for-nothing friends. She sighed, wondering what it would be like to feel his lips tease her neck while he whispered forbidden things in her ear. A strange thrill coursed through her before she forced the wicked daydream from her head. He was a scoundrel and not worth a second thought.

Digging her heel into Manfred's flanks, she drove him hard across the open ground, guiding him towards a hedge separating the fields. Pulling back on his reins, she sat forwards as he leapt and they easily cleared the bushes before landing on the other side.

'Well done, Manfred!'

She slowed him to a walk and, coming to another path, looked longingly east. A smooth mound stood out against the flatter fields, the ruins on top silhouetted by the rising sun. At a full gallop, they could reach the old fortress in a few minutes and she might spend a quiet hour picking through the high grass searching for relics. Her heel itched to tap Manfred, but she resisted, reluctantly directing him back to Knollwood. Emily expected her at breakfast. Why, she couldn't imagine. Neither Simon nor Annette, her stepcousins, had risen before noon since their arrival and when they were awake, they only complained about the country.

What could Uncle Edward possibly hope to accomplish by sending them here? she wondered, wishing he'd hurry up and recall them to London.

They trotted into the paddock, greeted by the fresh scent of hay and the sharper smell of horses.

'I see you've had another fine ride, Miss Howard,' John, the head groom, remarked, helping her down from the saddle. 'I've always said the two of you were made for each another.'

'That's because I believed in him when no one else did. Didn't I, Manfred?' Julia rubbed the horse's nose and he shook his head as if in agreement. 'John, please speak to the gamekeeper. I saw a poacher in the forest this morning.'

'A poacher?' He held Manfred's reins, disbelief deepening the lines of his forehead. 'We've never had such trouble before.'

'Well, I believe the man is a poacher, though it may have only been one of Mr Wilkins's guests.'

'Mr Wilkins has no guests, Miss Howard.'

Then who could he be? Julia tapped her riding crop against her palm, then handed it to John. 'No matter. Please ask the gamekeeper to take care of it.'

'Yes, Miss Howard.'

'Oh, and please don't mention it to Mother or Emily. They'll only worry and then Emily will lecture me if she discovers I went riding without you.' Emily had been married to her brother Charles for less than a year, but she'd prove his equal when it came to chastising Julia about proper behaviour.

'I won't say a word.' John laid a knowing finger against the side of his ruddy nose before leading Manfred inside.

Thank goodness for his loyalty, she thought, fastening up the long hem of her riding habit. Without him, she and Manfred might never be allowed to enjoy their solitary rides.

Walking up the path from the stables, she passed through a small grove of trees and into the large, open lawn. Crossing the wide space, she kicked the head off a dandelion, sprinkling her skirt with bits of grass and dew.

I must speak to Bill about bringing the sheep here to trim the grass, she reminded herself before passing through a gate in the low stone wall surrounding the garden on the other side.

Wandering down the gravel path through the semi-formal plant beds, she saw the house rise up in front of her, its many windows reflecting the morning sun. She removed her right glove and grazed the top of a large rosemary bush with her fingers before snapping off a sprig and inhaling the tangy scent. All the troubles she'd forgotten during her ride came rushing back, especially Charles's letter.

'His estate.' Julia threw the rosemary sprig on the ground, crushing it beneath her half-boot. 'What does he know of running Knollwood?'

She'd burned the hateful parchment after reading it, watching with delight as the neat script crumpled and charred in the flames. However, all the burned letters couldn't stop her brother from claiming his inheritance.

Pausing at the small pond in the centre of the garden, she stared into the dark water. Goldfish flitted beneath the glass surface, failing to disturb the reflection of the thick clouds passing overhead.

Why should he have Knollwood? Tears of frustration stung her eyes. *He's never taken an interest in it the way I have.*

Nor did he appreciate all her hard work to keep it prosperous. Only Father and Paul had ever recognised it, but with Paul serving with Admiral Nelson's fleet and Father—

No, she commanded herself, refusing to cry. Tears would not help her deal with Charles.

Heading up the garden path, she passed her mother's cherished rose garden, then hurried up the stairs of the column-lined stone portico leading to the back sitting room.

'Good morning, Miss Howard,' Davies, the butler, greeted, pulling open the large French door.

'Good morning.' She handed him her gloves and he held out a small paper-covered parcel.

'This arrived from Mr Charles Howard.'

'My book.' She tore off the wrapper to reveal a leather-bound copy of *The Monk*. 'I can't believe Charles sent it. He's always so concerned about not disturbing my delicate female mind. It's fortunate he doesn't know the half of what Paul tells me.'

'Yes, very fortunate indeed,' Davies solemnly concurred. He'd been Paul's valet when Paul still lived at Knollwood, making him well acquainted with her brother's nature and most of his escapades.

'Has Uncle George returned from London yet?'

'Captain Russell arrived a short while ago to collect Percy and speak with Mrs Emily How-

ard. He's returned to Creedon Abbey to see to
the repairs.'

'Uncle George was here and didn't wait for
me?'

'No, miss, but it appears we are to expect another gentleman.'

'Who?'

'Mrs Howard did not say, but she instructed
me to open Paul's room for him.'

Julia chafed at the news. 'When is he arriving?'

'This afternoon.'

'Thank you, Davies. Please tell Mrs Howard
I won't be joining her for breakfast.'

'Yes, miss.'

Julia walked down the hall to the study, determined to avoid the breakfast room no matter how
many lectures it might create. What right did
Emily have to make decisions at Knollwood? The
maids and footmen were stretched thin enough
with Uncle George staying here and all her stepcousins' demands.

Crossing the study's large, woven rug, Julia
sighed. Emily, as Charles's wife, had every right
to invite whomever she pleased, even if it did
mean additional work for Julia and the staff.
For a moment she imagined herself mistress of
her own home, free to make decisions and live
without her brother's censure, then dismissed the

thought. Once Charles took control, he'd soon realise the limitations of his estate management skills, or return to London for Parliament in the spring, leaving Knollwood in Julia's hands once again. Or so she hoped. Her brother had a habit of being very stubborn.

She sat down behind the large, mahogany desk situated at the far end of the study. High bookcases lined one wall while south-facing windows with a view of the garden dominated the other. A tall, wooden bookstand supporting a fine atlas stood guard near the window, flanked by two leather chairs. Her father had decorated the room, choosing every element down to each book. From here he conducted all family business, patiently bearing Charles's sermons about the proper education for Julia, dealing with one of Paul's many near scandals or teaching Julia to run Knollwood.

It'd happened by accident, after she'd fled here one day to avoid drawing lessons. Sitting with her father while he reviewed the figures, she'd asked questions and he'd answered them, noticing her interest. The next day, he'd invited her to join him again and it became their habit. In the afternoons, they'd ride the estate, speaking with the workers and learning their methods and the land. Then, one day, he told her to do the figures, allowed her to sit in the room while he met

with the overseer and gave her correspondence
to read and answer. No one in the family except
Charles questioned her strange education and Father would laugh him off, saying he wasn't about
to lose his best manager because she was a girl.

Julia smiled at the memory, then opened the
large, leather-bound ledger. Settling herself over
the accounts, she reviewed the figures, wrinkling
her nose at the increased expenditures brought
on by her stepcousins' visit. Closing the ledger,
she gathered up the large bundle of letters resting on the corner of the desk. She read through
the missives, the minute details of the dairy and
reports from the tenant farmers helping her forget the excitement of the morning.

Chapter Two

The study door swung open, startling Julia, and her pencil slipped, leaving a dark mark across two rows of figures.

'Yes?' she answered testily as Davies entered the room.

'Captain Russell and his guest have arrived.'

Tossing down the pencil, she sat back in the chair, needing just a few more minutes to finish balancing the accounts. 'They're early.'

'I believe they are on time.'

She looked at the windows, finally noticing how the sun and shadows had shifted in the garden and the room. 'How long have I been working?'

'All morning, Miss Howard.'

'Then I'd better hurry and join them or I'll never know a moment's peace with Emily.' Clos-

ing the ledger, she stood and started for the door.
'Though I know Uncle George won't mind my
being late. He isn't one for formality.'

'Excuse me, Miss Howard...' Davies coughed
'...perhaps a change of dress is advisable.'

She stopped, inspecting the riding habit skirt,
her loose hair falling over her face. Bits of leaves
stuck to the honey-coloured fabric, making
the damp hem noticeable and emphasising the
creases along with the habit's older style. She
hardly ever wore this habit, but she'd soiled her
better one yesterday by taking Manfred over a
fence and through the mud on the other side. Had
she seen the puddle, she wouldn't have jumped
him.

'I'll never hear the end of it if Emily catches
me greeting guests in such a state. Where are
they?'

'The morning room.'

'Do you think I can sneak upstairs and change
before she sees me?'

'It is quite possible, Miss Howard.'

'We shall see.'

She hurried from the study and down the cor-
ridor. Approaching the entrance hall, she crept
over the stone floor to the stairs, listening to
Uncle George's robust laughter followed by the
deep tones of the other gentleman in the morning room. The stranger's voice sounded oddly

familiar, but she didn't dare peek inside for fear of being seen. Stealing past the open door, she turned the corner to slip upstairs, coming face to face with her sister-in-law.

'What are you doing in your riding habit?' Emily demanded in hushed tones, her delicate eyes darting nervously to the morning room. 'And your hair? You can't welcome your guests looking like a dairy maid.'

'My guests?'

'Never mind. We'll say you were out riding and then you can meet the captain now before Uncle George drags him off for who knows how long.' Emily pulled her in front of the gilded mirror beneath the stairs and out of sight of the door.

'Did you say Uncle George's guest is a captain?' Julia winced as Emily untangled a small twig from her hair.

'Yes, Captain Covington.'

'Uncle George's friend from Tortuga?' Julia twisted around to face Emily before her sister-in-law gently spun her back to the mirror, dividing her hair into three sections, then working them into a braid.

'Yes, I believe so.'

Julia forced down a frustrated sigh. Single gentlemen were a rarity at Knollwood and Julia could practically see Emily's matchmaking machinations. It was the only explanation for why she insisted on this hurried first meeting. Apparently, she didn't know as much about Uncle George's friend as Julia did or she wouldn't be so excited, or eager to make the introduction. 'Well, if Captain Covington is to stay with us, I'd better instruct Davies to lock up the brandy.'

'Captain Covington isn't that kind of gentleman.'

'Then I'd better lock up the maids.'

'Julia!' Emily stared at her in the mirror, her pale face alight with shock. 'Young ladies shouldn't know about such things.'

Thankfully Paul thinks I should. If Emily and Charles ever learned the full extent of what Paul had told her, they'd probably chaperon their every conversation.

Emily smoothed the sturdy wool of Julia's habit, picking off stray leaves, her hands fluttering while she worked.

'You received another letter from Charles, didn't you?' Julia asked. Emily's concern for propriety always increased after a letter from her husband.

Emily blushed, pink spreading from her cheeks to her light blonde hair. 'Am I so obvious?'

'I'm afraid so.'

'It's only because we want to see you well settled.'

'No, it's because Charles thinks I don't act like a proper lady and such behaviour will cause a scandal and hurt his career in Parliament.'

Emily laid a motherly hand on Julia's shoulder. 'Your brother loves you and only wants to see you happy.'

Despite the well-meaning remark, Julia wasn't ready to concede defeat. 'I'm happy as I am.'

Emily moved behind Julia, fastening the braid into a small bun at the nape of her neck. 'I know, but time doesn't stand still. Some day you may want more.'

'What about Simon and Annette? They aren't greeting Uncle George. Why not censure them?'

'It's not my place to comment on their conduct.' Emily frowned and pulled her lips tight. 'They are both indisposed and will be down later.'

Julia bit back a sharp retort about the two of them always being indisposed when another idea came to mind. 'Perhaps I can speak to Captain Covington about Paul's promotion. Maybe he knows someone in the Admiralty who can arrange for Paul to get his own ship. I can't believe he didn't receive a command. If I ever find the man who wrote his bad recommendation—'

'I'm sure your brother is capable of managing his own affairs,' her mother interrupted, descending the stairs. Her grey eyes took in Julia, neither approving nor disapproving of her attire. Under her arm Charlemagne, her King Charles spaniel, panted, his pink tongue dangling from his mouth. Mother swept into the morning room, her plain dress whispering about her legs, her dark hair flecked with grey pulled neatly into a twist at the back of her head. Julia envied Mother's refined presence and decorum, wondering how many difficulties she could have avoided if fate had given her even a small portion of Mother's poise.

Emily, eager to fulfil her duties as hostess and, Julia thought, to fling her in the captain's path, guided Julia to the morning room. 'Come along. We've kept our guest waiting long enough.'

Inside, Mother exchanged pleasantries with Uncle George and the captain, who stood with his back to Julia.

'Your lands are some of the best I've seen,' he complimented, the rich, familiar voice vibrating through Julia. She noticed the dark hair curling just above the collar of his uniform and the way the sunlight falling through the window high-lighted the deep-red tones.

The stranger! A sudden rush of excitement mixed with fear jolted her and she froze just over the threshold.

'Are you all right?' Emily whispered and Julia shook her head, taking a large step back.

'No, I think I should change.' He'd seen her

riding without a groom. If he mentioned it to Emily, there'd be no end to the reprimands.

'It's too late now.' Emily gripped her arm tight to keep her from fleeing as she motioned to Uncle George.

'And here is the party responsible for Knollwood's prosperity.' Uncle George ushered the captain to them. 'Captain Covington, Miss Julia Howard.'

If she had thought him handsome in plain hunting clothes, he took her breath away in uniform. The dark coat with the gold epaulettes emphasised his wide shoulders and the powerful presence she had felt in the forest. Without the advantage of Manfred's height, she had to look up at him. Though not overly tall, he stood a good head above her. The fantasy of being swept into his arms filled her mind once again and she swallowed hard.

'A pleasure.' He bowed.

Her eyes travelled the length of him as he straightened. Well-muscled calves stretched his hose tight while slightly looser breeches could not hide his strong thighs and other unmentionable areas. Feeling her cheeks burn, Julia focused on his face as she held out her hand. 'Captain Covington, welcome to Knollwood.'

He wrapped his fingers lightly around hers, then swept his lips across the bare knuckles. Julia drew in a ragged breath, trying not to tremble. The white-trimmed collar of the coat framed his now clean-shaven face and she curled her fingers slightly around his to stop herself from tracing the smooth line of his jaw.

'Good morning, Artemis.' His breath tickled the back of her hand and her body tightened in shock. 'I assume I am no longer trespassing on your land?'

She leaned closer, inhaling the earthy smell of his lavender shaving soap. 'That remains to be seen.'

He squeezed her hand, then let go. Julia stepped back, very aware of Emily shifting from foot to foot behind him.

'Have you two met before?' Emily asked in a high voice.

'I had the privilege of encountering Miss Howard while she was riding in the forest this morning,' Captain Covington explained, oblivious to the trouble he'd just caused.

Julia braced herself for the coming scolding, wishing the captain had held his tongue.

'You were riding without the groom again?' Emily asked, the nervous quaver in her voice more irritating than a bur in a boot.

'No, the groom was with her,' James lied before Julia could answer. 'But I'm afraid I failed to properly introduce myself and she mistook me for a poacher.'

Julia gaped at him, surprised he'd lie for her after the way she'd addressed him in the woods.

'George left no detail untold regarding your management,' he continued. 'You have quite an estate. I'm very impressed.'

'Thank you,' she faltered, the compliment catching her off guard. Usually gentlemen scoffed at her unusual accomplishment. 'I'm quite protective of it, as you may have gathered.'

'Indeed. I've never met such a fearsome protector of woodland creatures in all my life.'

'I'm sure many innocent creatures need protection from Navy men.'

Emily inhaled sharply and Uncle George snorted out a laugh while her mother continued to pet Charlemagne, barely noting the exchange.

The captain's lips tightened in an attempt to keep from laughing and suddenly Julia regretted her impudent tongue. With all she knew of him from Uncle George's stories, to fire off such forward remarks, no matter how innocent, might give him the wrong impression and it wasn't very gracious, especially after he'd lied to help her.

'Shall we sit down?' Emily interrupted, nervously studying Julia and the captain.

'Yes, thank you.' He allowed Emily to escort

him to the sofa and chairs near the window, her mother following close behind.

Julia stayed by the door, hoping she could slip away without Emily noticing. Decorum dictated she stay and entertain the captain, but something about him unnerved her. It was one thing to speak so frankly to family, quite another with a stranger, no matter how well he knew Uncle George. Better to leave now than risk another slip.

'I see you hiding there.' Uncle George came up alongside her, thumbs hooked in his jacket lapel.

'I'm not hiding.'

'Then come and join us.'

Julia smiled half-heartedly, watching the captain as he answered one of Mother's questions, his smile steady as he spoke. Whatever the captain thought of her unconventional behaviour, he'd already forgotten it. Deep down, some part of her wanted him to notice her, the way he had in the woods. As if sensing her, he shifted in the chair, meeting her eyes, and she turned to Uncle George.

'No, I have business to attend to.'

'Leave it for later. I think you'll enjoy the captain. You two already have quite the rapport.' He tugged her ear playfully, the way he'd done since she was a child.

The friendly gesture usually made her smile.

Today it increased the irritation chewing at her. 'My work can't wait.'

'If you insist. But you can't hide at Knollwood for ever. Eventually, you'll have to get out in the world and live.'

'I'm not hiding,' Julia protested.

'Of course not. Silly of me to say it.' He patted her arm. 'Go back to the study. I'll make your excuses.'

Julia left, pausing a moment to listen to the muffled voices, suddenly feeling very alone. Walking through the back sitting room, she took in the sturdy walls of Knollwood covered in hunting prints and old portraits of well-dressed ancestors. Here she felt safe and, when not entertaining guests, confident in herself. Anywhere else she felt awkward and unsettled. What would happen if Charles took this away from her?

She slipped out of the French doors and crossed the garden to the far corner where the tall boxwood hedges hid her from the house. At the centre of this private courtyard stood a fountain of a man and woman locked in a passionate kiss, a copy of some nameless Greek statue. It had been a gift to their father from Paul after his first visit to Greece. Having no use for the statue in the house, her father had it made into a fountain, scandalising Charles, who insisted on hiding it in this secluded corner.

Julia plunked down on the stone bench in front of the fountain, watching the water run over the naked marble bodies. The polished stone glistened in the noon sun, intensifying the urgency of the lovers' embrace. The man's fingers dug into the hard flesh of the woman's thigh, his hands entwined in her hair as she pressed her naked form against his. Her long, gracefully carved fingers rested against the taut muscles of the male's well-chiselled back. Studying the lovers' embrace, their bodies so close not even water could separate them, Julia felt her chest constrict. What would it be like to inspire such passion in a man?

Picking up a small stone, she flung it into the pool at the base of the fountain, sending a large splash up and over the side. Reaching down for another rock, she heard the pitter-patter of paws on gravel as Charlemagne barrelled down on her. The small dog threw his front paws up on her knees, his wagging tail shaking his whole body as Julia stroked his soft fur.

'I thought I'd find you here,' her mother said, scooping up Charlemagne and sitting down next to her.

'Did Emily send you here to chastise me for not being a perfect lady?'

'Emily is a sweet girl, good for Charles and I adore her,' her mother remarked, settling the wiggling dog on her lap. 'But I seldom listen to her advice or Charles's. I suggest you do the same.'

'I've tried, but it only makes them more persistent.'

'Yes, he takes after your grandfather in that regard.' Charlemagne refused to be still and Mother put him on the ground. 'You're worried about Charles taking over Knollwood, aren't you?'

Like Uncle George, Mother could be very direct and Julia found it both helpful and at times hindering. She watched Charlemagne sniff around the fountain, jumping back when an errant bead of water landed on his nose.

'When he does, what will I do?' Julia choked, digging the toe of her boot into the ground.

'I think you'll find something. You're much more resourceful than either Charles or Paul.'

'But what else could there possibly be for me?'

Her mother took Julia's face in her hands, pushing a strand of hair off of her cheek. 'That's up to you to discover.'

She kissed Julia's forehead, then rose, snapping her fingers at Charlemagne.

'Do I hide from the world here?' Julia asked before her mother could leave.

'Who put such an idea in your head?'

'Uncle George.'

The older woman laughed softly. 'Since when do you take my brother seriously?'

Julia shrugged. 'Emily and Charles are always saying it, in their own way.'

'I think only you know the answer.' She strolled out of the garden, Charlemagne close on her heels.

The quick click of a lady's perturbed step drew James to the morning-room door. Miss Howard strode into the entrance hall, moving like a tempest, oblivious to everything but her own energy. Fascinated, he wanted to draw her out, but hesitated. Better to let her go than risk the blunt blow of her dark mood. However, something in the troubled frown on her pretty face prompted him to speak.

'Miss Howard?'

The stomping girl vanished, replaced by an awkward young woman conscious of the world around her. 'Yes?'

She stood on the bottom stair, one small hand on the oak banister, poised like a doe to flee. He wondered what had happened to make such an exuberant creature so timid. 'I want to apologise for this morning. You took me quite by surprise.'

'Yes, I imagine I did.' She moved to leave, but he wasn't ready to let her go.

'I don't usually meet young ladies in the forest so early in the morning.'

'Why didn't you tell me who you were?' she demanded with startling directness.

'You didn't ask,' he laughed, his mirth evaporating under her stern glare. 'Allow me to apologise. I should have introduced myself.' He offered a humble bow, but it did not soften the small crease marring her smooth brow.

'I wish you had for it might have saved us both a great deal of trouble.'

'I shall endeavour to be more agreeable to you the next time we meet in a forest.' The image of them alone among the trees, her hair loose about her naked shoulders, their bodies entwined came to mind. His hand itched to reach up and trace the gentle curve of her cheek, slip his fingers behind her long neck and draw her close.

'There will be no next time,' she corrected, ending the pleasant fantasy.

'I think it quite possible,' he teased. 'Judging by this morning, I assume it is your habit to ride out alone in the mornings.'

'Shh.' She stepped closer, waving a silencing hand and filling the air between them with the faint scent of rosemary.

'Your mother doesn't approve of you riding alone?' he asked in a low voice.

'Mother doesn't care, but Emily does.' She

stepped off the stair and stood in front of him, her face softening. 'Thank you for not telling her you saw me riding without a groom. You spared me a great deal of trouble.'

'It was my pleasure, and I'll gladly do it again if the need arises.'

'I hope it doesn't come to that.' She smiled, her face glowing with amusement.

'You're very pretty when you smile,' he offered without thinking, amazed at how much her pleasure delighted him.

Her smile disappeared and she raised one disbelieving eyebrow. Something of the confident Artemis he'd seen this morning flashed in her hazel eyes, rousing his blood.

'I know the country is lacking in diversions, but do not think to amuse yourself with me.'

James straightened, forgetting his desire. He should have been insulted, but he could hardly blame her for saying what he'd momentarily imagined. 'You misunderstood my meaning. I have never, would never behave as you intimate.'

She fixed him with the same scrutinising look he once used on seamen when they told him a tall tale to cover their misdeeds. 'I am not naïve, Captain. My brother and uncle tell me everything, so I know what Navy men are about.'

'Do you?' He struggled to keep the laughter out of his voice, still unable to believe a young woman with her hair pulled back like a dour nun could be so forward. He leaned against the wooden banister, bringing their faces much closer than intended. She did not step back. 'I may have to change your opinion of Navy men.'

'I'm afraid you have only worked to confirm it.'

Her saucy eyes teased him. Were this Tortuga, he would have covered her full mouth with his, allowed his fingers to free her hair from the bun as he pulled her close to kiss away the wry smile dancing about her lips. However, his good breeding, not to mention his status as George's guest, prevented such a blatant breach of etiquette.

'Julia!' Emily appeared at the morning-room door. Julia stepped back, her cheeks burning, awkwardness replacing her courage. Silently, she cursed her impetuous nature, wondering what it was about the captain that kept causing her to forget herself. A few minutes in the gentleman's presence and she was once again acting like a strumpet instead of a lady. How much had Emily heard? Hopefully nothing or she and Charles would feel vindicated in all their chastising.

Before anyone could say anything, baby Thomas's wail filled the upstairs hallway and the nurse appeared at the top of the stairs, carrying the infant. He was only two months old, but he'd been born early and Emily fretted over him like no other well-born mother in the county.

'Mrs Howard, it is time for his feeding,' the nurse called over the screaming baby.

Emily glanced from the captain to Julia to upstairs, weighing her desire to reprimand with the need to see to her child. Luckily, Thomas's cries grew louder, making the decision for her.

'If you'll excuse me, Captain, I must attend to my son.' Emily shot Julia a silent warning before hurrying up to escort the nurse to the nursery. For all of Charles's and Emily's priggishness, they were firm believers in Rousseau's ideas of breastfeeding. It was one of the few things Julia admired them for.

'Despite being born two months early, my nephew has a healthy appetite and powerful lungs,' Julia observed.

'His lungs will serve him well if he enters Parliament. Like his father, his opinions will always be heard,' Captain Covington teased.

Julia laughed, the captain's joke putting her at ease. She was about to respond when a small cough from the landing interrupted them.

'Good morning, Captain Covington.' Annette glided down the stairs, her blue eyes raking over him. Dressed in a fashionable walking dress of expensive yellow silk, she stepped in between Julia and the captain. Her haughty air irked Julia and she clasped her hands together to keep from smacking the chit on the back of her elegantly coiffed blonde head. Though they were the same age, they had nothing in common and had never been more than civil to each other since Annette's arrival.

'Miss Taylor, a pleasure to see you again.' The captain bowed over her extended hand, the relaxed Navy man from a moment before replaced by a proper gentleman.

Julia noted the change and her heart sank. Obviously, he respected the polished manners of a London lady to the questionable conduct of a country girl.

It doesn't matter, she told herself. *Neither of them will be here for ever.*

'How are your dear sister and mother?' Annette asked, her voice light and charming.

'My sister Charlotte is in Wiltshire with her husband. My mother is with them at the moment, though she returns to town next week. She prefers London to the country.'

'Who of us doesn't?' Simon yawned from the top of the stairs, his voice heavy with the Devonshire lisp so popular in town. Tall and lean, Simon wore a suit of the finest material cut tight to accentuate his slender body. He possessed the same sharp features as his sister, but the affected boredom of his dandified style softened them considerably.

Annette's face reddened at Simon's remark. 'You remember my brother?'

'Of course.' Both men nodded to one another, no affection lost on either side.

'We are going to the local town. Please join us for I'm eager for some society after such isolation.'

'Did I hear someone suggest a ride into Daringford?' Uncle George asked, coming up behind the captain.

'Yes. Care to join us?' Captain Covington invited.

While they made their plans, Julia started up the stairs, sure no one would notice her absence. They had each other; they did not need her. She froze when the captain called out to her.

'Miss Howard, would you like to join us?'

Surveying the waiting group, Julia wondered how much more of his company she could endure without gaining a reputation as a hoyden. Until she could learn to control her tongue in his presence, it was probably better to avoid him. She moved to make her excuses when Annette's condescending sweep of Julia's riding habit changed her mind. 'Yes, but allow me to change. I'll only be a moment.'

'Your dress is passable. Come and let's be off,' Uncle George impatiently called.

Julia reluctantly stepped off the stairs. Emily would have a fit if she knew Julia wore her old riding habit into town. Oh, well, what was one more reprimand? Besides, it was worth the rebuke to annoy Annette.

'Come, Captain Covington.' Annette motioned for his arm and like a true gentleman he offered it, leading her outside to the waiting carriage. Julia watched the way her stepcousin moved, the rich material and fine cut of her dress emphasising her willowy figure. A slight twinge of jealousy took hold and Julia wondered if things would be different if she made an effort to dress so well every day or demonstrate proper, genteel manners.

'My lady.' Uncle George offered her his arm with an exaggerated flourish.

'Why, thank you, sir,' she answered with equally false formality.

'What do you think of the captain?' he asked in a low voice as they strolled out to the waiting carriage.

'He strikes me as quite the man about town. He's already caught Annette's attention.'

'Any man with a pocketbook catches her fancy,' George huffed. 'You shouldn't let her have him.'

'I have no interest in a Navy man, especially one with a thin London polish.'

'He's no Simon, if that's what you're worried about. He's rich, too. Thanks, I might say, in part to many of my lucrative schemes.'

Julia suppressed a laugh, knowing how proud Uncle George was of the numerous profitable ventures he'd embarked on during his time in the Navy. 'Why did the captain resign?'

'George, stop gossiping and get in,' Captain Covington interrupted from beside the open carriage door. 'No need to give away all my secrets on the first day.'

'Not possible, Jim. You've got too many.' Uncle George chuckled.

'May I?' Captain Covington held out his hand, a playful smile lighting up his face. Julia reached for his upturned palm, hesitating a moment before pushing against the strength of it to step up into the carriage.

'Thank you.' She didn't dare meet his eyes, but slid across the squabs and settled in next to the far window, her hand still tingling from his touch. Uncle George sat beside her in an attempt to place some distance between her, Annette and Simon and she was grateful. The captain took a seat across from them, next to Annette, much to the chit's visible delight.

Simon paused to adjust his cravat, then carefully climbed into the carriage, moving like an old lady to avoid wrinkling his morning coat. The door closed behind him, but Simon wasn't fully seated when Uncle George rapped on the roof. The vehicle sprung into motion, throwing Simon into the seat next to his sister.

'I say,' Simon complained to George.

'Sorry about that.' George shrugged, unruffled by Simon's outburst.

'Men can be so silly, don't you agree, Captain Covington?' Annette laughed, reprimanding her brother with a look he pointedly ignored.

'Yes, they can be.' The captain allowed the conversation to drop, watching the countryside pass by outside the window, a strange melancholy clouding his face. Julia noted the way the afternoon sunlight spread over his features, highlighting a very small scar on his cheek and giving him a bit of mystery and depth she'd never seen in any London gentleman. Then his eyes darted to hers and she turned away, her heart fluttering, the heat in the carriage rising sharply.

What's wrong with me? she wondered, touching the warm skin of her neck. It wasn't like her to act so hen-witted in the company of a man, especially a Navy rake like the captain. Struggling to regain control, she concentrated on the river flowing in the gully below the road. No matter how much she focused on the clear water pouring over the rocks, the captain lingered on the edge of her vision. When she dared to look at him again, she found him still smiling at her.

'Captain Covington, were you at Lady Wellsingham's ball last month?' Annette asked.

'No, I'm afraid business kept me away,' he answered with a slight frown before covering it with a gracious smile.

Perhaps he's not so taken by London charms, Julia mused, sitting back to observe the conversation with a new interest.

'What a pity. You would have enjoyed it. All anyone could talk about was Lord Langston's comment on Napoleon. He said the Emperor's coat was too tight to suit a real gentleman, and if the Emperor had a better tailor, he might not be so fond of war.'

'I thought politics a taboo subject at balls?' Julia asked, more to annoy her stepcousin than out of any real interest.

'We were discussing Lord Langston's comment, not politics,' Annette arrogantly clarified. 'Surely you've heard of the earl, even here?'

Julia bit back a sharp retort, struggling through gritted teeth to remain cordial.

'Yes. Charles keeps me abreast of the latest London news, though I pay it no mind. I hardly feel the comments of a man who thinks only of clothes and dancing is worth the breath to spread it. Were he a man of actual accomplishments, such as Lord Nelson, I might take more interest in what he has to say.'

'Here, here, Julia.' George slapped his knee and Annette pursed her thin lips.

'Sounds like a rather American idea to me, Miss Howard,' Captain Covington asked.

'Have you been to America, Captain?' Julia asked.

'Yes, it's an interesting country.'

'I don't agree with the Americans. The French followed their example and all their patriotism and liberty turned out dreadful,' Annette interjected, but both Julia and Captain Covington ignored the remark.

'I'm a great admirer of Mr Jefferson. Are you familiar with his agricultural inventions?' Julia asked.

'Yes, I read one of his books while I was in London. I read quite a number of books while I was at home.' He paused, watching his left hand open and close before he looked up at her again. 'I don't recall the specific of Mr Jefferson's designs, but I remember them being quite innovative.'

'He devised a plough specifically for hills. It's proved most beneficial to Knollwood,' she volunteered, encouraged by his response. 'Like Mr Jefferson, I've discovered the best way to develop new techniques is to ask the workers. I regularly speak with mine to keep abreast of their progress and any potential problems.'

'How plebian to be so familiar with your servants,' Annette sneered.

Julia went silent, the conspicuous difference between her and her London cousin making her self-conscious.

'I agree, Miss Howard, servants are often aware of more than their employers realise,' the captain offered with a smile.

'Indeed, they know the land and conditions better than anyone else.'

Careful not to gloat over the obvious check to Annette's mocking remark, Julia continued her discussion of agriculture, encouraged by the captain's extensive knowledge. The bulk of it came from books, but he asked many questions about the practical application, eager to learn. While they spoke, Julia watched the way Annette hung on his every word, fluttering her eyelashes at him while praising his wit and intelligence. Each compliment brought a smile to his face and as much as Julia's opinion of him rose with their current discussion, his apparent infatuation with Annette lowered it. Perhaps the captain thought her cousin a better country amusement than Julia. After all, the way Annette fawned on him made her interest apparent. How typical of a man to fall prey to such a shallow woman.

The carriage rattled into town, coming to a stop near the centre of the High Street. James stepped out into the crisp autumn air and took a deep breath. Being confined for so long next to Miss Taylor reminded him of a tight gun deck on a humid day in the islands. Only Miss Howard's airy voice and sparkling eyes offered any respite from Miss Taylor's cloying company.

'What an exile,' Mr Taylor sighed, taking in Daringford's dusty streets lined with shops. 'I'll return shortly.'

'I thought you were going to stay with me?' Miss Taylor whined as James handed her out of the carriage.

Mr Taylor ignored her, strolling off towards the Sign of the Swan tavern, much to his sister's visible displeasure.

James turned back to the carriage to help Miss Howard out, only to see her alight from the other side before hurrying around to join them.

'I'm afraid I must leave you as well,' George announced. 'I have some business to attend to with my solicitor. Take good care of the ladies, Jim.' He went off in the opposite direction, leaving James alone with Miss Taylor and Miss Howard.

'Well, ladies, where shall we go?'

'The milliner's shop,' Miss Taylor decided. 'I must purchase some lace, though I doubt it will be of the same quality here as in London.'

'The milliner it is, unless Miss Howard has somewhere she wishes to go?'

Miss Howard shook her head. 'No, I'm simply here for the diversion.'

'One could hardly call this place a diversion.' Miss Taylor made for the row of shops lining the north side of the street, stepping gingerly around the dirt and mud.

'I suppose we must follow.' Miss Howard sighed.

'I suppose we must.'

Their progress across the square was slow, with Miss Howard stopping more than once to speak to some farmers' wives. He stood by while they conversed, noting how she addressed the women without arrogance or conceit. There were no signs of her former awkwardness and he thought it strange she should get along so well with these women, yet seem utterly out of place with people like the Taylors. It baffled him, but he enjoyed it, her friendly attitude a refreshing change from rigid London ways.

When they finally reached the milliner shop, James held open the door, then followed her inside. 'Do you come to the village often?'

'Yes, it seems I am always purchasing necessities for Knollwood.'

Miss Taylor ignored them in favour of the shopkeeper who hustled to help the London girl spend her blunt. Miss Howard did not shop, but loitered with him near the front window, as out of place here as Miss Taylor would be among estate labourers.

'You have no interest in lace?' James asked.

'I've come to town in my riding habit. I assure you, I have no interest in lace.'

He noted the older cut of the habit with its lower waist and fitted bodice. The style skimmed her flat stomach and accentuated her curved hips. He preferred the form-flattering shape to the high-waisted style dominating Rotten Row. 'I like your dress.'

'Do you?'

He heard disbelief in the question, but also a note of hope. 'I do.'

She played with a small piece of ribbon dangling off the table next to her, then nodded at Miss Taylor, who stood at the counter negotiating with the shopkeeper over the price. 'She certainly drives a hard bargain. I'm amazed she bothers to be so economical.'

'Perhaps her situation is not what it seems.'

Miss Howard's puzzled face indicated her ignorance of the London rumours regarding the

Taylors. However, before she could respond, a round matron followed by a blonde young lady with similar full features entered the store.

'Miss Howard,' the older woman called out, crossing to where they stood. 'What a pleasure to see you in here. I didn't think you one for the milliner's shop.'

Miss Howard's lips drew tight and James's ire rose at the belittling way the matron's eyes swept over Miss Howard, making her flush with embarrassment.

'Mrs Johnson, may I introduce Captain Covington.' Miss Howard motioned to him. 'He is a friend of my uncle and staying with us. Captain Covington, this is Mrs Johnson and her daughter, Miss Caroline Johnson.'

The two ladies curtsied to James, sizing up his value as a potential husband.

He bowed, unwilling to remain here or give this woman another chance to insult Miss Howard. 'If you'll excuse us, we were just about to step outside and leave you *lovely* women to your shopping.'

He offered Miss Howard his arm. She slipped her hand in the crook of his elbow and flashed the disbelieving Mrs and Miss Johnson a wide smile as he escorted her out of the shop.

'I see some mamas are as rude here as they are in London,' James fumed once they were outside. 'What did she hope to gain by being condescending to you?'

'I don't know, but please pay it no mind. I'm quite used to it.' Miss Howard withdrew her hand and placed a respectable distance between them. He brushed his fingers over the spot where she'd held his arm, missing the soft weight of her touch.

'You should make a habit of responding to rude people,' James suggested.

'Why? Emily and Charles would only hear of it, then chastise me for being ill mannered. It seems I must be civil to everyone while everyone may speak to me as they please.'

'There are many ways to appear courteous, yet still strike a cutting blow.'

'Then you must teach me some for I'm tired of putting up with such nonsense.' She laughed, the charming sound carrying over the noisy rattle of equipage in the street.

'It would be my pleasure. What sort of remark would you like to learn first?'

'James Covington,' the long-forgotten but familiar female voice called out from behind them, slicing through him like a sword and shattering his jovial mood. 'I can hardly believe it.'

He turned, watching Melinda Knight saunter up the street, a wicked smile decorating her full lips. A low-cut gown showed off her ample white bosom, much to the appreciation of the passing village men. Many paused to admire her, elbowing one another as their lecherous eyes enjoyed the well-displayed assets. They obviously deemed her a beauty, but James, who'd known her in his youth, saw the toll London indulgence had taken. Her dark-brown eyes seemed tired and dull while her once slender form had grown more stout, filling out her face and keeping away, for a few more years at least, the lines forming about her eyes and the corners of her lips.

'Miss Knight,' he greeted through clenched teeth.

'I'm Mrs Wilkins now, or have you forgotten?'

James's lip curled in loathing. 'So you married him?'

'Is that any way to greet an old friend?' Her seductive voice had once heated his blood; now it left him icy with disgust.

'I would hardly call us friends.'

She wedged herself between him and Miss Howard, her bosom brushing his chest. 'At one time you called me a great deal more.'

'That was a long time ago.' He stepped back, fighting the urge to push her away. The reaction unnerved him. He thought he'd forgotten her treachery years ago. Taking control of his surging emotions, he turned to Miss Howard, noting her stunned expression. 'May I introduce Miss Howard of Knollwood.'

Melinda faced Julia, taking her in and dismissing her all at once. 'We already know one another. My husband owns Cable Grange. My, what a pretty riding habit. Did you ride here?'

'No,' Miss Howard retorted, her dislike of Melinda palpable.

'Must be the new fashion. I find it so hard to keep up. You country girls have such different tastes.'

Melinda laid a gloved hand on James's arm and he pulled away, leaving her fingers hanging like talons before she lowered them. Far from being embarrassed, she seemed to take pleasure in his revulsion. 'You should come and visit us, James. I know Rowan would love to see you. Now, if you'll excuse me, I must be going.'

She swept off down the street, collecting more appreciative stares as she went.

'You know her?' Miss Howard gasped.

'I knew her once, a long time ago. It's of no importance.' He wondered how best to correct whatever false impression his acquaintance with Melinda left. He refused to be judged by a past mistake, but no proper explanation came to mind.

'Here comes George.' James motioned over her shoulder, thankful for the distraction.

George rushed along the road, the light of delicious news in his eyes.

'I can tell by the way he's hurrying, he's heard gossip,' Julia observed. 'He enjoys a story more than any old matron in Daringford.'

James laughed at the candid and accurate description. 'It is good to know some things haven't changed.'

'Julia, you won't believe what my solicitor told me,' George blurted out between winded pants when he reached them. 'Cable Grange is to be sold at auction in ten days if Mr Wilkins can't pay his London creditors.'

Chapter Three

Julia jumped from the carriage the instant it halted in front of Knollwood. Flying up the front stairs, she ran down the hall, throwing open her mother's sitting-room door, not caring what anyone thought of her very unladylike entrance.

'Cable Grange is to be sold by the bailiff in ten days. You must write to Charles and tell him to arrange for my inheritance at once.'

'Julia, do not stomp about the house,' her mother instructed without missing a stitch in her embroidery. Charlemagne watched from a basket at her mother's feet, his tail wagging lazily.

'Mother, did you hear what I said?' she demanded, chafing in the face of her apathy.

'You know he won't approve.' Her mother pulled a long, red thread through the fabric. 'He hardly approves of you running Knollwood in his absence.'

'That's why I need you to write him. Demand my inheritance, but don't tell him why. I can't have him buying Cable Grange out from under me.'

'I have little influence with Charles, especially in this matter.'

'But he has to give me the money,' Julia cried, pacing the room. 'This could be my only chance to secure an estate of my own.'

Her mother paused mid-stitch. 'Without a husband? He'd never allow it. You must be married first.'

'To whom? One of the many young men throwing themselves at my feet?'

'My dear, don't sound so despondent. Some day you will find a gentleman who loves you.'

'Not in time to purchase Cable Grange.' Julia sat down hard in the window seat.

'Perhaps George can supply the necessary funds?'

'Creedon Abbey is profitable, but not enough to finance another estate, especially not with the repairs from the fire.' She knew because she often helped Uncle George with his accounting.

'Then I'm afraid Cable Grange will go to another.'

Julia bit her thumbnail in frustration, feeling

like a rabbit caught in a snare. Though the money was hers, her father's will gave Charles control of it until she married or Charles died. At the moment, she wanted very much to kill her obstinate brother.

She picked at the gold thread on a pillow. 'Why did Father put Charles in charge of my inheritance? Why not Uncle George or even Paul? They wouldn't be so difficult.'

Her mother rose, sitting down next to Julia and taking her hands. 'It's what his solicitor advised. Your father intended to change it once George purchased Creedon Abbey, but his illness was so sudden—'

Silence heavy with grief settled between them. Outside, birds chirped in a nearby tree and Julia heard the distant bark of Uncle George's hunting dogs.

'It's not fair.'

'No, it isn't, but don't fret, my dear. Nothing is hopeless. Now, go and change for dinner.' Her mother kissed her gently on the forehead, then returned to her embroidery stand.

Julia wandered down the hall to her room, her mind working over the current dilemma. She had to have Cable Grange. She refused to be shoved aside at Knollwood by Charles or to let him control her life. Paul would never do such a thing if it were up to him.

Closing the door behind her, she wondered if Paul could arrange for the money. Knowing how freely he spent while in port, she doubted he possessed the means to buy an estate and his failure to gain command of his own ship hindered his ability to make his fortune. Even if he could help, there was no way to reach him before the auction.

Julia paced her room, her mind working to think of a solution. The only way to buy Cable Grange was to obtain her inheritance. The only way to get her inheritance was to marry. At present, she had no suitors. To be honest, she had never had suitors, not here or during her one Season in London.

Julia stopped pacing, her mind seizing on an idea. What if she was only engaged? If Charles thought she intended to marry, surely he'd give her the money in time to purchase Cable Grange. Even he could see the benefit of making Cable Grange part of the Howard lands. But what gentleman could she possibly convince to make her a false offer?

Through the window overlooking the garden, she spied Simon strolling among the roses. It wasn't like him to be awake at this time of day. Usually, he napped in the late afternoon in anticipation of an even later evening. How a man could spend all night gambling was beyond her comprehension.

The idea hit her like a bolt of lightning. Simon. As a gambler, he must need money. They could make a deal, pretend to be engaged and once she had her inheritance and Cable Grange, she'd give him a few hundred pounds to jilt her.

She rushed to the door, eager to strike the bargain, when a terrifying thought froze her hand on the doorknob. If he accepted the deal, could she buy his silence at the end of the engagement? If not, it would create a scandal, then who knew how Charles or even Mother would react. Charles might force her to go through with a ruinous marriage to avoid disgrace.

Julia resumed her pacing, desperate for a solution. Simon was no different from other London peacocks. How hard could it be to use her money, or the future possibility of money, to snare him? Instead of entangling herself in a potentially shocking agreement, she'd flaunt her wealth, then allow his greed to lead him to her. Once she had her inheritance and Cable Grange she could easily dismiss him. Simon would suffer no more heartbreak than the other London pinks who proposed to every unmarried rich woman who entered a ballroom. Even if breaking the engagement labelled her a jilt, it wouldn't matter.

She'd have her inheritance and Cable Grange and everything else could go to the devil.

Standing at the wardrobe, Julia tore through the dresses, selecting one of her better frocks. Slipping off the habit, she put on the light-blue dress, then sat at her dressing table to do her hair. The sight of herself in the mirror dampened her enthusiasm. Though the cloth of her frock was fine enough, the cut was unflattering and her hair, which was still fastened in the simple braided bun at the nape of her neck, did nothing to improve her features.

'If only I were pretty enough to catch Simon without my money.' She sighed and then dismissed the ridiculous notion. 'I might as well wish for gold to fall from the sky.'

Pulling out the bun, she brushed out her hair. A man like Simon couldn't resist the allure of money and she'd parade herself in front of him like a fat cow at market. Dignity be damned. She had to have Cable Grange for if she ended her days as a spinster aunt, she'd do it on her terms in her own house.

'I never thought I'd see Melinda again.' James smacked the cue stick hard against the white ball, sending it skipping over the slate, off the table and across the library's wood floor.

George picked it up, laying it back on the

table. 'You aren't still chewing on that, are you? Let it go. No good can come of it.'

'Except an estate. I wasn't planning it—I couldn't have planned it—yet here it is, in my lap. I only have to wait for the bailiff to act, then I'll watch them go and be done with it.' Revenge coiled inside him with unnerving force. Even in the days after Melinda betrayed him, he hadn't felt this much hate, but things were different then. His naval career had stretched out before him to blunt the disappointment and at sea he'd been too focused on succeeding and surviving to dwell on lost love. Now, with his career a shattered heap, his whole life crushed and bruised with it, there seemed nothing to distract him from old wounds. He flexed his left hand, cursing the dull pain. How he hated it and the way it made him hate everything.

George shook his head. 'That's not the Jim I remember.'

'A lot of things changed last year.'

'No, you just think they have. Look to the future. Don't concern yourself with some past offence that no longer matters.'

'You think it doesn't matter?'

'I think Rowan did you a favour, showed you who she really was before she leg-shackled you.' George leaned across the table and took a shot, scoring another point. 'Of course it's your decision and Cable Grange will suit you, but you'll need something more or you'll be bored in a fortnight.'

'You thinking running an estate won't be enough?' He reached for his glass of brandy sitting on the edge of the table.

'Not for a man like you. You need adventure and what better adventure than marriage?' George announced.

James stopped drinking mid-sip. 'Marriage?'

'Yes, marriage.' George hooked his thumbs in his coat, quite pleased with himself.

'What new scheme are you planning?' He didn't trust George's happy manner.

'Scheme? I never scheme.'

'Never scheme?' James laughed. 'What was all that business with the rum in Jamaica?'

'Merely an investment.'

'And the plantation owner's wife in Barbados?'

'One could hardly fault me for such an escapade.'

'Except the escapade's husband.'

George shrugged, unrepentant. 'You're a man of your own mind. I never forced you to participate in the rum venture or follow me to the plantation.'

'I followed you to save your hide and keep her husband from running you through.'

'Perhaps.' George fingered his cue stick, then levelled it at James. 'But you went along with the other ventures because you wanted to, making a handsome profit on more than one occasion if I remember correctly.'

'Yes, I have a great deal of my current fortune to thank you for.'

'So why distrust me now?'

It wasn't George he distrusted. It was himself. He hadn't seen Miss Howard since returning from Daringford, but following George through Knollwood, he kept searching for her in every room, hoping she might appear. Her presence touched a place deep inside him he thought destroyed with his career and the feeling left him wary and unsettled. One woman had already preyed on the weakness of his youth. He couldn't allow another to take advantage of his ruined life.

George fixed him with a stern, superior officer's stare. 'Seriously, Jim, you had a bad run last year, but you can't live in the past. You're young, full of possibility. You need a good woman by your side.'

'I suppose you have someone in mind? Your little Artemis, perhaps?'

George leaned towards James, the glint of mischief in his eyes. James knew this expression all too well. How many times had he followed it into a tavern, or the heat of battle? 'Now that you mention it, perhaps Julia is just the kind of woman you need. Sizeable inheritance. Brother in Parliament. Adept at running an estate. She's a good match.'

James shook his head as he readied his cue stick. Is this what his life had come to? Discussing marriage over a billiard table? Country life must be very dull to lead an old salt like George to such a pastime. 'Interesting suggestion—however, it has two flaws.'

'And they are?'

'One, I have no desire to marry, which you well know.'

'At the moment, yes, but there's always the future.'

'And two, your Artemis doesn't like me.'

'Of course she likes you. She's just an awkward girl. Spent too much time in the country, odd relatives and all that.'

'Odd indeed.' James hit the cue ball and it sailed past the red ball. 'I see a great deal of Paul in his sister.'

'There you are with the past again. Forget it. Paul was young. You were young and both of you stupid.'

'I'd hardly say stupid.'

'Stubborn, then, if you like. You'd be surprised to see him now.'

'"Surprised" is not the word. Does your Artemis know I wrote to the Admiralty against Paul's promotion?'

'I didn't see the need to inform her and I suggest you don't either if you wish to have a pleasant visit. You don't want to be on the wrong end of my niece's temper.'

As if I needed the warning. 'You don't think she'll find out?'

'He's off at sea and you're here, not likely to meet.'

James had to admire George's devil-may-care attitude. Here was a man who always believed everything would work out swimmingly and somehow for him it always did. What James wouldn't give for even a small measure of George's optimism, but the last year had left him anything but optimistic. The long days of his recovery followed by the even longer days of stalking the Admiralty, asking, then begging for another commission, had taken their toll.

During the year of his recovery, younger, fitter men with more prestigious connections had passed him by, and not even his loyal years of service were enough to secure him another ship. He could almost smell the oil on the wood panels of Admiral Stuart's office the day he told James there would be no more commissions and encouraged—insisted, one might say—James enjoy his fortune while he still could.

In the end, despite his disappointment, he'd secretly been relieved. It shamed him to admit it, but he couldn't lie to himself. Death had passed over him. Ten years ago he'd have shrugged it off and raced to face the devil once more. This time he couldn't. He wanted to live free of violence and risks, to take care of his family and see his sister's future children grow up, but without his command he saw nothing, no meaning or activity, just an endless set of days stretching out before him.

James refilled his drink from the small decanter of brandy on the table near the window. He hated this emptiness. It made him feel like a ship in a storm with a broken rudder at the mercy of driving winds and an unforgiving sea. He took a deep drink, careful not to enjoy too much the burning in the back of his throat. He'd seen other men come home and lose themselves in gin, women and cards, their energy wasted by a lack of duty and direction. He put the glass down, knowing his future wasn't at the bottom of a bottle, but was it really as close as Cable Grange? Perhaps an estate would give him a sense of purpose again, a chance to do something more than grieve for his past and the future he'd planned for himself.

James watched while George calculated his

next shot. 'Why isn't your little Artemis already married?'

'Says she's not interested.'

'A woman not interested in marriage? Next you'll tell me you believe in mermaids.'

'I do. I saw one off the coast of Florida once. She's not interested in marriage. However, a man with an estate could change her mind. If you're determined to buy Cable Grange, she's the woman you need to run it.' George took his time lining up his shot, looking quite proud of himself for what he considered a brilliant idea.

James couldn't resist the opportunity to rib his old friend. 'So your niece is only interested in marrying a man for his estate?'

George whiffed the cue ball then straightened up, indignant. 'She's not that kind of young lady. She's clever, a real woman of substance, made running Knollwood her life, but the place isn't hers. Charles plans to assume control when he comes home at the end of the month. Where will she be then?'

'You could leave her Creedon Abbey.'

'I probably will…' George floundered. Clearly he hadn't thought of this and James enjoyed watching the older man work to recover himself. 'But I'm not at death's door yet. I plan to live at least another twenty years. Spend some time with her, get to know her, you'll see what I mean.'

James walked to the window, noticing the threatening clouds gathering overhead. Their darkness layered the hills with damp shadows, making the hour feel late. Somewhere across the hills and valleys sat Cable Grange. Watching the wind shake the tall hedges of the garden, he tried to picture himself as lord of the manor, spending his days in land management with all its hundreds of concerns, but he had trouble imagining it.

Reaching up under his jacket, he felt for the jagged, raised scar. Yes, he was lucky to be alive and sometimes it made him think he wanted a wife and a family. What would it be like to enjoy the kind of happiness he'd witnessed between his parents before his father died or the love he saw in his sister's eyes when she walked with her husband? He'd tried so many times while convalescing to imagine the future, but always it remained shrouded in a grey fog of uncertainty. The sudden end to his naval career made the years before him seem meaningless while old wounds and betrayals arose from the past to dominate his mind.

A bolt of lightning split the distant horizon and the image of Miss Howard atop that beast of a horse commanding him like a common seaman seared his mind. Tight desire coursed through him at the memory of her tongue tracing the line of her lips and the curious need illuminating her face. Her free spirit and courage reminded him of Caribbean ladies, bringing a smile to his face at the memory of warm afternoons and even warmer nights in the islands. Those days seemed like a lifetime ago yet today, in Miss Howard's presence, their carefree ease sparked deep inside him for the first time in over a year.

The feeling made him uneasy. He'd experienced something like it once before, allowing it to guide him, and he'd come to regret it.

He downed the last of the brandy, forcing back the encroaching sadness. He wasn't ready for another life-altering change and certainly had no intention of courting Miss Howard.

As James examined the cut-crystal glass, an idea suddenly came to him, so simple yet brilliantly amusing. George was determined to meddle with yet another scheme. Why not catch him up in one of James's devising, give him a friendly taste of his own medicine?

'Perhaps you're right. I should give more thought to the idea of marriage,' James announced, strolling back to the table and scrutinising the position of the balls.

George's smile broadened. 'Indeed.'

'A man needs a woman to make a comfortable home for him.'

'One with a sense of how to run things properly.'

'The perfect mistress to complement him.'

'Exactly.'

'A woman like Miss Taylor.'

'Annette?' George sputtered. 'You must be joking.'

'I'm quite serious. She's well brought up and pleasing to view.' James leaned over the table to take a shot, pretending not to notice George's stunned expression.

'But there's nothing there, no substance.'

'Good. It makes life less complicated.' James hit the cue ball, sending it bouncing off the side to hit the red ball. Straightening up, he worked to contain his laughter as George stared slack jawed at him.

'Annette?'

James smiled to himself, realising just how much fun this harmless revenge would be.

Chapter Four

The clock in the hallway chimed six times as Julia rushed across the marble floor, late for dinner again. Stopping outside the dining-room door, she ran her hands over her hair, tucking a loose tendril into her *coiffure*. Mary, her lady's maid, had been too busy with Annette to arrange Julia's hair so she'd done it herself, pulling it back into a more flattering bun and allowing a few curls to hang about her face. The *coiffure* was far from stylish, but it framed her features much better than Emily's plain creation. Pulling the bodice of the light-blue muslin dress lower, she hitched up the pink sash in an effort to make it appear more fashionable. The ribbon refused to co-operate, slipping back down to her waist. With a sigh of frustration, she gave up, knowing she'd dressed as well as could be expected for dinner at Knollwood, which was never a formal affair.

Until tonight. The instant Julia stepped into the dining room she remembered Emily's instructions to dress for their new guest. She'd been so distracted by planning her tactics with Simon, she'd completely forgotten.

'I'm so glad you could join us. I was afraid Knollwood business would keep you away.' Emily's high, nervous voice pulled Julia out of her momentary shock and she took in everyone's attire. Mother's deep-maroon mantua, though of an older style, suited her matronly frame while Emily and Annette's dresses were the height of London fashion. Simon wore a coat of the finest material and Uncle George and Captain Covington looked dashing in their uniforms. Plain muslin in the face of so much silk only emphasised her lack of fashion. For a moment, Julia contemplated making her excuses, feigning a headache or some other feminine nonsense, then changed her mind.

I've already made a fool of myself. No sense starving now. Throwing back her shoulders, she strode into the room.

'Yes, Knollwood business can be quite exacting, but I wouldn't dream of missing dinner.' She took her place next to Simon, across from Annette and Captain Covington.

'You look very lovely this evening,' the captain offered across the table.

'Thank you.' Was he teasing her? It was difficult to tell. His beguiling smile reminded her of the one Paul always used to flatter pretty ladies at the assembly hall.

'The affairs of Knollwood must be very demanding to make you lose track of time,' Annette mocked.

'No, I was quite aware of the time,' Julia replied coolly, annoyed by her stepcousin's condescending tone.

'Perhaps you could learn a thing or two about managing your affairs, Annette,' Simon suggested, dabbing the corners of his mouth with his napkin.

'Now you prefer bluestockings?' Annette frowned. 'I thought you felt education was wasted on women?'

'I do. It leads a woman to interfere too much in a man's business.' He fixed an icy stare on his sister, who coloured under the remark, but said nothing.

Julia sensed more to this conversation than a simple debate of female education, but having no interest in the intricacies of the Taylors' personal business, she concentrated on enjoying her meal.

'Julia, Jim was telling us the latest news from London regarding Napoleon,' Uncle George announced. 'It appears Admiral Nelson will face him before the month is out?'

The food turned to dirt in her mouth. 'Do you think so?'

'It's a very real possibility,' the captain answered with measured words, fingering the spoon next to his plate.

'Paul's ship, *HMS Pickle*, is with Admiral Nelson's fleet. He could be injured, or worse.' Her voice quavered with worry and she didn't care who heard it or what they thought.

'Even if there is a battle, *HMS Pickle* is a small ship used to send messages or fetch supplies. She won't see much action.'

'But there's still a chance Paul will be involved in the fighting?'

'There is, but let's hope if Admiral Nelson and your brother face him, the battle is quick and decisive in Britain's favour.'

His sympathetic eyes touched her and she wished they were alone so she could pour out all her worries to him. He would understand, perhaps even take her in his sturdy arms and, with tender, reassuring words, drive away all her fears for Paul.

'Admiral Nelson will lose more than a battle if he continues his indiscretion with Mrs Hamilton,' Annette added, indifferent to Julia's concerns. 'Don't you agree, Captain Covington?'

'I'm afraid I don't follow town gossip,' he answered, but Annette refused to relinquish his attention or the table's.

'Don't you find his indiscretion scandalous?'

Julia noticed the way his fingers tightened on the stem of his wine glass. 'Great men are always granted some leeway.'

'If society shunned him, then who would lead the Navy against France?' Julia demanded, irritated by Annette's prattle. 'Or would you prefer the French on our shores? Perhaps they would be more delightful in the drawing room.'

'How droll to discuss politics at dinner,' Annette sniffed. 'Captain Covington, you must tell me all about your sister's wedding.'

With a twinge of regret, Julia left the captain to Annette and focused on the dandy beside her. How could she possibly capture his interest? She couldn't simply announce the size of her inheritance and hope he took the bait. Conversation seemed the key, but since his arrival they'd barely exchanged ten words. Now she had to captivate him with witty repartee? It seemed a Herculean feat, but one she had to accomplish.

'Simon, do you ride?' she asked in her most pleasing voice. The young man turned his pointed chin over his starched cravat, staring at her as though she possessed three heads.

'Of course,' he sneered.

Julia clamped her hands together in her lap, screwing the smile on her face. 'I suppose no country ride could compare to the fashionable hour in Rotten Row?'

'On at least that point you are correct,' he lisped, returning to his meal.

Her cheeks burned with the strain of holding her smile. For a moment, the game felt like more trouble than it was worth, but the thought of having her own estate urged her on. 'You must be an excellent horseman.'

Simon's knife and fork clanked against the plate. 'I prefer the elegance of a phaeton—surely you've heard of them, even here in the country.'

She resisted the urge to empty her plate in his lap, continuing to remain charming as though nothing was amiss. 'Oh, yes. When I receive my inheritance I plan to purchase one. Perhaps you can help me select the best?'

'Your inheritance?' His bored eyes almost sparkled at the mention of money. She leaned towards him, dropping her voice.

'Yes, I receive it as soon as I'm married. Tell me about your phaeton. I imagine it is one of the finest in London.'

Just as she suspected, flattery worked. Simon puffed up at the opportunity to discuss himself. 'It's second only to the prince's.'

Despite the loss of her appetite, Julia soldiered on. 'Oh, you know the prince? How wonderful.'

'He complimented me on my rig.' Simon's voice dripped with pride.

'Please, tell me all about it.'

What followed was the most boring and tortuous hour of Julia's life as Simon described, in minute detail, his phaeton. From the corner of her eye she noticed Uncle George and Emily exchanging baffled looks. Even Captain Covington threw her a sideways glance and for a brief moment she felt ashamed of her plan. Only her mother seemed indifferent, slipping bits of food to Charlemagne, who sat on the floor next to her chair.

'The squabs are far more comfortable than the average phaeton. I had the leather dyed dark green,' Simon continued and Julia gazed up at him through her lashes, mimicking the way Annette flattered the captain. If only her dress were cut as deeply as Annette's. However, such a ploy might make her scheme too obvious.

After what felt like an eternity, Emily rose, ending dinner. 'Shall the ladies retire to the drawing room?'

Julia forced herself not to jump up and run into the adjoining room. Instead she smiled coyly at Simon as she rose. 'Perhaps we can discuss it more later?'

'Perhaps.' He didn't seem enthusiastic at the prospect.

Massaging her aching cheeks, Julia followed the other women into the drawing room. Taking *The Monk* out of her dress pocket, she situated herself on the sofa to read, hoping the others would leave her in peace. Her hope was short lived when Emily walked over to the card table near the window and shuffled the deck. 'Ladies, would you care for a game of piquet?'

'I'd love to play,' Annette announced, choosing her place at the table and taking the deck from Emily. 'I'll deal.'

Julia buried her nose in her book, pretending not to hear the invitation, even when Emily cleared her throat to gain her attention.

'Come play, Julia,' her mother gently ordered.

With a sigh, Julia put down her book and joined the others at the table.

'We're always playing in London and the stakes are often very high. Sometimes gentlemen lose a great deal at the tables,' Annette explained, dealing the cards.

'Perhaps the men of London are not very sensible, for it takes only a tiny amount of sense to know one should not bet what one cannot afford to lose.' Julia laid down a card, then chose another.

'No gentleman worth his salt would dare refuse a wager.'

'Then there must be many poor fools about the London ballrooms.'

'Do you consider Captain Covington a fool?'

Julia shrugged, trying to imagine the captain dancing, but she could only picture him gambling in some tropical den of iniquity. She fought back a laugh, struggling to keep her face a bland mask of uninterest. 'I haven't known the captain long enough to comment on the merits of his wit—however, if he lives in London, the odds are against him not being a fool.'

'I assure you, Captain Covington is no fool,' her mother interjected. 'He has proven himself a hero on more than one occasion.'

Julia didn't respond, wondering what her mother would think if she knew about the captain's involvement with the Governor of Bermuda's widowed sister. She'd overheard Uncle George telling Paul about it once. It was quite shocking.

'How long has George known Captain Covington?' Annette asked.

'Ten years,' Mother answered. 'Captain Covington was a lieutenant on George's ship in the war against France during the First Coalition.

His service was so distinguished he was given command of his own ship. He's very well travelled, Julia.'

'Is he now?' Julia barely heard her. She was too busy concentrating on which card to play next so she could lose and end the game.

'George tells me Captain Covington is a very sensible man when it comes to money, much like you, Julia,' her mother remarked, attempting to draw Julia into the conversation.

'Interesting,' Julia mumbled, disappointed by her excellent hand for it made losing very difficult.

'Captain Covington and I spoke a great deal this afternoon and it was as if we've known each other for years. We have a great deal in common for we both adore cheese,' Annette continued.

Julia selected another card and scowled for it was a good one. 'Most men in London adore food. That's why there's so much gout in town.'

Emily coughed disapprovingly.

'London is a gourmand's paradise,' Annette insisted. 'I advised Captain Covington to hire a French chef. All the best houses have them. He's a very affable man. I'm surprised he's not married for he'd do well with a wife.'

'A man of thirty with a sensible head is a rarity these days,' Emily said more to Julia than to Annette.

'He's very handsome,' Annette added.

'Yes, he is, don't you agree, Julia?' Mother entreated.

Julia took another card and smiled to find it a bad one before she noticed the three women waiting for her response. 'Pardon me?'

Emily scowled at Julia's inability to follow the conversation. 'Captain Covington is very handsome, don't you agree?'

Yes, she did, but she was not about to admit it. 'I hadn't thought on the matter.' She rearranged her cards, needing only another bad one to lose.

'I'm told he's a very accomplished horseman,' Emily added. 'Perhaps, Julia, you could accompany Captain Covington on a ride tomorrow?'

Julia watched the rain hit the window, streaking down the panes. Without his afternoon ride, Manfred would need a good gallop. She did not relish the idea of trying to control him in a gentle trot alongside Captain Covington's mount. Hopefully the weather would clear by morning and she could take Manfred out before duty intruded on the day.

'I'm sure Uncle George will escort him if he wishes to ride.' Julia continued to study her cards, avoiding Emily's chastising scowl. 'He's better company for the captain than I am.'

'Of course nothing can compare to Rotten Row at the fashionable hour. Captain Covington promised to join me there when we return to London,' Annette said, drawing another card. Julia judged from the smile on her narrow face that Annette had a good hand. It was only a matter of moments before Julia could lose the game and put an end to this tiring conversation.

'I won. I won,' Annette announced much to Julia's great relief, though she pretended, like Emily and Mother, to be disappointed. They slid their sovereigns across the table and Annette swept the coins into her palm, making Julia wonder how someone from London with a carriage and four could covet a few crowns.

'Shall we play again?' Annette shuffled the deck and the entrance of the men saved Julia the trouble of declining.

'Ladies, we're here to amuse you,' Uncle George announced, making his way to the card table. Simon didn't come in with the men and Julia wasn't the only one who noticed his absence.

'Where's Simon?' Annette asked, dealing the cards.

'It appears he had some pressing business in Daringford,' Uncle George explained with obvious disdain, taking Julia's place at the table.

Julia stood behind Uncle George, drumming her fingers on the back of the wooden chair, watching him arrange his hand. She felt disappointed, but also relieved at being spared another hour of Simon's pompous chatter. Unable to charm a missing man, she decided to learn more about gambling, thinking it might be the only real way to capture her stepcousin's very small heart.

James stepped into the room, his eyes seeking out Miss Howard. She didn't acknowledge him, but stood over George's shoulder watching the play. He resisted the urge to join her and initiate the intelligent conversation he now craved after a dinner spent listening to Miss Taylor's vapid gossip. However, showing Miss Howard too much attention would only make George more determined in his matchmaking efforts. Instead he walked to the sofa and picked up the small book lying open on the cushions.

James examined the cover of *The Monk*, then held it up. 'Miss Taylor, I believe you left your novel here.'

'That is mine.' Miss Howard crossed the room, gesturing for the book.

'I wouldn't have guessed you one for Gothic novels,' he quipped. He expected her to read dry tracts on crops, not notorious novels. What other passions lay hidden beneath her quiet exterior?

'You think a woman who manages an estate can't enjoy novels?'

She took the offered tome and her fingers brushed his, sending a shock through him. She must have felt it, too, for he noticed the slight hint of a blush under the scattering of freckles across the bridge of her nose.

'Not at all. What other books have you enjoyed?'

She sat down on the sofa, looking as though she wasn't sure if she should tell him. A single ringlet teased the soft sweep of her jaw and the flickering candlelight caressed the fine line of her cheeks. 'I recently finished Edward Ive's *A Voyage from England to India.*'

He sat on the sofa across from her, leaning against the padded back. 'An excellent book.'

Her face brightened. 'You've read it?'

'You think a man in the Navy can't enjoy books about travel?' he teased, delighted by the easy smile it brought to her lips.

'Not at all.'

He sat forwards, his elbows on his knees. 'I read a great deal last year. Have you travelled?'

'Only as far as Portsmouth. But with the way Mr Ives describes India, I know one day I will have to see it.'

Her face lit up at the prospect of visiting India, the passionate response striking his core. She might dress like a stern governess, but he'd seen too much of the woodland nymph to be fooled.

What would it be like to make her blaze with more sensuous emotions, his fingers stoking the heat simmering beneath her compliant exterior? He shifted on the sofa to cover the sudden fullness in his loins. What a powerful effect this curious young woman had on him. 'Then why not set out for Bombay?'

She laid the book on her lap with a sigh. 'A woman does not have the freedom of a man to travel.'

'Perhaps you need an adventurous husband.'

She raised one disbelieving eyebrow. 'No such creature exists.'

'Then you'll have to go alone.' He couldn't resist teasing her, delighting in the honest reaction it provoked. 'Someone of your pluck would prove quite the explorer.'

She glanced at the card table and, satisfied the others were too busy playing to notice, leaned forwards, bringing them much closer than decency allowed. He smelled the crisp scent of rosewater, noticed the slight curl of her long lashes. He chanced a brief peek at her breasts. Though well hidden by the dress's high bodice, they pressed against the blue fabric, offering a hint of the creamy skin beneath. The heaviness in his manhood increased and he dug his fingers into his thigh to keep from leaning forwards to claim her full, teasing lips.

'Do you assume because my accomplishments are unusual that I have a flagrant disregard for convention?' Her mischievous eyes dared him to respond.

He leaned closer, dropping his voice, eager to meet her challenge. 'I very much admire your accomplishments. And your disregard for convention.'

'You like unconventional women?'

'Indeed. It gives them a certain mystery.'

'Really?' She leaned closer, her heady voice and smouldering eyes tightening the desire coursing through him. 'I suppose you've met many mysterious women.'

'I've known a few.'

'Yes, your time in the Navy must have acquainted you with many ladies in many ports.'

'Julia!' Emily exclaimed.

They both turned to see everyone staring at them. He'd forgotten about the others and obviously she had, too. He expected the rebuke to make her retreat back into a compliant, self-conscious miss. Instead, she rose with all the composure of a lady of the first water.

'It was a pleasure debating with you, Captain.' Ignoring her sister-in-law's stunned face, she dipped a slow, graceful curtsy, then strode from the room. He watched her leave, captivated and impressed. Here was no Artemis, but Venus waiting for the right man to draw her out.

'She's a real spitfire, Jim.' George laughed.

'A bit too forward, if you ask me,' Miss Taylor remarked and George snorted.

'No one did, Annette.'

Julia closed her bedroom door, leaning against the smooth wood to catch her breath. Her fingers felt beneath the doorknob for the brass key and, turning it in the lock, a sense of relief accompanied the click.

What had just transpired? She didn't know, but it thrilled her as much as riding Manfred at a full gallop across the hills. What had she seen in the captain's eyes? Desire, excitement and a few more dangerous emotions she felt along the back of her spine.

She hurried to the window seat, her hands shaking as if she'd almost been caught rifling through Charles's private papers. Leaning her forehead against the cool glass, she watched the rain falling in sheets, running down the window and blurring the view of the garden. If Paul were home, she could tell him about the captain and the taunting riot of emotions tightening her stomach. He'd put a name to them, help her understand why the captain ignited her senses.

Fingering the books strewn about the upholstered window seat, she pushed aside a pamphlet on crop rotation to reveal a large book on India. Flipping through it, she examined the coloured plates of Indian gods and goddesses and the dark ladies with their almond eyes, veils and jewels. Pictures of the Mughal emperors riding their elephants, accompanied by exotic animals and splendidly dressed courtiers, decorated the pages.

The women in the paintings of the palace stretched their arms out towards the men, their breasts taut against crimson saris, their round hips hugged by the delicate fabric. The image of Captain Covington's sharp eyes, the rich tones of his voice and the heat of his fingertips brushing against hers filled her mind. There'd been a moment during their discussion when she thought he meant to kiss her.

No, I must have imagined it. The captain couldn't possibly possess an interest in her and if he did it was an entirely dishonourable one. The idea should have scandalised her, but deep down she felt flattered.

As she turned the pages, thoughts of the captain continued to dominate her mind. She imagined him sitting atop an elephant, inspecting the fields of an exotic plantation as the monsoons overtook the land, the heat and spices all coming together in his skin, hair and eyes. She pictured herself beside him, standing on a veranda over-looking the jungle. With steam rising from the hot earth, she'd run her hands up over his chest, push the jacket off his shoulders, then follow the line of his back to his waist and hips. She'd tug the white shirt from his breeches, trace the hard flesh and muscles of his stomach with her fingers, then dip lower to more sinful places.

Abandoning the book, she hurried to the wardrobe and pulled the doors open. Dropping to her knees, she felt around the bottom, behind shoes and old quilts, to a plain box near the back. She took off the lid and removed a shimmer-ing red-and-gold silk sari, a present from Paul many years ago after his first trip to India. Slip-ping off her frock and the cotton chemise, she wrapped the shiny silk around her naked body. It felt glorious next to her skin and she could al-most smell the curry in its deep-red sheen. She imagined the cool feel of the silk to be the mon-soons washing over her, rinsing away the dust and heat of Bombay.

A flash of lightning caught her eye. She turned to see her reflection in the window as the thun-der rolled overhead. She pulled her hair out of its bun and it fell over her shoulders, their creamy white colour further whitened by the dazzling sari. The way the fabric traced the curve of her thighs, hugging her breasts and hips like the alluring women in the pictures, delighted her.

Is this what the captain meant by mysterious? Her skin tingled to discover his meaning and she wondered if the weight of him on top of her would feel as heavenly as the silk? Perhaps he'd run his hands over the firm, round line of her hips? Cup her breast like the men in another, more wicked book she'd once seen.

Suddenly the other book came to mind, the one she'd found a few years ago hidden in Paul's wardrobe. Those pages held the same almond eyes, voluptuous women and robust men, only the pictures were more intimate, sensual and forbidden. What would it be like to delight in some of those illicit poses with the captain?

She shuddered, simultaneously excited and embarrassed. What would Charles or Emily think if they knew she had such wicked thoughts or acted like a Cyprian in private?

Unwinding the sari from her body, she folded the fabric, then returned it to the box and the back of the wardrobe. She slipped on her shift, blew out the candle and settled into bed. Staring up at the dark ceiling, she wondered if she should have set her cap at the captain instead of Simon. Lightning flashed, branding the twisted shadow of the oak tree outside across the ceiling before the room went black. Like the shadow, the idea of pursuing the captain gave her a small shock of fear. He acted on her nerves like no man had ever done before, the effect both thrilling and terrifying. If she played her game with him, could she jilt him? Would he let her?

Sitting up, she bunched the flatness out of her pillow. Of course he'd let her jilt him. Hadn't he spent the entire meal entranced with Annette, making his preference for her stepcousin clear? He'd only showed an interest in her when she'd acted like a strumpet. In the future, she must behave like a perfect lady in his presence.

She rolled over, pulling the blanket up under her chin and nestling into the warm mattress. Another bolt of lightning illuminated the room, followed by a deep roll of thunder. The steady plunk of rain hitting the window lulled her to sleep, weaving into her dream about monsoons falling on thick jungles, swelling the river roaring past the grassy bank where she stood, Captain Covington at her side.

Chapter Five

'Thoughts of a certain someone keep you up last night?' George nudged James as they made their way down to the stables. The clouds had cleared overnight and though everything was wet, there was no hint of rain in the brisk morning air.

James laughed, pulling on his riding gloves. 'I never thought you for a romantic.'

'We all have our secrets.'

'What secrets are you hiding?'

'Never mind.' George adjusted his white cravat. 'What exactly were you two so intently discussing?'

'Travel.'

'Who knew it was such an engrossing subject.'

'Very.' James didn't elaborate, for once not wanting to discuss a lady with George. His tête-à-tête with Miss Howard had disturbed him far more than he wanted to admit. He'd seen her surprise when she realised she wasn't properly dressed for dinner and had expected her to flee the room. When she'd determinedly crossed the threshold, he'd silently applauded her decision to stay. Then, during their exchange, the low cadence of her voice and her irrepressible enthusiasm made him feel again like a carefree young naval officer.

James slapped the riding crop against his tall boot. What was he now? A crippled man fit only to languish in the country, the past hounding the unfilled hours, the future torturing him with its emptiness. He'd come so far since his first days in the Navy, the prospect of advancing to commodore discussed more than once with the Admiralty. Not until the bullet struck him had he realised how fast fate could crush a man.

Near the stables they came upon Mr Taylor. Dark circles hung under his red eyes and his clothes, normally as fine as five pence, were ruffled as if he had spent the night in them.

'Simon, fancy a morning ride?' George asked, much to James's surprise. He planned to inspect the Cable Grange land and didn't want any additional company. But sensing George's eagerness to give his stepnephew a difficult time, James didn't object to the invitation.

'I have no interest in a ride,' Simon sneered,

trying to slink past them, but George refused to be put off.

'Come, some fresh air will do you good.' He threw his large arm around Simon's slight shoulders, directing him back to the stables, much to Simon's visible displeasure.

The stables occupied a flat parcel of land hidden from view of the house by a small grove of trees. Crossing the paddock, George led them inside where the groom sat polishing a saddle.

'John, please help Simon find a suitable mount,' George instructed, pushing Simon at the man.

'Yes, Captain Russell,' John answered. 'If you'll follow me, Mr. Taylor, I have just the animal for you.'

'Happy to see me, Percy?' George stood at the first stall, running a hand over his horse's chestnut mane. 'Choose any you like, Jim. They're all some of the finest horseflesh in the county. Another of Julia's accomplishments.'

'Yes, an impressive collection.' James walked down the line of horses, trying to decide which to ride. All the stallions impressed him, but none so much as the black one in the last stall. Here was the darkest, largest, most sinister horse he'd ever seen. He recognised it as the animal Miss Howard had ridden when she'd surprised him in the woods.

'That's Manfred. Miss Howard's horse,' John offered with pride. 'She jumps him when she has a mind, too.'

James moved to rub the horse's massive neck, but it backed up, its eyes wide and wild. 'If I hadn't seen her riding him myself, I'd say he's too much animal for such a young lady.'

'If he's truly too much animal, Captain Covington,' a soft female voice sang from behind him, 'I'm sure we can find an even-tempered gelding for you.'

James turned to see Miss Howard watching him, a challenging smile decorating the corners of her full lips. She wore a stylish dark-blue riding habit, well tailored to her petite figure. The same saucy air she'd captivated him with last night made her cheeks glow, igniting his blood. The image of her beneath him on a fresh mound of hay, the golden morning sun illuminating the pink tones of her flesh while his fingers undid the long row of buttons on the back of her habit, teased his already aching body.

'I'm sorry if I've given offence, Miss Howard. It's not my intention,' he apologised, letting the image of the soft velvet sliding from her shoulders linger for just a moment longer before forcing it away. 'I'm merely surprised such a beast is suitable for a lady.'

She walked past him, rubbing the horse lovingly on the nose, taming the fire in the creature's eyes.

'Or do you think the lady is unsuitable for the horse?' she challenged with a sly grin, the playful curve of her lips exciting him more than he cared to admit. 'Would you like to ride him?'

James examined the beast, hesitant. One throw might undo the last year of recovery. However, something in the way the little Artemis challenged him made the risk irresistible.

'May I?'

'If you think you can handle him. He'll need a firm rider since he didn't have his afternoon exercise yesterday.'

James flexed his left hand, feeling the loss of strength more keenly than ever before. He shouldn't ride. He should admit he couldn't handle the beast and decline like a reasonable man, but this morning he didn't feel like being reasonable. 'I've handled a ship in a storm. I can handle a horse.'

'If you like.' She stepped back, motioning for John to take control of Manfred.

'Good luck to you, sir. Thrown off everyone who's tried to ride him, 'cept Miss Julia and Mr Paul Howard,' John remarked, leading Manfred out of the stall. The horse strained against the harness with pent-up energy and James balled his left hand.

'Shall we?' James waved towards the paddock.

Following Miss Howard outside, he admired the gentle sway of her hips as she strode into the sunlight, realising there was more to her than exuberant youth. She possessed a firm determination he admired, even if others in society did not.

John led an agitated and now saddled Manfred into the yard, ending all of James's pleasant thoughts. George, sitting astride Percy, shot him a questioning look, but James brushed it aside, his attention firmly focused on the beast. He'd never shrunk from a challenge, but if the horse proved too difficult to manage, the idea of being thrown in front of such an audience held no appeal. Unconsciously, he touched his shoulder.

'You aren't afraid, Captain? Are you?' Miss Howard teased, her capricious smile steeling James's resolve.

'What's to fear? He's only a horse and I've certainly faced worse.' James took the reins and Manfred shook his head, pawing at the packed dirt. 'Easy, boy.'

He stroked the horse's neck, cautious of the animal's dark, wild eyes. Manfred settled down long enough for James to step into the saddle. Ignoring the throbbing in his left shoulder, he gripped the reins with both hands in an effort to hide his weakness. Once comfortably astride, James shot Julia a surefire grin.

'I told you I could handle him.'

No sooner were the words out of his mouth than Manfred, contemptuous of a foreign rider, bucked. James clamped his thighs tight against the animal, determined to stay in the saddle. Manfred landed hard on all fours, then bolted, shooting out of the paddock. The countryside flew by, the wind more cutting than the pebbles and mud kicked up by Manfred's hooves. James sat back in the saddle, choked up on the reins and pulled hard, but the beast fought him. Gritting his teeth at the searing pain tearing through his shoulder, James seesawed the reins until Manfred, tired from his exertion, had no choice but to relent. Slowing down, Manfred trotted in a circle, breathing fast and snorting before finally coming to a halt.

James bent over in the saddle and closed his eyes, the pain in his shoulder making him dizzy. His right hand shook from fatigue and his thighs burned when he eased his hold on the beast's flanks. With a deep breath, he straightened and allowed his body to relax. The throbbing in his shoulder subsided to a dull ache and he opened his eyes, amazed by how much ground they'd covered.

'Well done, Manfred!' James shouted, his excitement echoing off the nearby hills. He laughed hard for a long time, the thrill of the ride charging him like St Elmo's fire. He'd experienced the same feeling once before during a hurricane off Barbados when he'd manned the helm after the rigging broke loose and knocked out the helmsman.

'Now I see why your mistress enjoys riding you. Perhaps there is some excitement in the country after all.' Still laughing, he slapped Manfred on the neck. 'Come, let's return to your lady. I think she'll be surprised.'

The horse's ears twitched and the animal settled into a challenging but manageable trot. They returned to the paddock, greeted by the cheers and shouts of the gathered crowd. Word of his daring ride must have spread among the servants for there were double the number of grooms and stable hands than before and James noticed a fair bit of blunt changing hands. Even George caught a coin flipped up from John. It wasn't the first time James had found himself the subject of a wager, but today it held a certain triumph intensified by Miss Howard's impressed eyes.

She stood away from the others in the shade of the stable, clapping her gloved hands in congratulations.

He manoeuvred Manfred next to her, clucking him to a stop. 'An enjoyable beast, Artemis. No trouble at all.'

With an impish smile, she tapped his right

hand with her riding crop. 'Then perhaps you should loosen your grip.'

Releasing his tight hold, he knew she'd caught him out, but he didn't mind. Having controlled the horse and proven his mettle made the experience worth the agony he'd surly endure tonight.

Manfred snorted, stepping back and forth. 'Whoa,' James soothed, calming him with a quick tug of the reins.

'Jim, if you're done playing with Manfred, then let's be off,' George joked, guiding Percy towards the bridle path. Simon's gelding fell into step behind Percy, much to its rider's visible displeasure.

James nodded at Miss Howard, who curtsied in return, her upturned face and playful smile calling to him. He wanted to pull her up behind him, dash off across the countryside with her clinging to his back, the two of them alone together. Unfortunately, such daydreams were better left to poetry and he kicked Manfred into a walk, directing him next to Percy.

'Never thought I'd see the day when anyone but Julia or Paul took Manfred's reins,' George said, impressed.

'I still can't believe the woman rides this beast.' Manfred tensed as if intending to rear, forcing James to concentrate on the animal beneath him. This would be no leisure ride for the horse would throw him if James ever let his control wane. No, he had to keep working Manfred to make him behave.

'I'm surprised to see you taking such a risk.'

'So am I,' James admitted, feeling something more than pain, bitterness and anger for the first time in months. He was careful not to revel too much in the feeling, knowing it might not last.

George led them along a path circling the woods, past newly planted fields and pastures full of grazing sheep. A wide valley stretched out around them. Beyond it, woods surrounded by neat rows of well-ploughed fields extended up into the hills. Labourers worked while the overseers stood nearby giving directions.

'They rotate the four fields to get a better crop. Julia introduced the idea after reading about it.' George turned in his saddle to face Simon, who'd fallen behind. 'You could learn a lot from Julia, Simon.'

'I doubt it.' Simon hunched over in the saddle, shielding his eyes from the morning sun. 'I have no interest in riding further.' He turned his horse around and cantered off to the stables.

George moved to recall him, but James stopped him. 'Let him go. Looks like he's been in his cups all night.'

'You don't know the half of it.'

'Why not put a stop to it, or speak to your brother about ending it?'

'If Simon wants to ruin himself, so be it.'

'What about Miss Taylor? Shame to let him drag her down.'

'She has a small inheritance from her mother and will probably catch some poor fool with a sizeable income.'

'I hardly call myself a fool.' James puffed up with mock indignation.

'You aren't for her.' George scowled.

They rode for some time, George relaying London gossip as they crossed meadows, streams and fields. James listened to George's tales with half an ear, enjoying the crisp air and the steady gait of the horse. A few wispy clouds hung in the sky, which shone a rich shade of blue like many he'd seen during still days at sea. The chill of autumn filled the air, but it wasn't sharp or biting, and James hoped the winter cold would come late this year. After spending so much time in the dirty air of London, he craved more days like this.

'We're on Cable Grange land now,' George announced after they'd ridden a good distance.

James took in the sudden change in the landscape. The topography was the same, but the meadows showed the lack of the prosperity so evident at Knollwood. Thin, ragged sheep grazed in the meadows while the fields, many of which should have been well ploughed, stood fallow and full of weeds.

They moved from the small path to a wide country lane. The road split, one branch winding down the hill, the other sloping up to the iron gates of Cable Grange. Stopping at the fork afforded them a view of the rutted and muddy drive leading up to the main house. Even from this distance the neglect was evident in the dingy grey capstones, dirty windows and ivy-choked walls.

'Quite a difference,' James remarked.

'No revenge you could have exacted would have done what they've done to themselves.'

James didn't answer. He'd expected to find satisfaction in seeing Melinda's ruined estate. Instead he felt a certain pity for her, the emotion taking him by surprise. Maybe George was right. Perhaps the past didn't matter now.

'Let's go before someone sees us.' George turned Percy around and James followed. They had started down the road when a curricle came over the hill, slowing as it approached. James's stomach tightened at the sight of the driver and his female companion.

'Well, well, well, now of all times James Covington gets on his high horse to pay me a visit,' Wilkins sneered from his seat, taking in James and Manfred. Rowan still possessed the greasy features of a scoundrel and his dark hair, cut short, failed to enhance his thin face or hide the hard lines under his red eyes. As with his wife, London living had taken its toll. 'Here to kick me while I'm down?'

'You brought this on yourself, Wilkins.'

'Still the moralist. You'd think killing all those foreign soldiers might have taken it out of you. But I suppose you didn't come to see me.'

'No, he's not so hard-hearted, Rowan, though he's not above bragging,' Melinda answered with a sweet smile that turned James's stomach. 'He's come to flash his blunt at the auction, show me what I missed out on all those years ago.'

'Shut up, you. We're not going anywhere,' Rowan spat.

'Of course we aren't.' Melinda laughed, then blew James a kiss. 'Have a lovely ride.'

Rowan flicked the reins, setting the curricle into motion. It tore down the drive, pitching when the wheel caught a rut before righting itself.

'Now you've seen it, do you still want it?' George asked.

'Yes.' Memories of a summer in Portsmouth twelve years ago when he'd loved a woman and she'd thrown him over for lack of a fortune taunted him. He'd been a fool to lose his heart to someone like her. Studying the crumbling stone walls and overgrown fields, he knew her decaying life should vindicate him, but he wasn't cruel enough to delight in her misery, only his own.

'It won't suit you,' George said.

'What won't?'

'The peace of the country. It'll do for a time, but eventually you'll need more adventure than just what crops to plant and when.'

'I'm done with adventure.'

'Says the man riding Manfred.' George laughed, turning Percy around.

The desire to return to sea hit him with the force of a hurricane. He craved the peace of the ocean, the gentle roll and pitch of the ship, his only concerns their position and the strength of the wind. Feeling under his jacket for the scar, bitter bile rose up in his throat, choking out everything except the throbbing in his shoulder before he forced it down. He would not let anger and longing torment him. No, he would command his feelings like he'd commanded his crew, setting a course and not allowing the fickle winds of emotion to drive him about. The sea was no longer his life and there was no use pining for it.

The small china clock on the mantel chimed the noon hour. Julia sat at her dressing table, knowing there was no way to avoid nuncheon today. Mary stood behind her, arranging her hair into a simple style. Out of the bedroom window, Julia watched Uncle George and Captain Covington ride across the meadow towards the stables.

'Are you all right, miss?' Mary asked, hearing Julia sigh.

'Yes, thank you.' *I'm having my hair done while the captain is riding Manfred.* This would be her permanent lot if Charles and Emily had their way.

Mary hummed a soft tune while she worked and Julia's mind drifted back to the stables and Captain Covington. She hated to admit it, but he was dashing atop Manfred. She'd almost taken John's wager that the captain would be thrown, but the captain's tenacious eyes matched with the steady, fluid way he pulled himself into the saddle made her hold on to her coin. His daring reminded her of Paul, but he possessed a seriousness and maturity her brother lacked. Unlike Charles's self-imposed austerity, the captain's seemed more contemplative, as if something weighed on him. It only appeared in small flashes when he thought no one was looking, but she'd seen it more than once. Whatever it was, it failed to dampen his deep humour. She enjoyed his wit, even if she was jealous of his ability to act and display his talents without fear of rebuke. How often was she able to display hers?

'What do you think, miss?' Mary asked.

Julia examined herself in the mirror. The hairstyle was simple, but not fashionable, and the white muslin dress with the pink check obscured all hint of her figure. Even with the promise of money, dressing like a frump would not help Simon imagine her decorating his arm at a London ball. She might not want to marry him, but she had to make him believe her suitable for society or he'd never make an offer.

'Mary, please bring down my London dresses from the attic,' Julia instructed. The gowns were no longer the height of fashion, but they'd suit her better than her current attire.

Mary's stunned eyes met Julia's in the mirror before the older servant caught herself and dipped a quick curtsy. 'Yes, Miss Howard.'

James watched Miss Howard enter the dining room, Miss Taylor's idle chatter fading away into the background. She glowed like a white sand beach on a sunny island, the sight of her as welcome as land after a long voyage. She took in the room, briefly meeting his eyes. Her face lit up, making the breath catch in his chest. He leaned forwards in his chair, ready to rise, cross the room and feel her hand on his arm while he led her to her seat. He didn't care who saw them or what they said. Let George rib him; it would be worth the teasing to enjoy the sound of her light voice.

The image shattered when her eager eyes went to Mr Taylor and she took her place next to him. James picked up his ale glass and took a long sip to cover his near move, all the while watching Miss Howard over the rim.

'Simon, did you enjoy your morning ride?' she asked.

'It was far from pleasant.' He picked at the food on his plate, his lips turned up in exaggerated disgust.

Her smile faltered before she bolstered it, but her irritated eyes betrayed her true feelings. James wondered what she was about and why she worked so hard to appeal to the dandy. Perhaps Mrs Howard desired their better acquaintance, though from everything he'd witnessed Miss Howard rarely complied with her sister-in-law's requests.

'Captain Covington,' Miss Taylor interrupted his thoughts. 'I would be happy to paint your portrait.'

'Thank you.' He continued to watch Miss Howard, feeling Miss Taylor's irritation. He tossed her a charming smile, exhausted by the constant effort involved in foiling George's matchmaking plans.

Miss Taylor started to say something and

James put down his glass, leaning towards Miss Howard. 'Thank you for allowing me to ride Manfred.'

Miss Howard paused in a comment to Mr Taylor. 'You're welcome.'

'I'd like to ride him again if you don't mind.'

'Of course,' she replied off-handedly, turning back to the fop.

'Tomorrow, perhaps?'

Her perturbed eyes snapped to his. 'Any time you wish.' She returned to Mr Taylor, but James refused to let her go.

'Tell me, how did you come by such a beast?'

'Ah, now there's a story.' George laughed from the end of the table.

Miss Howard forgot her irritation, flashing what James sensed was her first genuine smile of the meal, Mr Taylor forgotten. 'It's Uncle George's fault. He bought Manfred in London.'

'I had a mind to breed warhorses when I first left the Navy,' George added between bits of meat. 'He's a Friesland and who knows what else, but steady as a rock around gunshot.'

'Certainly explains his colour and height,' James remarked. 'But how did you end up with him, Miss Howard?'

'Manfred may be steady as a rock, but he has a temper.'

'Horse dealer failed to mention it,' George admitted.

'The price alone should have made you wary,' she chided.

'Horse dealer did seem awfully eager to be rid of him, but it's my own fault. What do I know about horses? I'm a Navy man.'

'And not one to think through any scheme.' James laughed.

'Perhaps there's some truth to it.' George clapped his hands together. 'Well, none of my men could control him, and after a fortnight I had a mind to put him out to pasture.'

'But this time, he asked my opinion first. I observed Manfred with the grooms and something about him just called to me. Uncle George's men were trying to make him behave, but they were going about it all wrong. Manfred needed a patient hand and a gentle but strong voice.'

'And you possessed both,' James complimented.

'I suppose I did, but I prefer to think it was because I believed in him when no one else did and he thanked me for it.'

'You may be right.'

Miss Howard smiled and he delighted in the dimples at the corner of her lips. For a moment, there was only the two of them in the room. Her amber eyes met his and he felt their heat deep in his body, but the moment was short lived.

'How wonderful you're such an amazing horsewoman,' Miss Taylor interrupted. 'Are you also a skilled painter?'

'I'm adept at no art except running an estate,' Miss Howard admitted with confidence and James silently cheered her for standing up to the ridiculous criticism.

'Yes, I forgot. I plan to draw in the garden this afternoon. I've asked the captain to accompany me. He even volunteered to carry my easel for it can be such a cumbersome thing.' She smiled at James, who shifted in his seat, having forgotten about his offer and wondering how he could extricate himself from it without being rude.

'I think some time outside would do us all a world of good,' Emily announced, trapping James in this bland game.

Half an hour later found everyone in the garden enjoying the unusually warm autumn weather. Even Mr Taylor deigned to drag himself outside, much to Miss Howard's visible delight.

James listened in disbelief when she complimented Mr Taylor on his excellent description of his last evening at White's.

What is she after? he wondered. Was she playing him for his money? Surely she knew he had nothing more than the ready extended by his London creditors. James shifted restlessly, hating the way she nodded, enraptured by the pretentious pink's description of a card game. He refused to admit his anger was jealousy, but there it sat, gnawing at him.

Swallowing it back, he watched Miss Taylor arrange Emily and George into a formal pose on the opposite side of the fish pond. Was this really his life now? Garden parties and flattering London chits? He kept glancing at Miss Howard. Here was a woman who would keep life interesting—if only he could tear her away from the damned coxcomb.

'Should I pull my arm in my sleeve?' George joked once Miss Taylor returned to her canvas. 'I may not be as handsome or slender, but I think I might make a good Nelson.'

Everyone laughed except Miss Taylor, who sketched with her charcoal, and Mr Taylor, who took a pinch of snuff from his silver snuffbox with an affected flourish.

'Rather shameful, the Admiral continuing in such a ruined state,' Mr Taylor lisped. 'Hardly speaks well of Britain to have such a specimen leading our Navy.'

James almost leaned over and punched the idiot in his pursed mouth. If they'd been at White's he'd have called him out, but for the ladies' sake he allowed the comment to drop.

Miss Howard, despite her newfound infatuation, refused to let it stand. 'I think it very fitting he continue. It shows weakness in a man not to carry on after an injury, if he can.'

The remark hit James like a cudgel to the chest. 'Do you extend that opinion to all Navy men, or just Admiral Nelson?'

'All Navy men. If every sailor with a cut or scrape retired we'd have no hope of winning any war.' There was no malice in the statement, just a simple declaration. He wondered if George had told her about his wound.

'What of duty to one's family? Is an only son to die at sea for no other reason than to prove he's not a coward, leaving the future of his family to the cruel whims of fate?'

'A man who chooses the Navy knows the dangers. If his family truly faces ruin then perhaps he should apprentice himself and enter a safe trade, such as tailor.'

'What if he comes home wounded to find responsibility for his mother and sister upon his shoulders?' James flexed his left hand, the memory increasing the pain in his shoulder.

'I cannot speak for every man's situation, but if Admiral Nelson soldiers on then so can other brave men.'

'I think you speak a great deal about something you know nothing about,' he chastised, but she refused to back down. He had to admire the girl's courage, despite her infuriating views.

'And I think you, like most men, dislike opinionated women.' She didn't wait for his response, but turned on her heel and strode off.

'Julia, where are you going?' George said, but she didn't stop.

'I have some urgent business to attend to,' she answered over her shoulder, then disappeared inside.

Mr Taylor coughed as he took another pinch of snuff. 'As I said before, bluestockings always get in a man's business.'

James turned a hard eye on the dandy, who wilted under the harsh gaze. He had a mind to thrash the man, but even with his weak arm it wouldn't be a fair fight. Instead, he decided to enjoy the fine afternoon and have his portrait done as a Christmas present for his sister. He leaned over Miss Taylor's shoulder to admire her sketch, but, unable to keep still, he began pacing, chewing over Miss Howard's remark.

Had she just called him a coward? Did she even know about his injury? Maybe George hadn't told her. Despite George's love of gossip, he had an annoying habit of conveying worthless stories while forgetting to relay critical information, such as Melinda living next door or just how close Miss Howard was to Paul. It was a wonder George had thought to tell him about Cable Grange before the actual sale took place.

'What do you think, Captain?' Miss Taylor asked.

He paused long enough to watch her apply the first colour to the sketch. 'Excellent portrait.'

Why did he care so much about Miss Howard's opinion? It was only the assumption of an ignorant country girl with no real understanding of the world. Let her think him a coward. Once he returned to London, he'd never be troubled with her again.

'Jim, what's wrong? You're acting like a nervous hen,' George called and James finally noticed everyone's curious eyes.

'I just remembered a matter I must attend to.'

'But your portrait,' Miss Taylor protested.

'Another time, perhaps. Please, excuse me.' He bowed, then headed into the house.

Julia scratched out the last line of figures, marring the ledger page with yet another mistake. Outside, Uncle George laughed and her temper flared. Throwing down her pencil, she leaned back in the chair, watching the others laugh and pose for Annette and noticing Captain Covington wasn't with them. After this morning, she'd thought him a different type of man. Just now, he'd proven himself exactly like all other men, dismissing her opinion, then getting angry when she refused to defer to his better judgement. Of all people, he should have supported the logic of the argument, not defended a London fool.

Outside, Simon sat on the garden bench swatting at a fly.

To think my future lies in the hands of such a pathetic specimen. Reluctantly, she closed the ledger and rose. She'd allowed Captain Covington to interfere with capturing the dandy's affection. If she wanted Cable Grange, she had to continue her pursuit and secure a proposal before the auction.

The door clicked open and Captain Covington stepped into the room.

'If you mean to bait me further, please refrain. I'm in no mood for arguments,' she snapped, tense at the idea of facing him so soon after their disagreement.

'I have no intention of baiting you. I thought I might read. George said you have an excellent book on crop rotation.'

'Crop rotation?' She eyed him suspiciously, doubting his interest in the subject.

'Yes.' He fingered a small wooden figurine on the table near the door.

'It's there, on top.' She pointed to a stack of books on the table next to a large leather chair, then sat back down. Opening the ledger, she expected the captain to thank her and leave, but instead he lingered.

'Do you mind if I browse your other books?'

Julia waved her hand at the bookshelves without looking up from the ledger. 'You're more than welcome to anything in my collection.'

'Thank you.'

He walked along the row of bookshelves, examining the spines, his tension evident by the way he kept tapping the crop book against his hand. Julia tried to ignore him, shaking her head at a miscalculated line of figures. He stopped at the large, coloured atlas on the bookstand, flipping through the pages before marching to stand in front of the desk.

'Do you really think a man is a coward for retiring after being wounded?' He stood before her the way a superior officer stands in front of a line of sailors.

She fixed him with a hard stare, refusing to be cowed. 'I told you I won't be baited.'

'Surely you don't believe it applies to all men?' He walked back and forth across the carpet as though on the deck of a ship, hands behind his back, every inch the Navy officer. 'What if your brother was wounded and forced to resign his commission. Would you call him a coward?'

Julia opened her mouth to answer, but the captain raised his hand, stopping her. Irritation flared, but she forced it back. Shouting at a guest, no matter how rude he might be, was definitely a breach of etiquette.

'What if the man's father died a few years ago and the investments he left to support his wife and daughter failed, leaving his son responsible for his sister's dowry and his widowed mother's affairs?'

The strange conviction in his eyes warned her off meeting the challenge. 'I respectfully decline to answer. We obviously have a difference of opinion so I see no reason to continue the debate.'

'Then you'd insist he return?'

Julia stayed silent, the lingering sadness in his piercing eyes hinting at the truth. Had he been wounded? Is that why he'd resigned? No, it wasn't possible. Running her eyes up the length of him, admiring his trim waist, flat stomach and wide chest, he was too strong to be injured. Surely if he were, Uncle George would have said something. Perhaps he'd lost friends or maybe his father had died in debt? Whatever drove him, it emanated from somewhere deep inside and she knew to tread carefully.

'Each man must decide what is best for him,' she answered in an even voice. 'It's not up to me to make such decisions.'

The tightness in the captain's jaw eased while the feverish hunger to debate faded from his eyes. 'This is quite a room for a young lady,' he remarked, his voice softer, but no less strained than before.

'A great many people have said so,' she agreed, relieved at the fading tension. 'It was my father's. He did his business here. I saw no reason to change it.'

'Do you think your father would approve of you hiding yourself away from the world in here?'

The anger rushed back and she jumped to her feet. 'And where do you hide, Captain?'

'I don't hide.'

'Then why are you here in the country?'

He turned to the window, staring past the garden with a sense of loss she could feel. 'London wearies me.'

'Ghosts have a way of haunting a person to exhaustion,' she observed, more to herself than to Captain Covington. Why else was she so desperate to stay at Knollwood if not to hide? Who outside its walls had ever accepted her or her talents? If she lost Knollwood, she lost her life's meaning for she could see no other. Unless she secured Cable Grange.

'You think I'm haunted?'

'I can't pretend to know the full measure of your mind. I only know everyone has fears.'

'We must face our fears to overcome them.'

'Then neither of us is hiding, are we?' No longer interested in his company or conversation, she made for the door. There was work to do outside, the prospect of which suddenly tired her.

James watched her leave, stunned, the full impact of her accusation striking him. He walked to the large atlas near the window and turned the coloured pages until he came upon the familiar maps of the Atlantic and the Caribbean. With his finger he traced the shipping routes, the miles of ocean once so familiar to him. England to Africa, Africa to Jamaica, Jamaica to America, America to the coast of Spain.

He slammed the book shut. He'd faced pirates, angry colonists, hostile natives and the French. He did not hide from his problems.

'There's one.' James pointed at a duck flying up out of the tall grass along the edge of the lake.

George took aim and fired, but the bird continued its ascent and flew off. 'Missed another one. I think I'd do better with a cannon and grapeshot today.'

'Perhaps,' James concurred, finding little humour in the joke. He'd joined George in the hopes the fine afternoon would take his mind off his shoulder and his irritation. After more than an hour of walking through tall grass or watching the sun reflect off the lake, he still felt tense and plagued by pain.

George handed the empty gun to a waiting footman and took a new one. 'Are you sure you won't shoot?'

'Not after this morning's exertion.' He rolled his shoulder, trying to ease the ache, but it didn't help. No doubt he'd strained it by showing off this morning and it nagged at him as much as Miss Howard's comments in the study.

They picked through the mud and damp of the marshy bank before George aimed at another bird rising from the reeds and fired. The duck crumpled in midair, falling with a splash into the lake. A dog bounded past them, flinging itself into the water and swimming excitedly towards the carcass.

'Excellent shot,' James muttered, unable to rouse much enthusiasm.

'What's got you so glum?'

'Nothing.' James stomped off, his boots sinking in the soft dirt, George close on his heels.

'If you say so.'

'Did you tell Julia about my injuries?'

'No.'

'Why not?'

'It's not my place to choose who to tell. That's your decision.'

So she didn't know. It explained her strong

opinion, but not her remark about him hiding. 'Would you say I hide from problems?'

'I've never known you to back down from a challenge.'

'But do I hide from them?'

George thought for a moment. 'Other people's or your own?'

'My own, of course.' He didn't like the sound of this last question. 'Miss Howard is under the impression I hide from problems.'

'Do you?'

'Of course not.' George's inability to directly answer led him to believe Miss Howard might be right. 'Though I suppose it depends on the problem.'

George laid his gun over his shoulder and stared at the ground, thinking while he walked. 'Jim, a man goes to sea for a number of reasons. I was a second son, I had to make my way and the Navy appealed to me. You joined to avoid a career in law.'

'You know I had no interest in it.'

'But your mother did.'

'She thought I'd make an excellent barrister. There was quite a row the night I informed her I'd purchased a commission. Mother is very formidable once she sets her mind to something.'

'Yes, I know.' George chuckled.

'How do you know?'

'From everything you've told me, of course,' George stammered, tugging on the sleeves of his coat. 'So you escaped the law.'

'You could say that.'

'And you accepted my invitation to the country to escape London.'

'I wouldn't say "escape".' James ran his hand over the back of his neck, seeing George's point all too clearly. 'But two instances hardly make me a coward.'

'You're no coward. I've seen you in enough battles to know. But what man doesn't sidestep a problem now and then? I've been known to turn tail a few times myself. Why do you think I never married? But seriously, there's a lot of unpleasant business in life. We deal with it as we can. You and I have seen enough of it in all corners of the world. Julia, she's seen her share here and in London. A brave man faces what he can, but no one has the strength to face it all. You're no coward, but, like all men, you have your weaknesses.'

James flexed his hand, admiring the peaceful green hills of Knollwood rising in the distance. 'Is my weakness so obvious?'

'I wouldn't call it a weakness and I'm amazed Julia mentioned it, though of all people she'd be the first to recognise it.' A suggestive twinkle replaced the pondering thoughtfulness in George's eyes. 'Why do you care what my niece thinks? I thought you had no interest in her?'

The urge to escape suddenly gripped James. 'I don't. I only wondered at what she said, nothing more.'

'Then it's settled. You're no coward and you have no interest in my niece. Now, let's head back. I have business to take care of before dinner.'

James followed George through the high grass to where the horses stood tethered to an old post, his mind far from clear. Why did he care so much about Miss Howard's opinion if he wasn't interested in her? He couldn't lie to himself. She intrigued him with her disregard for convention and her bold, adventurous spirit. However, her interest in Mr Taylor, combined with her disdain for wounded naval officers, infuriated him.

Would she change her opinion if she knew about his shoulder? He flexed his left hand. It was useless to ponder. She had no interest in him and there was no point pursuing such a woman. Besides, Miss Taylor now expected his attention and, despite her annoying simpering, he couldn't be rude.

He mounted Hector, the stallion he'd chosen to ride, and gritted his teeth with the effort of pulling himself into the saddle. Once astride the brown horse, he settled into the seat, his grip light on the reins. The animal was so well trained, it took little but a tap of his foot or pressure from his legs to control it. With such an easy horse beneath him, he couldn't resist the solitude and freedom of wide open fields.

'You go back to the house. I'm going for a ride.'

'I think a storm is coming in.' George pointed at the dark clouds hovering on the horizon.

'It doesn't matter.' James dug his heels into the stallion's sides and the animal tore off over the grassy field.

Julia hurried across the paddock, the wind playing with the bottom of her habit and scattering leaves across the path. She'd made absolutely no progress with Simon. The minute she'd returned to the garden, he'd pleaded a headache and went to his room to lie down. Emily then cornered her with an impromptu drawing lesson from Annette. It resulted in nothing but a mangled green blob meant to resemble a tree and the urge to dump the paints in her sister-in-law's lap.

Thankfully, baby Thomas's nurse appeared with the crying infant, freeing Julia from Emily's attempts at female education. Pleading the same headache as Simon, Julia fled to the quiet of her room to read. However, with the weather holding and the daylight fading, she knew this would be her only chance for a ride before dinner.

'Good afternoon, Miss Howard,' John greeted, brushing down one of the horses.

'Saddle Manfred,' Julia called out, hurrying past him down the line of stalls. 'Use the standard one.'

'Yes, Miss Howard.'

While John went to work, Julia slipped into the small closet at the back of the stable. Pushing the lid off the large chest on the floor, she pulled out the horse blankets to reveal an oil-cloth-wrapped bundle. Untying it, she lifted out the special riding habit crafted of dark-blue wool. Removing her regular habit, she donned the other garment. When walking it hung like a skirt, but the excess fabric hid the trouser-like design sewn into the dress. Julia had paid John's wife to sew it and for a tidy profit she also kept it laundered and mended.

Once dressed, she grabbed *The Monk* from the regular habit's pocket and hurried to where John stood holding Manfred.

'Watch the clouds,' John advised, helping her up into the saddle. 'You don't want to be caught out in a storm.'

'I'll be careful.' Julia kicked Manfred into a steady gallop, directing him east.

They followed the valley down to a small

brook and across a crude wooden bridge constructed to herd sheep back from pasture. The land on the other side flattened out, leading to another higher hill visible in the distance. Julia pointed Manfred at it and horse and rider moved seamlessly past a large lake, another small forest, and through a herd of sheep scurrying to make way for them.

During afternoon rides, Julia and Manfred usually ambled so she could take in the condition of the sheep, the walls, the fences, the height of the river, all the things so important to running the estate. Today she had no interest in business, only the desire to be alone.

They approached the next hill and she slowed Manfred to a walk, guiding him up the rocky path to the stone keep commanding the top. It was a Norman relic, abandoned ages ago by men who no longer mattered. She loved coming here for its lichen-covered stone walls offered a solitude she sometimes failed to find at Knollwood. Guiding Manfred alongside a large stone wedged into the ground, she slid off his back, her boots gripping the coarse surface. Pulling *The Monk* from her pocket, she tossed the reins up over his back, leaving him free to graze on the sweet grass covering the ancient site. He never wandered far and she was safe to steal an hour alone among the ruins.

Inside the old tower, she picked her way up the narrow stone staircase, her left hand clutching the book, her right hand tracing the wall as it rose up towards the battlements. At the top, she stepped out on to the last of the rampart, taking in the view of Knollwood and some of Creedon Abbey. Thick, menacing clouds covered the horizon while birds criss-crossed her view, arching and rolling as they chased each other.

A small alcove in the stones sheltered her from the wind and she settled in with her book, tucking the length of the riding habit about her legs for warmth. She opened *The Monk* and began to read, the sound of Manfred's whinny mingling with the warble of birds and the whistles of the wind through the grass. She devoured the descriptions of far-off places she'd probably never see, and frustration plagued her, subtly at first, but growing stronger with each new line. She snapped the book shut and tilted her head back to look at the sky, breathing in the heavy smell of rain and noting the dark clouds floating overhead. Today, her future seemed dim and bleak, the chances of obtaining her inheritance in time to purchase Cable Grange an impossible feat. What future could she hope for without her own estate? Perhaps she could live with Paul and keep house for him? Even then she wouldn't be free, but tethered to the whims and demands of Navy life and open to the gossip of vicious people who would wonder why she wasn't married.

Why is everyone so concerned with what I do? she thought, picking a piece of moss off the wall. She'd never crossed the lines of propriety and in public she always acted like a proper young lady, even if she did occasionally wear her riding habit to town. Yes, she preferred riding to the pianoforte, but Father had always encouraged the exercise and besides, every unconventional thing she did was always done among family who understood her. Or did they? Obviously Charles and Emily didn't. No, in their minds she was a veritable Jezebel for riding without a groom or preferring the business of an estate to the latest fashions. They were more concerned with the opinion of the few local families who laughed at Julia's strange habits, but dismissed them as nothing more than eccentricities. After all, her father and mother were, in their own ways, eccentric. Why should Julia be any different?

A hawk screeched and she watched the bird float on the up draught, searching the field for prey. If only she could be more conventional and refined like the other young ladies in the county. How many times had she tried and failed? After all, she couldn't spend days painting screens when the entire fortune of an estate rested on her shoulders.

The hoofbeats of an approaching horse echoed through the keep.

Am I never to have a moment's peace? she fumed, peering over the battlement and spying Captain Covington approaching. Ducking down behind the stone, she cursed her luck. Of all the people to happen upon her, did it have to be him?

'Manfred? Where's Miss Howard?' he asked in an anxious voice.

She thought of staying hidden, but she didn't want him to worry. Gripping the rough wall, she pulled herself into view. 'I'm here.'

He looked up at her, his dark hair falling back off of his forehead. Her heart skipped a beat at the sight of him atop the chestnut stallion. Dressed in the same hunting clothes he'd worn in the forest, their brown tones warmed his face and softened the line of his jaw. For a brief moment she wished she could draw so she could capture the way the greying light caressed his features.

'What a relief. When I saw him alone, I thought something had happened.' He rose up in the saddle to dismount.

'Stop there,' Julia demanded. 'If you're as contentious as you were at nuncheon, then leave now. I've had enough of irritable people for one day.'

Instead of sitting, he swung his leg over the

horse and dropped to the ground. 'You're a very direct young lady.'

'And quite serious.' She crossed her arms over her chest.

'I promise to be pleasant and cheerful.' He placed his hand on his heart, bowing deferentially, then snapping up into a formal military stance. 'Permission to come aboard.'

The stories she'd heard about him demanded a refusal, but they also fuelled her curiosity. If nothing else, here was her chance to discover the truth behind Uncle George's tales. Emily would faint if she discovered them alone, but if the captain kept this meeting a secret, then what was the harm in conversing? 'Granted. Tie Hector to the post.' She pointed at the ruins of an old fence near the keep's entrance.

He wrapped the horse's reins around the mouldering wood, then made his way inside, taking the stairs two at a time before stepping out on to the rampart. Julia admired the steady, sure way he crossed the ledge.

'I'm surprised to find you here,' he remarked.

'I often come here to be alone.'

'Then I apologise for intruding on your solitude.'

'It does not matter.' Julia leaned against the short wall, admiring the view and struggling to appear indifferent despite the strange nervousness creeping through her. The captain leaned next to her, resting his elbows on the stones, the nearness of him making her jittery excitement worse.

'This is an impressive place.' His eyes scanned the landscape and for the first time she noticed the small lines about his mouth.

'Indeed.' She moved closer into his circle of warmth and for a brief moment considered slipping into the crook of his body, out of the wind and damp air.

'Are all Uncle George's stories true?' she asked, eager to break the awkward silence and distract herself from Captain Covington's warm body.

'What do you know?'

'I know about his liaison with the plantation owner's wife, the rum running and your dalliance with the governor's sister.'

Captain Covington threw back his head and laughed. 'Yes, it's all true and then some, for I doubt he told you everything.'

'He told me enough. You have quite a reputation, Captain.'

'Me? No, I take no responsibility. It was all George's doing.'

'Including the governor's sister?'

The corners of his lips pulled up. 'I assure you, the story was exaggerated.'

'Why didn't you marry her?'

He sobered, but not enough to remove the wicked smile. 'We were not suited for marriage. Nor was the lady inclined. It seemed she'd had enough of husbands and very much liked her freedom.'

For a moment Julia envied the woman, especially her intimacy with the captain. What she wouldn't give to have such control over her life and enjoy someone like him without censure. 'What of your other adventures with Uncle George?' she asked, trying to distract her wandering mind.

'Some were true. I leave it to you to discover which ones.'

'Then you admit you went along.'

'Only to keep a very good friend out of trouble.'

'And to make a bit of profit.'

'In that regard I am guilty.'

'I envy your grand adventures.'

'Do not envy them. They weren't all grand.' He straightened, rubbing his left shoulder, a scowl darkening his features.

A gust of wind hit the keep, pulling a strand of Julia's hair loose. Tucking it behind her ear, she noticed the thickening clouds moving faster across the sky. It was time to ride back, but she wasn't ready to leave. Emily would scold her if they got caught in the rain, but she no longer cared. What did any of it matter—propriety, etiquette—if one were always confined to this small corner of the world? Julia sighed and the captain turned a curious eye on her.

'Something troubles you?'

She shook her head, wondering how much to confide in him. In many ways he reminded her of Uncle George or Paul, of someone who would listen without judgement. But for all his resemblances, he was still a stranger. 'I wish I could be more like Annette,' she admitted, throwing convention to the wind.

'Do not envy her. She has nothing you don't possess.'

'Except perfect manners.'

'Your manners are not so very imperfect.'

'But they're not polished enough for my brother or Emily or most of the countryside.' She picked a small stone off the ledge and hurled it over the edge. It arched in the air before dropping to the grass with a soft thud. 'I don't shun propriety, Captain. I do my best to follow Emily's suggestions, only—'

'—they're always at odds with your nature.'

Yes, he was very much like Paul and Uncle George. 'It was different when Father was alive. He didn't mind if I wore the wrong dress or went riding alone in the mornings.'

'And your mother?'

'She's quite content with her roses and Charlemagne. She loves me, but doesn't fret like Charles and Emily. They don't realise how much I try to behave. They think I'm like Paul and being contrary for the sake of being contrary. Charles believes because it's so easy for him to be proper that it's easy for everyone. He's turned into a dreadful, puritan bore.'

'I wouldn't call Charles a puritan,' the captain snorted.

'What do you mean?' What did he know about Charles that she didn't?

'Nothing. I was only thinking of your brother Paul. I'm sorry if I confused the two.'

'Oh, yes, well, Paul certainly doesn't follow convention. But he's a man and allowed to do as he pleases.' She turned back to the view, her world suddenly feeling small. 'Paul is out there having adventures and Charles is in London, making great speeches and deciding my future.'

'No one decides your future unless you let them.'

'Those are the words of a man who can make his own choices and live as he pleases.' She reached back, tucking the waving strand of hair into the loose bun.

'Men don't always live as they please. Sometimes they live as they must,' he responded with some resignation.

'Even then you have choices,' she encouraged, willing him to be strong. If a man like him gave in to fate, what chance did she have?

He moved to object before his lips spread into a smile. 'You don't strike me as a young lady resigned to someone else deciding her future.'

She picked at the stone wall. 'Perhaps, but for the moment, here I am.'

James watched her work loose a pebble, her face bereft of a smile. No, she was not a woman to give up, no matter what she might say. She would continue to strive, to struggle, to fight for what she wanted. 'Where would you be if you could be somewhere else?'

'India. Paul gave me a book about it once. It seems so magical. Have you been to India?'

'Once, a long time ago.'

'Was it magical?'

He turned to her, admiring the excitement of youth and innocence reflected in her eyes. While he pined for what he'd lost, she waited to hear about what she might never experience. Suddenly his sadness seemed self-indulgent, giving him a new appreciation for his past. 'Yes, it was. Blazing white palaces crowded with men and women in dazzling colours. The air so thick with curry and moisture, you feel as though you could slice it with a sword.'

'Paul brought me curry powder once. I gave it to cook and she didn't know what to do with it. She put it in the chicken and the house reeked of it for days. It's like nothing I've smelled or tasted before. Would you go there again?'

He watched a pair of deer race through the high grass before disappearing into a thick clump of trees. Would he go back? There was nothing to stop him. He could go there and a hundred other places he longed to see. He thought of Paris, Vienna and Venice and for a moment pictured himself walking through the ancient city, Miss Howard by his side. The image startled him though it wasn't an entirely unpleasant idea. 'Yes, I would.'

'I wish I could go.' The wind pulled a small curl across her cheek.

'Perhaps some day you will.' He tucked the strand of hair behind her ear, allowing his fingers to linger at the nape of her neck. She didn't pull away. Instead her eyes held his with nervous anticipation. He stepped closer and her head tilted up invitingly. He felt her rapid pulse through the warm skin beneath his fingertips and was close to claiming her soft, parted lips when a loud clap of thunder broke overhead.

A sudden gust of wind pungent with rain swept past them, ruffling the skirt of her habit.

She stepped away from him, an awkward blush colouring her cheeks. 'We'd better get back before it rains.'

He didn't want to leave, but he couldn't object. Staying alone together here was dangerous and he possessed no desire to expose her to vicious gossip or her sister-in-law's criticism. To compromise her in such a way would only confirm Julia's previous suspicions about him and he very much wanted her good opinion.

Julia followed the captain down the stone steps, watching his broad shoulders lead the way through the tower's deep shadows. He'd almost kissed her. She'd almost allowed him to kiss her. She stopped in the middle of the staircase, fear gripping her. How could she have been so weak? It was unlike her to lose her head over a gentleman, especially one with questionable intentions.

At the bottom he hopped off the last step, turning to help her down. 'Is something wrong?'

'No, not at all.' She hurried down the stairs, taking his offered hand and allowing him to help her. She delighted once again in the feel of it, the strength and warmth. Their eyes met as a bolt of lightning cracked overhead followed by a deep roll of thunder.

'We'd better hurry.' He pulled her towards the horses.

Julia grabbed Manfred's reins and led him next to the large stone. She saw the captain's surprise when she threw her leg over Manfred's back, revealing the trousers in the riding habit.

'Very clever.'

'Please don't tell Emily.'

'Your secret is safe with me.' He winked, then swung into the saddle, pain flashing across his face before he settled his feet in the stirrups.

She was about to ask if he felt well when another heavy blast of wind hit them, flattening the tall grass and scattering bits of earth and leaves.

'Do you think we can outrun the storm?' he called over the gust.

'I think we should try.' Digging her heels into Manfred's flanks, she shot off down the hill. In seconds the captain was next to her, leaning over Hector's neck, spurring him on. Remembering the way he'd ridden this morning, she pushed them hard, guiding them around trees and boulders and over the crest of hills. She avoided the hedges, not knowing the captain's capacity for jumping, but she couldn't resist leaping the small gully. Though Hector was no match for Manfred, the captain never let up or veered off course. He urged the stallion up and over the rushing water, meeting her on the other side, his wide smile revealing his excitement. Her heart skipped a beat at the sight of his exuberant face and she kicked Manfred back into a gallop. The captain followed, his body matching Hector's gait with satyr-like fluidity.

The horses were fast, but the storm moved faster. She could have ridden for ever with the captain, but the icy rain fell hard, pouring down her hair and soaking her back. With visibility declining, she guided them on to a wide country lane. Racing around a bend in the road, the horse's hooves kicked up mud from the deep puddles, the rain matting their manes against their necks. The captain's speed did not waver as he kept pace with her. Water dripped from his chin and his keen eyes watched the road, at intervals meeting hers with an intensity as highly charged as the lightning.

The glowing windows of Knollwood came into view through the deluge and the captain followed Julia down away from the house to the stables. She pulled Manfred to a halt in the yard, the captain drawing Hector up alongside them. She breathed hard, every inch of her wet, her fingers aching with cold, but she didn't care. The exhilarating ride warmed her, as did the captain's blazing eyes. Large drops of water dripped off the wet hair matted against his forehead, sliding down his cheeks, tracing the fine sinew of his neck before disappearing beneath his collar. His charging pulse beat against the exposed skin, echoing the steady rhythm in her chest. She wrapped the reins around her fingers as he leaned hard on one hand, tilting towards her and she leaned closer, noticing the small beads of water sticking to his eyelashes. He was exactly as she'd imagined him in her dream about the monsoon, his chest rising and falling with each deep breath.

The wind cut a sharp line through them and Julia shivered.

'We'd better get inside,' the captain yelled over the pounding rain. Julia nodded, water running into her eyes as she walked Manfred into the warmth of the stable.

'I'm glad to see you back. I was getting worried.' John rushed to take Manfred's reins and help her down.

'I'll only be a moment,' she called to the captain, then slipped into the small room. Stripping off her soaked riding habit, she hung it on a hook, knowing John's wife would see to its cleaning like she always did. She wrung out the bottom of her chemise then pulled the dry habit over her damp stays and hurried out of the room to where Captain Covington waited by the open stable door. Water dripped from his coat, pooling on the hard-packed dirt.

'Should we wait it out?' he asked, pushing the wet hair off his face. The rain fell in thick sheets on the paddock with no sign of letting up.

'No. Wet or dry, I'm sure to receive a tongue lashing for this.'

'Then we'd better hurry. The sooner it begins the sooner it may end. After you.'

She ran past him into the downpour and in two large strides he was next to her. They rushed up the small hill, but she stumbled, her boot sticking in the mud. He grabbed her by the elbow, pulling her free and into the grove of trees. Lightning split the sky and the air crackled with electricity, the deep roll of thunder vibrating in Julia's chest.

'Perhaps we should go back to the stable until it passes,' the captain suggested, pulling her closer, his hand protectively on her arm.

Julia gauged the distance between the house and the stable, seeing no safe, clear path in either direction. 'No, we're halfway there. We might as well keep going.'

'Come along, then. I have no desire to be struck by lightning.' He slipped his hand in hers and pulled her out of the trees. She hung on tight, his strength soothing some of her fear during their mad dash over the gravel path and up the back portico.

Another lightning bolt cracked overhead as

the captain closed the French door behind them. He followed Julia laughing and dripping into the hall at the front of the house, wet footprints trailing them across the stone floor.

'Maybe we should have stayed in the stable.' Julia smiled, shaking the water off her skirt.

'No. I enjoyed our adventure, even if I won't dry out for a week,' he laughed, wiping his hands on his soaked trousers.

'Julia, Captain Covington.' Emily's voice echoed off the walls. Julia whirled around to see her standing at the top of the stairs, her delicate face red and her pale eyes dark. 'What is the meaning of this?'

'We were caught in the rain.' Julia shifted from foot to foot, her stockings squishing in her half-boots.

'Forgive me, Mrs Howard. It was my fault. I allowed Miss Howard to dally on our ride and the storm came upon us faster than we anticipated.'

'And was the groom with you? No, he wasn't because John came to the house looking for Julia after it started to rain,' Emily answered before he could. 'He was worried about her—we all were.'

Emily flew down the stairs, her stern face fixed on the captain. 'Such behaviour from Julia does not surprise me. She is young and not well versed in the ways of the world, but not from you,

Captain. If you wish to remain in my house, I insist you behave like a gentleman.'

'My apologies, Mrs Howard. It was not my intention to offend you or place your sister-in-law's reputation at risk.'

'I certainly hope not. Now come along, Julia.'

Julia resisted the urge to unleash a torrent of words as Emily hustled her up the stairs and into her room. Inside, her mother sat on the small sofa by the window, petting Charlemagne, a slight smile raising the corners of her mouth.

'How dare you speak to the captain like that, or me? How dare you make such accusations?' Julia said sharply.

'Don't you see how compromising such behaviour is? To be out alone with a man who knows where doing who knows what.'

'Out riding and doing nothing. Why do you and Charles always believe the worst of me? What have I done to make you think I might do anything compromising?'

Emily twisted her hands in front of her, some of her anger fading. 'Even a young woman of solid character may slip and cause herself a great deal of grief.' From the adjoining dressing room, baby Thomas let out a wail, nearly drowning out the nurse's soothing coos. 'Besides, your mother was worried about you.'

Her mother stopped petting Charlemagne,

shocked to find herself pulled into the conversation. 'No, my dear, I was not worried for this is not the first time you've been caught out in the rain.'

Emily stared at her mother-in-law in frustration. 'She was alone with a gentleman.'

Mother rose, tucking Charlemagne under her arm. 'As I said, I was not concerned.' She left, closing the door behind her.

'See, it is only your own fear playing on you.'

Emily placed her hands on Julia's shoulders, her face softer than before. 'I am only trying to help. Others will speak badly of you if they witness such behaviour.'

'You're the only one talking now.'

'But think of the Taylors. What would they say?'

'I don't care what they think and I'm tired of enduring Annette's foolishness.'

'Please try to be more cordial to her. There are things concerning the Taylors of which you are not aware and they may have a direct impact on Annette's current mood. She can be a very sweet young lady.'

Julia crossed her arms with a disbelieving huff. 'Annette constantly derides me, points out my faults to all and yet you describe her as sweet. I do nothing and you treat me like the whore of Daringford.'

Emily pinched the bridge of her nose, the dark circles under her eyes made deeper by the candlelight. Julia knew Emily was tired from nursing Thomas through the night in keeping with Rousseau's ideals and Charles's instructions, but at the moment she had no sympathy for her sister-in-law. 'You must learn to get along with people. Life is not all deferential servants and friendly tenant farmers.'

'Of this you and the Taylors have made me very aware,' Julia fumed through clenched teeth, barely able to stand still with the anger coursing through her.

'Forgive me. I was not clear.'

'No, I understand perfectly,' she seethed, balling her fists at her sides. 'Despite everything I've done and can do, you two are ashamed of me. I'll have no peace until I become a simpering wet goose or marry and leave. Why not simply send me to Paul, then you might never be bothered with such an embarrassing sister?'

'Julia, please…'

'No, I've heard quite enough for one day.' She left, afraid of what she might say if she stayed longer.

Once in her room, her hands shook so hard with anger she could not undo the buttons on her habit without Mary's help.

'You are soaked through, miss,' the maid

giggled, dropping the soggy garment in a large china bowl along with her wet hose and gloves.

'I'm quite aware of my current state of wet-ness.' Julia bristled, then instantly regretted it. 'I'm sorry, Mary. I don't mean to be cross.'

'It's all right, miss.' Mary smiled, lacing the dry stays, then helping Julia into an afternoon dress. 'An exciting run with a man like the cap-tain would be enough to send any woman into a state.'

'I wish it was the captain who'd put me in such a state,' she let slip, then caught herself as Mary shot her a knowing glance. Snatching the towel from the washstand, Julia rubbed her soaking hair, eager to do anything to relieve her agita-tion. 'That will be all, Mary.'

Mary curtsied, then left. Julia threw down the towel and braided her hair, fastening it with a rib-bon at the base of her neck.

How could Emily say such a thing to me and the captain? She flipped the braid over her shoul-der and, determined to put the incident from her mind, headed for the study, craving the solace.

Once inside, she took a deep breath, hoping to gain some measure of calm from the familiar surroundings, but for once not even this comfort-able place made her feel better. The fire had been allowed to burn out, taking with it all remain-ing warmth and leaving only the ashen tones of the rain-drenched light from outside. It made the room cold, the books heartless, the large mahogany desk uncaring. Despite the chill, she loved it all, but it wasn't hers, as Emily had made abundantly clear.

'Her house,' Julia snorted. Emily might be Charles's wife, but since her arrival she'd never lifted a finger to do more than arrange dinners or fuss over Thomas. The urge to march upstairs and hand the accounts to Emily was overwhelming. Let her manage the estate if she was so quick to call it her own. Instead Julia sat down at the desk and took the pencil in her shaking fingers. If nothing else, she still loved Knollwood and owed it to Father to keep it prosperous.

Lightning lit the room and a hard wind drove the rain against the window. Julia watched the heavy drops bounce off the stone patio. Her thoughts wandered back to the captain and their mad dash across the garden. Was this the kind of life he offered? Turning a rainstorm into an adventure, a ride into an energetic race? Chewing the end of the pencil, she remembered his face when he'd leaned close to her at the keep, the way his fingers brushed her neck sending chills of excitement racing along her skin. She'd wanted him to kiss her, to taste him, to give in to the urges swirling inside her. It might be worth compromising herself to live in such a daring way.

No, a man like the captain might make her forget herself, but he'd also make her regret it.

Tapping the pencil against the desk, she debated calling a footman to relight the fire, then decided against it. She didn't feel like being alone. On rainy days when he was with them, Uncle George usually played billiards in the library with a warm fire and a glass of port. She hesitated, knowing Captain Covington would be with him. The thought of his company appealed to her as did the desire to spite Emily, though it would hardly be spite with Uncle George playing the chaperon.

'I wondered when you'd join us,' Uncle George greeted when she stepped into the library, the crackling fire and friendly faces a welcome contrast to the lonely study. 'Will you play?'

She caught the captain's eye. He offered an apologetic smile before disappearing into a glass of port.

Julia shook her head. 'No, finish your game. I'll join the next one.'

'She's quite the player, Jim. Takes after me.' George leaned over the table, taking aim at the red ball and striking it with the cue ball.

'She also has your spirit of adventure.' The captain strolled to the scoreboard standing near the fireplace behind her. 'I'm sorry to have caused you trouble,' he whispered, sliding a tally along the line.

She ran her fingers over the smooth-wooded side of the billiard table. 'It's not your fault. Emily has a great concern for propriety.'

'Which is surprising considering,' Uncle George commented, sipping his port as James took his shot.

'Considering what?' Julia asked.

George turned a strange shade of pink, then pulled on the sleeves of his jacket. 'Nothing.'

'Tell me. You know you can't keep a secret.'

'Of course I can keep a secret.'

'No, you can't.'

'Name one secret I've failed to keep.' Uncle George leaned over the table, practising before he took his turn.

'Only one?'

'One will do, thank you.'

Julia thought a moment, studying the wood-beam ceiling, debating whether to reveal a certain scandalous and unladylike bit of knowledge. With Emily's rebuke still ringing in her ears, she decided to be bold. 'The woman you visit in London.'

Uncle George whiffed the cue ball and jerked up straight. 'You know better than to distract a man when he's taking a shot. You'll ruin his game. Besides, how do you know about her?'

'Paul, of course.'

'Did he tell you who she is?'

Julia sighed in frustration. 'No.'

'You see—' he pointed his cue stick at her '—I can keep a secret.'

'I'm sure it's the only one.'

'Who is she, George?' the captain joined in. 'Miss Howard is right, you know. You can't keep a secret.'

'Don't think the two of you will get me to reveal it.' He was about to say more when Davies stepped into the room.

'Captain Russell, the foreman from Creedon Abbey is here to discuss the progress of the repairs.'

'Excellent.' George straightened, his smile wider than Julia would have liked. 'If you'll both excuse me.'

'You can bring him in here if you'd like,' Julia offered, uneasy about being left with the captain.

'No, I'll return shortly and tell you all the details. In the meantime, please continue my game.' Uncle George handed her his cue stick, then left, the proud way he carried himself making her suspect there was no foreman for him to meet.

She gripped the cue tightly, worry creeping through her. Despite her previous desire to spite her sister-in-law, the very real threat of Emily catching her alone in a room with a gentleman worried her.

'So, who is this woman George is seeing in London?' the captain asked, the mischief in his eyes dissolving some of her concerns.

'I don't know. I wasn't even sure she existed until just now.'

'Clever.'

Julia swelled her chest with mock pride. 'Paul taught me well.'

The captain leaned far over the table to execute a difficult stroke and Julia admired the way his breeches pulled over his backside. She wanted to run her hands from his hair, over the length of his back to the snug breeches, feeling every contour of his body.

A small medallion slid out from beneath his shirt, glinting in the candlelight and stopping her mind from wandering too far.

'What's that?'

'A reminder.' He fingered the pendant, his voice more measured than before. Distant thunder rolled outside, the storm moving off deeper into the countryside. 'I had it on the last time I was aboard ship. We were off the coast of Spain when we came across a French frigate and it opened fire.'

He unclasped the chain from around his neck and handed it to her. She examined the bronze surface, running her thumb over the dent with its worn and nearly illegible letters.

'It stopped the bullet?'

'Yes, but there were two.' He took the medal back, fastening the chain around his neck and tucking it into his shirt.

'And the other?'

He hit the cue ball with such force it rolled around the table, bouncing off the sides and missing the red ball. 'It struck me in the left shoulder.'

Their eyes met and she realised why he'd reacted so vehemently to her comments about Admiral Nelson. No wonder he'd been so intent on challenging her reasoning. What must he think of her? Would she never learn to control her tongue? Embarrassment overwhelmed her accompanied by the urge to make her excuses and flee. 'Is that why you resigned?'

'Mostly.' He picked at the end of his cue stick. 'But I had other responsibilities. My father died four years ago, while I was at sea. He left a large share in a shipping company to maintain my mother and sister, but the company faltered after losing a number of ships to storms. My mother tried to manage as best she could, but neither she nor my sister possess your business acumen. I discovered the troubles a few weeks into my recuperation when a bailiff appeared to collect the debts. I instructed my solicitor to pay them and once I was sufficiently recovered, took over Mother's affairs and saw to my sister's dowry.'

'Once everything was settled and you were well, couldn't you have gone back to sea?'

'I wanted to, but it seems the Navy is quick to forget a man once he's away from active service.'

'Didn't they know you were recuperating?'

'They did, but there are always younger, eager men craving ships and, unlike me, those men have not been badly wounded.'

'But Admiral Nelson was wounded and he commands the fleet.'

'As Admiral Stuart was kind enough to point out, I am no Nelson.'

She gasped. 'How could he be so cruel?'

'He wasn't cruel. He was honest. Admiral Stuart and I have known each other a long time and, despite a mutual respect, we both know the way of things. I just needed someone to state it plain enough for me to acknowledge it.' He laid the cue stick on the table and traced the polished wood with one finger. 'The Navy isn't an easy life. George is one of my oldest friends, but I've lost too many others to sickness or French bullets. Most men pursuing commands need to face those hardships to make a living. I'd made a handsome fortune and the Admiralty knew it.

Thanks to Admiral Stuart's honesty, I have the chance to enjoy my rewards instead of suffering who knows what fate.' He touched his shoulder, a far-off sadness filling his eyes before he jerked his hand to his side and turned to face her. 'It wasn't easy resigning my commission and it still troubles me, as much as my shoulder.'

Julia stepped back, rolling the cue ball, wishing lightning had struck her on their run, allowing her to avoid this embarrassment. 'I'm sorry for what I said about wounded men. I shouldn't have been so callous or spoken so freely.'

He slid his hand along the table's edge, allowing it to rest very close to hers. 'Don't berate yourself for your views. It's a brave person who does not bend under pressure to others' opinions.'

His fingers brushed the tops of hers, sending a shiver through her body. All of this was inappropriate, his touch, the seclusion but she couldn't bring herself to leave. He stepped closer, his expression more tender than she deserved. She met his soft eyes, anxious, wanting, eager to follow him down whatever road he led her.

The clock on the mantel chimed, the tinkling bells bringing her back to reality.

Cursed interruptions. It was almost time for dinner. If she wished to avoid her *faux pas* from the night before, she needed time to prepare.

'Please excuse me. I must dress for dinner.' Sliding her hand out from beneath his, she noticed his fleeting disappointment as she hurried from the room.

Chapter Six

'Are these all of them?' Julia stared at the dresses draped over every surface, her room resembling the inside of a milliner's shop.

'No, miss. I left the three formal dresses in their trunks.' Mary laid an assortment of gloves on the writing desk. 'Should I bring those down, too?'

'Yes, for heaven knows I may have use for them yet.' Julia fingered the hem of a pink-silk pelisse.

'Which dress would you like to wear tonight?' Mary asked, arranging a few fans on the bedside table.

Julia circled the room, examining each one, trying to remember which one had looked the best on her. She barely remembered the ensembles, having banished them to the attic the instant they'd returned from her horrible Season in London. She'd have gladly given it all to Mary, but her mother had stopped her, insisting she might one day need it. Tonight, Mother would discover how right she'd been. 'Which do you suggest?'

'The green one, it was so pretty on you in town.'

Julia nodded, allowing Mary to help her out of the simple afternoon frock and into the fancy, green-silk creation. The dress highlighted her amber eyes and showed off her curves to their best advantage. However, the low-cut bodice made her feel exposed and very self-conscious. Examining herself in the mirror, she felt all of her London awkwardness come rushing back.

Her embarrassment increased when, half an hour later, after patiently bearing Mary's many attempts at a fashionable *coiffure*, Julia curtly dismissed her. As she stared at the lopsided style in the mirror, tears of frustration stung her eyes. How could she possibly hope to capture Captain Covington's interest with dishevelled hair?

Not his interest. Simon's, she corrected herself, furiously combing out the style, then tossing the brush down on the table where it rattled against a small vase with a lone rose. *Obviously my money isn't enough to attract him. The stupid peacock.*

Despair crept along the edges of her irritation,

but she shook it from her head with the last of the hairpins. She couldn't afford to lose hope now.

I will catch Simon's eye. I have to. With renewed determination, she twisted her hair up the way Mother did, fastening it with a tortoiseshell comb while leaving the front curls, Mary's sole accomplishment, to fall about her face.

James trailed his fingers on the marble mantel, wincing at another of Miss Howard's hollow laughs. Twice today he'd nearly kissed her. Twice he'd allowed the wanting in her eyes to overcome his better sense, yet there she sat on the sofa next to Mr Taylor, seemingly enthralled by the twit. What game was she playing in her London finery, her white, round breasts well displayed by the curving neckline of the green dress? What hold did Mr Taylor have over her? He wondered if she knew about his affair with the dowager baroness or the wager at White's as to whether or not they would elope to Gretna Green? Surely she must know, having previously claimed a broad knowledge of London gossip.

Flexing his left hand, he leaned his elbow on the mantel, pretending to study a small horse figurine. He'd watched her throughout dinner, noticing the way her eyes lost their sparkle whenever Mr Taylor turned away. This was not the same woman who'd dared him to keep up with her on the downs or challenged him in the library.

He thought of asking George what his niece was about, but it would only make his feelings obvious. What where his feelings? He'd struggled against them ever since they'd met, yet this afternoon at the keep he could no longer lie to himself. She enchanted him, amused him. She was an original in every way, fresh and free spirited, tethered by a prudish brother and an indifferent mother. How she'd blossom if she ever cut herself loose from Knollwood. Yet she clung to it like a man clings to a sinking ship, praying against all odds it might still save him.

Miss Taylor's voice accompanied by the tinkling notes of the pianoforte drifted to him from the far corner of the room. She flirted with him from across the instrument's polished surface, dropping her head coquettishly, her eyes betraying her true intention. James knew he could not go back to such women. However, it was a fool's errand to chase after a young lady who held no real interest in him. Melinda had taught him that lesson years ago. He must find some way to draw Miss Howard out and drive thoughts of Mr Taylor from her mind.

While Simon spoke of his London house at length, Julia stole a number of glances at the captain. He stood by the fire, watching the flames consume the log with a sense of distant wondering. He wore his blue uniform, the high collar framing his strong chin. The firelight danced in his dark hair and blue eyes. For a moment she pictured him on the deck of a ship as it sailed into Bombay, watching the far-off coconut trees on the rolling hills sway in the warm breeze, just as Mr Ivers described in his book. Only the strange sadness surrounding him interrupted the lovely dream. Seeing the way it darkened his eyes, she wanted to take him in her arms and caress it away, but with so many people around them, she couldn't even entreat him to tell her what troubled him.

'It is such a bother to turn one's own music,' Annette remarked from her place at the pianoforte. 'Captain, will you turn the pages for me?'

'Simon can turn the pages for you,' George responded.

Simon stopped his chattering long enough to heave a small sigh. 'She knows the tune by heart and can play without the sheet music.'

Annette's face went pale before she fixed a charming smile back on her lips. 'How silly you are, Simon, to make such a joke. You know very well I do not know this piece.'

Julia caught Uncle George's eye. He glanced from her to Simon, scrunching his brow with a silent question. Julia flicked her hand in his direction, waving the question away, but she could tell he wasn't deterred. Panic stole through her. Uncle George didn't believe her sudden interest in Simon and suspected something. Had he guessed her scheme? She hoped not. She didn't need any more obstacles.

'Mr Johnson told me Mr Wilkins is hosting a game at the Sign of the Swan tonight,' Uncle George announced with a sly grin.

Drat, Julia thought, wishing they were still at dinner so she could kick him under the table. She didn't need him working against her, but she also wasn't ready to let him in on her plan.

'A game, you say?' Simon asked, taking his gold chronometer out of his pocket and checking the time.

'Quite a large one from the sound of it. A man could make a lot of money. It seems Mr Wilkins is very keen to win back some of the blunt he lost last night. Though I doubt he'll succeed. He's a terrible player.'

'Simon, tell me more about your horses,' Julia implored in a feeble attempt to outmanoeuvre Uncle George, but it failed. Simon rose and sauntered over to the card table, quite forgetting their conversation.

'You've played the man?' he asked.

'Once or twice. He has no face for the game.

Reveals his hand—hardly a challenge.' George laid a card on the table and drew another.

'Where's the fun in an opponent who gives away the game? A real gentleman wants a challenge, a chance to truly flaunt his talent,' Annette chided Simon, who, for the first time since their arrival, didn't respond to his sister's rebuke. Instead he stood, fingering the button on his coat, appearing to weigh Uncle George's announcement with Annette's comment before the gambler in him won the debate.

'If you'll excuse me, I believe I'll retire for the evening.'

'But it's only nine. Stay,' Annette pleaded. 'I'm sure George can make room for you at the table.'

'The country has tired me. Goodnight, ladies.' He bowed to Mother and Emily, then made his way out of the room. He didn't fool anyone with his excuse and Julia knew it would only be a matter of minutes before they heard him sneak out of the front door.

Annette's hands lingered over the keys and she looked torn between following him and returning to her pursuit of Captain Covington. It took only a moment for her to reach a decision and she resumed her pretty playing.

Julia sat on the sofa, clutching her hands in her lap in frustration. Beyond a few dinner con-

versations, she hadn't made any progress with
the dandy.

'Captain Covington, would you mind turning
the music for me?' Annette sang to him.

'Would you care to accompany me across
the room?' The captain stood in front of Julia,
his hands behind his back. She had no desire
to watch Annette fawn over him, but with no
Simon or interest in cards, annoying her stepcousin seemed the only thing left to do.

'It would be my pleasure.'

'Perhaps Miss Howard and I may play a duet,'
Annette suggested with false gaiety when they
approached.

'You are quite aware I don't play.' She was in
no mood for another discussion of her accomplishments.

'You don't play. And you don't draw.' Annette's fingers paused, giving her astonishment
the most effect before she resumed her piece.
'How do you expect to find a husband without
such accomplishments?'

Julia restrained her urge to slam the keyboard
cover on Annette's pale fingers and wipe the
pompous look off her face.

'I think many gentlemen would be pleased to
have a wife skilled in running an estate for he
would never have to agonise over his purse or

hers,' Captain Covington offered, coming to her defence against Annette again.

'Even without a gentleman, it's a comfort to handle one's own affairs instead of trusting them to men who only gamble them away,' Julia added, staring down her nose at Annette.

Annette struck a sour note, then stood, turning hard eyes on Julia. 'Do not be so proud. A lady's fortune is always in the hands of her male relations, no matter what her accomplishments.'

Her words rang more of sad bitterness than malice and Julia's spirits fell, the realisation striking deeper than any other comment Annette had ever made about her. For the first time, Julia felt sorry for her stepcousin, thinking they had more in common than she knew.

'If you will excuse me.' Annette pushed past them towards the door, disappearing upstairs.

'If I had an estate, I would wish for a wife like you to run it,' Captain Covington offered and Julia responded with a weak smile, unwilling to accept his pity.

'But you have no estate. And neither do I.'

'Perhaps in time that will change for both of us.'

'Yes, you will buy an estate and I—well, I'll wait for my brother to return and then I can be the spinster aunt.' She meant the comment to sound like a joke, but it fell flat. Desperate for something to occupy her hands, she sat down at the despised instrument and began picking out the tune in front of her. She tried to concentrate on the black notes in their cosy lines and not the captain standing close behind her.

'No, you will not be a spinster. Do not listen to the likes of Miss Taylor. There are many gentlemen who want a lady with a head for business.'

'Then they must all be married for I've never met such a gentleman.'

She came to the end of the stanza and he reached over her shoulder to change the page, his cheek tantalisingly close to hers. She closed her eyes, listening to the sheet music rustle, hearing his heavy breath in her ear. She only had to turn her head to sweep her lips across his skin, bury her face in the warm crease of his neck while reaching up to lace her fingers in his dark hair.

'I am not married,' he whispered, his breath teasing her neck.

Her hands dropped to the keyboard, the clanging notes snapping her out of her daydream. Going back over the stanza, she tried to make her awkward fingers behave, but they kept tripping over the keys. She glanced at the card table, noting the way Emily watched them before Uncle George distracted her with some comment. She also felt the captain's eyes lingering on her. Why did he insist on staring? Julia hit another wrong note, increasing her agitation until she could no longer bear it.

'If you'll excuse me, Captain, I'm tired.' She stood, closed the keyboard, then fled for the door.

George leaned back in his chair. 'Retiring so early, Julia?'

'Yes, goodnight.'

She hurried from the room before Uncle George could compel her to stay. Reaching the top of the dimly lit stairs, she heard a faint noise, like someone crying. She followed the sound, tip-toeing over the carpet, expecting to see a maid in one of the small chairs situated near the window. Moving past the cushioned retreat with a view of the garden, she found it empty. Down the hall, light slipped out from beneath Annette's door. Cautiously approaching it, Julia heard her step-cousin's muffled sobs. She felt sorry for the girl and raised a hand to knock, then thought better of it. If Annette was rude downstairs, Julia could only imagine her fury if she interrupted her now.

Once in her own room, Julia sat in the win-dow seat, snatching up the agricultural report in an attempt to lose herself in the dry pages. She read the first two lines, then tossed it aside, too frustrated to concentrate. Leaning her forehead against the cool glass, she watched a few stars peep out through a break in the moving clouds.

What did the captain mean by suggesting gentlemen wanted women with a head for business? Did he mean he wanted such a lady? No, he was not interested in a sensible wife, only a country fling, no matter how much tender sincerity filled his eyes. Paul had warned her about a man's ability to charm a woman for purely dishonourable reasons. She could not let herself fall into the captain's trap, no matter how easily her body reacted when he stood so close.

The idea that she might be too weak to resist him scared her as deeply now as it had at the keep and in the library. Pulling her knees up under her chin, she wrapped her arms around them in an effort to ward off the sudden cold. Everything felt so uncertain, as if the captain's arrival had changed more than just the place settings for dinner. Not even Knollwood or her own conviction to buy Cable Grange seemed steady any more.

If only Paul was here. He'd know what to do about the captain, the Taylors and Cable Grange. However, he was at sea and about to face unimaginable dangers. Even if she could get a letter to him, it wasn't right to burden him with her concerns at a time like this. She would have to solve these problems herself.

James lay in bed, staring at the white plaster ceiling, his aching shoulder preventing any chance of sleep. He'd gritted his teeth more than once during the ride back to Knollwood, but the pain seemed a worthy price to pay for the excitement he experienced racing Miss Howard. Outside, the wind rattled the window, knocking a tree branch against the house. Thoughts of Miss Howard continued to torment him despite all attempts to drive them from his mind. He could not care for her. He would not. What did he have to offer her but a weak body and a meaningless life?

As he pulled the medallion back and forth across its chain, those old familiar protests sounded hollow tonight. Over the last few days, he'd felt freer than he had since being wounded and dreams of the future crept into the long hours of the night. Perhaps he'd travel to Rome, inspect the ruins, then carry on to Greece or Constantinople. He might even return to India and explore more than the port cities. Miss Howard's eyes would flash at the sight of the palaces and market places.

James twisted the chain tight around his finger until the metal bit into his flesh. How many times had he lain here, distracting himself from his painful shoulder with dreams of her young, supple body? He'd almost groaned when she'd appeared in the dining room tonight, her low-cut gown displaying the delicate curves of her body. He wanted nothing more than to slip his hands beneath the green silk, to feel the soft flesh of her thighs, taste the sweet hollow of her neck while his hands caressed her stomach. Did she know how she teased him and made him ache with need? She wanted him as much as he wanted her. He'd seen it in her eyes at the keep, felt it in the way she'd held his hand when they'd run through the rain. Yet still she went back to the dandy.

Smacking his fist against the sheets, he tried to ignore the subtle throbbing in his member as it overcame the sting of his shoulder. He'd placed his happiness in the hands of a woman once before, only to be cruelly disappointed. What did Melinda matter now? George was right; she was in the past where she belonged. Thinking about her did nothing but weaken his spirit. No, there were other, more pleasant things to consider, such as the taste of Miss Howard's lips. He'd been tantalisingly close so many times today, yet she continued to elude him.

Shifting on the bed, he searched for a more comfortable position. Guilt filled his mind. He couldn't ruin George's niece, not for simple need, nor could he ask for her hand. Or could he? A woman with her talents would be an asset and he could well imagine her accompanying him to India or on any other whim. But were these reasons good enough to tie him to a woman for life? Miss Howard would certainly keep things interesting, assuming she'd have him. He remembered George's suggestion that a man with an estate could capture her heart. He'd wanted Cable Grange for revenge; now he had another, sweeter reason. For once the idea of marriage didn't seem distasteful, but was he ready to spring the parson's mousetrap? If so, he'd need a tempting bit of cheese to catch this mouse.

Chapter Seven

Julia ambled back from the stables, the cold, early morning air chafing her cheeks. Stifling a yawn with the back of her hand, she tried to blame last night's restlessness on Annette or the problem of Simon, but it was Captain Covington who'd kept her up until almost sunrise. With the auction date drawing closer, it was time to put such foolishness aside and be serious about her pursuit. She calculated again the ready locked in the desk drawer, wondering how much it would take to buy Simon and his silence. Father had always kept the money at hand, mostly to send to Paul when one of his frequent letters arrived asking for more. She'd left it there out of habit; now she could use it to her advantage. She'd corner Simon once he finally awoke and came down to eat, assuming he'd even returned from his rousing night at the Sign of the Swan.

A flash of pink caught Julia's eye and she noticed her mother, parasol in hand, inspecting her roses. Charlemagne trotted beside her, his tail wagging in happy excitement. The rose garden was her mother's domain, the one area of Knollwood off limits to both Father's and Julia's management, and she coaxed from it flowers of amazing beauty. Watching her with her precious bushes, her hem wet, feet encased in sturdy shoes instead of slippers, she knew her mother played a small part in her own love of the land.

In no mood to risk a serious discussion, Julia slunk past the garden, hoping her mother wouldn't turn around. She was nearly to the house when Charlemagne let out an excited yip.

'Come here, dear,' her mother called in a voice Julia could not ignore.

She wondered if Emily had told her about their conversation yesterday. It wasn't in her mother's nature to scold, but she was not above the occasional reprimand. 'Yes, Mother?'

'Do you have feelings for Simon?' She turned over a leaf, searching for signs of disease.

Julia hesitated, hating the blunt questions. It made evading it difficult. 'He's an affable gentleman.'

Her mother stared hard at her. 'The truth, please.'

'No, certainly not,' Julia admitted, knowing it was better to level with her mother than continue the charade.

'Then why show him so much preference?'

'I thought if I could make him ask for my hand, then an engagement would be enough for Charles to give me my inheritance in time to purchase Cable Grange.'

'I suspected as much.' Her mother plucked off a wilted bloom and tossed it over the wall. 'Even if he did propose, Charles wouldn't allow it. Simon has too much of a reputation in town.'

'Must my entire life be governed by what Charles does and does not like?'

'I thought you didn't care for Simon?'

'I don't, but I hate Charles's high-handed meddling.'

'Be kind, dear. He does love you and only wants your happiness.'

Julia didn't agree, but held her tongue. Arguing with her mother would get her nowhere and with the plan to entice Simon unravelling, she needed her help. 'What am I going to do?'

'Have you considered Captain Covington?'

Julia fingered a stem, snapping off a thorn with her thumb. During the long hours without sleep she'd considered the captain many times, in many different ways, none of which was suitable to discuss with her mother. 'I chose Simon because I thought the promise of a fortune would be enough to attract him. I won't have the same influence with the captain. Besides, he's infatuated with Annette.'

'I don't believe he is. I've watched him and I think he tolerates her simply to be courteous.'

Julia knew she was right. At certain unguarded moments, the captain did appear bored or annoyed with Annette.

'I'd have to tell him directly of my scheme and what if he told others?' She knew he wouldn't, but she felt the need to make some kind of protest. If she agreed too speedily to the idea, her mother might suspect something more, something Julia didn't even want to admit to herself.

'I don't think he'll reveal your secret. He's honourable, possesses a good reputation and George can vouch for him. Charles is more likely to accept him. And think of Paul. A friendship with the captain may help his career. He must know people in the Admiralty and he might be in a position to bend their ears.'

Despite her mother's reasoning, Julia hesitated. Such a game with the captain would prove far more dangerous than with Simon. Could she trust herself to spend enough time with him to give the appearance of genuine affection without compromising herself? Of course she could. Couldn't she? 'I'll think about it.'

'If nothing else, imagine how it will annoy Annette,' her mother suggested with a wry smile.

Julia gasped. 'I never knew you were so wicked.'

'I'm your uncle's sister, am I not?'

'Indeed.'

'Now come along, for I believe George has a surprise for us about nuncheon.'

Uncle George's nuncheon plans did come as a surprise. Somehow, without Julia discovering it, he'd arranged for an outdoor picnic on a grassy hill near Knollwood. He'd ordered a number of oilcloths spread on the still-wet grass and brought over from Creedon Abbey a large canopy acquired during a visit to India. From their high vantage point, they could see Cable Grange perched on a distant hill and one turret of Creedon Abbey peeking above a far-off line of trees.

Julia sipped her tea, studying the captain and Annette over the rim of her cup. Annette served him a slice of cake while leaning over to reveal the tops of her breasts pushed up by her low-cut bodice. Uncle George had advised them to wear clothing appropriate for the cool autumn weather but she'd ignored his advice, dressing instead for husband hunting.

'Annette will catch her death of cold pursuing the captain,' Julia whispered to Emily, noticing the chit's goose bumps from across the oilcloth.

'You shouldn't laugh at people,' Emily chided, popping a small sandwich into her mouth to cover an agreeing smile.

Julia focused on the captain, noting how often he turned away from Annette's charms to take in the view. After a moment, his eyes met hers and she concentrated on her tea cup, sipping the tepid liquid with as much ease of manner as she could muster. The idea of revealing her scheme to him and asking for his help terrified, yet intrigued her. Would he go along? If she kept the mood light, made him understand it was all a game, why wouldn't he? After all, he'd participated in many of Uncle George's schemes.

If it all seemed so simple, then why was she afraid of asking him? She'd almost risked her reputation on a dandy. Why did a man like Captain Covington frighten her?

Deep in her heart she knew the reason. His dashing features and the easy way they laughed together would make it difficult to jilt him and jilt him she must. As a single woman, Cable Grange would be hers completely. Married, the property would belong to him, leaving her in a position no better than her current one with Charles. Though she doubted Captain Covington would act like her brother, it was still risky to gamble her future on a man she barely knew.

She turned towards Cable Grange, watching the sunlight dance off the dirty sandstone, trying to imagine it clean, the sheep well fed and bred, the fields high with wheat and barley. The thought of such a beautiful estate left to moulder broke her heart. No matter what her fears, she had to face them and get Cable Grange.

Julia put down her tea cup and stood, smoothing her dress with her gloved hands. 'I think I'll go for a walk.'

Catching the captain's eyes, she nodded in the direction of the woods. He met it with a questioning frown before comprehension dawned on his face, bringing with it a roguish smile. Julia, confident he understood, turned and walked off down the hill. What exactly he understood she wasn't sure. He certainly wouldn't expect her proposal, but he couldn't anticipate a sordid rendezvous, not with everyone sitting only a few hundred feet away.

'More tea, Captain Covington?' Miss Taylor asked, forcing James to stifle a smile. He'd seen the signal, the same one George used to use when they needed to escape a room and discuss their next move. What did Miss Howard wish to tell him that the others could not hear?

'Annette, leave the captain alone. He'll float away if you ply him with much more tea,' George chided.

'I'm sure Captain Covington is quite capable of knowing when he has and has not had enough tea,' she snapped and James seized the chance to leave.

'I think I'll join Miss Howard.' He hurried after her before Miss Taylor or anyone else could offer to join him.

The hill quickened his pace and his feet fell hard on the firm dirt. Miss Howard watched him approach from where she sat on the twisted trunk of a fallen tree, standing once he reached her. A strange sort of nervous anticipation decorated her face and he wondered what serious secret made her so eager to speak with him in private.

'You've set their tongues wagging by following me.' She walked deeper into the woods and he followed, leaves crackling beneath his boots.

'George's tongue is already wagging.'

'What do you mean?'

'He's playing the matchmaker and would like very much to see us married.'

She stopped and her fingers flew to her lips in fearful surprise. 'Really?'

'You didn't know?'

'No.' She resumed her languid pace, her face more tightly drawn than before.

'As much as I enjoy teasing him, if I have to spend one more minute eating out of Miss Taylor's hands just to see the stunned expression on his face, I may expire from fatigue,' James admitted with a smile.

'Thank heavens,' she breathed, sounding more nervous than amused. 'I was afraid you'd succumbed to her fake charm.'

'I might say the same of you and your present infatuation with Mr Taylor,' he countered, eager to get at the truth of her relationship with the dandy.

'You can't believe I'm interested in him.' She picked up a stick and smacked a brown leaf off an overhanging branch. 'He's weak and useless and no woman wants such a man. Like you, I was merely pretending.'

James flexed his left hand, resisting the urge to feel under his shirt. 'Why would you feign interest in a man? You aren't after a husband, are you?'

She stopped abruptly and turned to him. 'No, I'm in search of a fiancé, or, more correctly, someone like you who can pretend.' The words came out in such a winded rush he almost missed their meaning. He stared at her, waiting for a laugh, smile or some other indication of a joke, but she only watched him with the same nervous fear as before.

'You're serious?'

'It's my intention to purchase Cable Grange with my inheritance, but I don't receive it until I'm married. However, if Charles believes I'm engaged—'

'—he'll give you the money.'

'Yes. Once I've purchased the estate, I'll cry off the engagement and you'll be a free man.' She broke the stick in half and tossed it aside.

James stepped back, unsure how to respond. An engagement for Cable Grange? It seemed impossible, yet exactly like something a girl of her pluck would suggest.

'I'd hoped to entice Simon into an engagement,' she continued when he didn't answer, 'but the gentleman is thicker than mud and, according to Mother, quite unsuitable. Charles isn't likely to approve of the match. But as an old friend of Uncle George's you're—'

'—perfect.'

'Well, I wouldn't say "perfect", but you'll do.'

'Will I now?'

'You have a fondness for schemes.'

'So it seems.' James leaned back against a large oak, crossing his arms over his chest in amusement. The woman was unbelievable.

'Please. It's the only way. I have to have Cable

Grange.' The desperation in her voice and the
dejected way she drew the pelisse's satin ribbon
through her fingers touched him. He wanted to
take her sad face in his hands and kiss away
the small line between her brows. The idea was
doomed to fail. He knew something of Charles.
Her brother was exacting and wouldn't simply
give her the money on a promise. If James agreed
to the scheme, it could only end in either their
marriage or her ruin. He might have contemplated marriage in the middle of the night, but in
the light of the day, under such dubious circum-
stance, it was quite a different prospect.

She bit her bottom lip in anticipation of his
answer. Did she care for him? Sometimes, when
he caught her observing him, he suspected some
interest. However, she was a determined girl and
she'd set her mind on Cable Grange. She'd never
admit any feelings for him if they interfered with
her plans.

'What will you tell your brother when you end
the engagement?'

'I don't think Charles likes Navy men, so I
doubt he'll be too put off by the idea.'

'Or he might insist.'

'You're a free man—refuse him.'

'It's that important to you?'

'It's the only future I have.'

If this were any other woman, he'd think she

was trying to trap him, but the way she admitted her situation with such raw agony told him she had no designs. Like him, the realities of life frustrated her and she did her best to overcome them. It took courage to reveal her situation and propose the plan and he respected her bravery. An engagement would force them together, giving him a chance to know her better, perhaps convince her not to jilt him if his feelings and hers proved true. If he was wrong and there was no interest, they'd break the engagement. It all seemed so uncomplicated, but he knew it wasn't. Was he ready to agree to her arrangement and risk the very real possibility of marriage?

'You have George's talent for schemes,' he said.

'So it seems,' she agreed.

'You know about most of the plots I was entangled in?'

She nodded.

'Then I'll have to tell you the rest during our engagement.'

'You'll do it?'

'I followed George. It seems only fitting I follow his niece.'

'Thank you, Captain, thank you.' She threw her arms around his neck, hugging him close. He breathed in the clean scent of her soft hair, felt the warmth of her neck so close to his lips. He moved to wrap his arms around her, put his hand on the small of her back and draw her deeper into the arc of his body. His member eagerly responded to the sudden rush of desire, but knowing his breeches wouldn't hide it and in no mood to embarrass himself, he removed her arms from around his neck. Her eager eyes met his and he saw more in her happy expression than a scheme. He released her wrists, afraid of what might happen if he held her for too long.

'We must play the role of courting couple,' she explained matter of factly, covering the lingering tension. 'Give ourselves time to develop an attachment and for the others to see it. Charles must believe it is real. When would you like to begin?'

'Now, my little Artemis, before we change our minds.' He offered her his arm and she took it, allowing him to walk her back through the woods.

Was it his pulse or hers she felt racing beneath her fingers? Pausing for him to hold back a branch, she moved forwards, barely able to keep her body from trembling. Up ahead, the trees began to thin, the green hill just visible beyond the forest's deep shadows. Once they stepped out together, the game was on and would not end until she either had Cable Grange or—or what?

She stopped, nervousness making her whole

body vibrate. 'You could turn back now,' she offered, more to herself than the captain.

'I wouldn't dream of it.' He took a step forwards, but she didn't move. 'You aren't afraid, are you?'

'Of course not.' *I'm terrified*, she thought, but didn't say it. Having her scheme turn real in so short a time was overwhelming.

'Good.'

He pulled her forwards, out of the trees and she blinked against the sunlight. He kept a tight grip on her arm, escorting her up the hill. Julia could almost feel the shock rippling through the group at the sight of them in such an intimate attitude. Annette's jaw dropped, Uncle George choked on a biscuit, Simon inspected them through his quizzing glass and Emily's eyes went large. Only her mother appeared not to notice, doting on Charlemagne in an attempt to hide a knowing smile.

'I think we've made an impression,' Julia whispered, her fear fading in the face of this small triumph.

'I believe we have.'

They sat down together on the oilcloth, a short distance from the others who continued to watch them in silence. Not even Uncle George had recovered enough to ask questions or do anything more than stare. Julia acted like nothing was amiss and for the first time in days felt hope for her future. Neither Annette's sour face nor Emily's dumbfounded expression could ruin the feeling.

'Tea?' Captain Covington offered, holding up the small teapot.

'Yes, please.' She held out her cup. When it was full she exchanged it for a small plate of tarts. 'Would you like one?'

'Thank you.' He reached for a delicacy, but Julia pulled it away, then held it out for him to taste.

'Subtlety,' he whispered, taking the treat from her fingers and breaking off a small bite.

'Why?' Julia whispered back. 'If I'm going to do this, I'm going to do it well.'

'George, you've outdone yourself with surprises today,' James congratulated when they returned from the picnic to find a game of battledore and shuttlecock arranged on the lawn.

'I'm not the only one,' George remarked as James took two battledores from the footman and handed Miss Howard one with all the tender flourish of a smitten suitor.

'What do you mean?'

George scowled in answer, then turned to Miss Taylor. 'Annette, you should play.'

Miss Taylor's pinched eyebrows drew closer

together. 'I have no intention of remaining out-side. My shoes are already soaked through.'

Holding up the wet hem of her thin gown, she marched inside.

'I believe I'll join her,' Mr Taylor added and no one tried to stop him.

James and Miss Howard began their game while the others fell into furious whispering. He noticed the volley of looks thrown their way, but the ping of the shuttlecock hitting Miss Howard's battledore forced him to focus on the game.

He ran for the wispy target, smacking it back to her and sending her running. She whacked it inches from the ground and it sailed through the air towards him. Lunging for it, he ignored his stinging shoulder, enjoying the lively play. With a quick swing, he shot the shuttlecock over her head and into the tall grass.

'You're an excellent player, Miss Howard.'

'You're trying to flatter me.' She laughed, re-trieving the shuttlecock and preparing to serve.

'I never offer a compliment I don't mean.'

Their vigorous game continued, Miss Howard chasing the shuttlecock, her face flushed with ex-citement, hair slightly dishevelled and eyes vivid from the exertion. It reminded him of the mo-ment they'd first met in the forest. What would it be like to drive her to such a state by the play of his fingers along her skin? Hopefully, he'd get the chance to discover it, but for now vigorous exercise must suffice.

James played with equal enthusiasm, chasing the shuttlecock all over the field. Then, in the middle of one challenging set, something over Miss Howard's shoulder made him pause. He let the shuttlecock drop to the ground, watching the stable boy run up the lawn towards them.

'What's wrong?' She turned and at the sight of the boy, threw down her battledore and rushed to meet him. 'Samuel, what is it? What's happened?'

'There's been trouble, Miss Howard.'

James hurried to her side and the flustered stable boy, breathing hard from his run, warily took them in.

'What? Tell me,' she demanded.

He hesitated, visibly torn between telling his mistress and getting in trouble.

James knew whatever he'd come to report had happened under suspicious circumstances.

'Tell her what happened,' James commanded, ignoring the disapproving glance Miss Howard tossed his way.

'There was a fight in the clearing near the lower pasture,' he explained, James's order loosening his tongue. 'Mr Wilkins's man was knocked out and Bill's bleeding badly.'

'I must put a stop to this at once. Come along, Samuel.'

'Can I stay here, miss?' the boy stuttered.

'Whatever for?'

'I believe the lad is afraid of losing face,' James offered, sensing the boy's predicament. He'd seen it many times aboard ship. 'Whatever's going on is a secret and the others might hold it against him if they learn he told you.'

'All right, Samuel, you may stay. But when I return I'd better find you working, not dallying or daydreaming.'

'Yes, miss.' He dashed off in the direction of the stables.

Miss Howard turned to the others, who watched from their place along the edge of the court. 'Mother, send John to fetch the medicine chest. Emily, have Davies send two men and a stretcher to the clearing near the pasture.'

'Where are you going?' Emily asked in a heavy, warning tone.

'To deal with this incident.' Miss Howard turned, striding off.

'I insist you let the farm manager deal with it,' Emily called after her to no effect. Miss Howard kept walking, pretending not to hear her sister-in-law.

'I'll go with her.' James knew the hot tempers

of fighting men. He couldn't imagine the diminutive Miss Howard facing them alone.

'Me, too,' George offered.

Despite her quick clip, James easily caught up to her, his long legs giving him an advantage. Behind them, George huffed and puffed, struggling to keep pace with their steady strides. 'What will you do when you find them?'

Miss Howard didn't slow, but kept on down the rutted path. 'I don't know.'

'Do you think this is wise?'

'Is it wise to allow workers to neglect their duties?'

'Perhaps there is a better way to handle the situation.'

'How? By letting you command them? Perhaps you would like to oversee their wages as well or direct them where to plough?'

'The boy talked, didn't he?'

'That's not the point.'

'Then what is?'

'I have no wish to discuss it at this time.'

They walked a fair distance from the house, across one large field and down a rolling slope to where the land flattened again. Sheep watched them march by until they reached another clearing.

'What's going on here?' Miss Howard took the lead, her voice carrying across the grass to the circle of men. They turned, guilt washing over their faces. James stifled a laugh as the gruff field hands dropped their heads like a bunch of schoolboys caught cheating. He recognised a number of men from Julia's staff. The others appeared to be Mr Wilkins's men for they leered at Miss Howard, making James very glad he'd decided to come.

An unconscious man lay on the ground. Another, larger man sat next to him, holding his bloody arm. The two fighters were naked from the waist up, but Miss Howard seemed not to notice as she strode into the thick of things.

'I said, what's going on here?' she demanded again upon reaching the circle, her hands balled against her hips. All the men had strapping builds from years of labour and towered over their employer. James might fear for her safety, but he had to admire her spirit. She reminded him of a certain well-known tavern owner in Tortuga who didn't tolerate fighting in her establishment.

When no one answered, she turned to the bleeding man on the ground. 'Bill, tell me what happened.'

He blinked against the sun, his face long with shame. 'It was a friendly wager, Miss Howard. Tim said I could beat Mr Wilkins's man, and you know I can. But he had a knife. Cut me before I laid him out.'

'You lie,' one of the greasier men challenged, his lascivious eyes raking Miss Howard, making James's blood boil.

'It's the truth,' Bill challenged, sparking a round of heated accusations.

'Bloody liar—'

'He cheated—'

'Can't trust a Wilkins servant—'

'That's enough!' Miss Howard shouted, her voice lost in a swirl of angry shouts and jabbing fingers. The jabbing rapidly escalated to shoving with Miss Howard caught in the middle. James pulled her from the centre as the first punch swung close to her head. Pushing her towards George, he summoned all his years as a commander and addressed the tangled rabble.

'Attention!' The men with military experience straightened up while the others stopped arguing long enough for him to take control of the situation. 'I want silence this instance. You men there, get back to Cable Grange.'

'And who are you to be ordering us around?' the greasy one sneered.

James stepped toe to toe with the man. 'What's your name?'

'Mark.' He spat on the ground at James's feet.

James fixed him with an insolent-wilting glare. 'Then get back to Cable Grange, Mark, and take your companion with you.'

The men slowly crept across the pasture towards Cable Grange. Mark and another man pulled up their groggy friend and with his arms over their shoulders dragged him off through the high grass.

'The rest of you listen to Miss Howard or you'll have me to answer to.' He stepped aside, waving his hand at the workers. 'Your men are ready.'

Her angry eyes flashed at him before she stepped forwards to face her servants.

'You know I don't condone fighting. I should dismiss every one of you for what you've done.' Alarm swept through the men, but they did not answer back. Watching her walk up and down the line of servants, she reminded him of a petite captain. It was strange to see a lady in such a position, but it boded well for a woman who, depending on how their scheme played out, might accompany him throughout the world under who knew what circumstances.

'I know you men all have families and you're all good, hard workers, so I'll forgive you today,' she continued. 'But if I ever catch any of you doing something like this again, you'll be instantly dismissed. Now, return to your duties at once, except you, Bill. We must see to your arm.'

The men filed past, thanking her profusely. She nodded sternly at each and when they were gone, turned to Bill. Behind her, John and two other servants appeared with the stretcher and a small wooden medicine chest.

'Well, Bill?' Miss Howard asked, standing over the injured man.

'Am I to be dismissed?' he asked, shamefaced.

'No, I think you've been punished enough for today.' She knelt down beside him. 'I want to see your arm.'

She motioned for it, but he held it fast, drops of blood seeping out from between his fingers.

'It's no sight for a lady.'

'Let me see it,' she insisted.

He removed his hand, revealing a gaping cut. It was small but deep and bleeding heavily. She didn't blanch, but examined it with care, then motioned for the chest.

'You need the surgeon.' She pulled off one glove and removed a bandage roll from the medical box, winding it tightly around Bill's wound. 'John, please fetch the surgeon. You two, help Bill back to the stable. Uncle George, can you accompany them?'

'Yes, but I want James to escort you back to the house.'

'I can find my own way.' She started to rise and George took her by the elbow, helping her to her feet.

'I insist he see you back.'

'Very well.'

George joined the servants making their way back to the house, leaving James alone with Miss Howard.

'That was very brave of you. I don't know another lady with such command of her staff and quite the strong stomach.' He kicked loose dirt over the small puddle of blood on the ground. 'I think you'd be very good in any crisis. You have a way with authority.'

'And you, Captain, have a way of interfering when you shouldn't. Kindly remember you are a guest at Knollwood, not its owner.'

Julia pushed past him, making for the path to the house. She heard the heavy fall of his boots on the ground as he caught up to her and she quickened her pace, nearly breaking into a run.

'Julia, wait.'

She whirled to face him, closing the short distance between them. 'How dare you address me in such an intimate manner?'

'I think it only fitting since we're engaged.' There it was again, his knowing smile, the one she found so infuriating. What was it about this man who annoyed her with such charm?

'Yes, engaged, and not even that, yet you already act like a husband.'

The comment wiped the smile from his face. 'Is this my thanks for helping you?'

'You weren't helping. You were undermining my authority, giving orders and interfering with my management of Knollwood.'

'If I hadn't undermined your authority, some servant would have pummelled you.'

'I do not wish to discuss it.' She continued on up the path, too worked up by the fight, the wound and the captain to stand still. A small pang of guilt needled her for being so cross. Yes, if he hadn't stepped in she might well have been injured, or worse. But she couldn't bring herself to thank him. She suddenly wished she were at Cable Grange with all of this ridiculous business behind her.

'Julia, please stop.'

The tender request held more power than any of his commands, bringing her to a halt. He walked around to stand in front of her, but she refused to meet his face. She kept her head down, studying his boots, noting the mud stuck to the sides and a small scuff on the toe.

'Whatever you think of my interfering, I only meant to help and whether our engagement is real or fake doesn't matter. I had no desire to see you hurt.'

She pulled on her glove, fumbling to fasten the small button at her wrist, unsure how to continue. He was right. She shouldn't be angry and she had insulted him again without good reason.

Would she never learn? 'Perhaps we shouldn't play this game.'

He took her hand, his fingers slipping the ivory button through its hole.

'I very much enjoy this game, my little Artemis.' His thumb stroked the inside of her palm, firm and warm through her glove. Her heart raced and she worked to breathe evenly.

'Don't call me that.'

'But it suits you.'

Her anger, the fighting men and all her troubles faded away and she was aware of nothing but his hand on hers. 'I'm sorry if I seem ungrateful. I shouldn't be, especially after everything you've agreed to do for me. I do thank you for your help.'

'We all need help sometimes.'

'I'm not accustomed to asking for it.'

'You didn't ask. I offered.' He swept her into his arms, covering her lips with his. All the stories Paul had told her about Navy men urged her to pull away, but she didn't. Instead she went soft in his arms, falling into him as he pulled her close. His warm, firm lips drove everything from her mind: Cable Grange, the fighting servants, Charles. A thrill coursed through her, like riding Manfred over the hills on a sunny day. Her heart raced, her mind spun and then suddenly it was over. He stepped back, and she smiled as she stared at him, resisting the urge to throw herself into his arms and demand he continue.

'I think we should return to the house,' she stammered. What else did one say after allowing a gentleman to take liberties?

'Indeed.' He offered her his arm and she took it.

She hadn't been able to command one coherent thought on the walk back. So much had happened so fast she couldn't make sense out of any of it. Only when they entered the garden to find her mother and Emily waiting on the stone patio did her head finally clear. Emily's lips were drawn tight with worry, but her mother only raised a curious eyebrow at the sight of them walking so close together. Julia's grip on the captain's arm tightened.

'What's wrong?'

'I'm going to hear a great deal from Emily about being so rash. I don't suppose you wish to help me again?'

'If only I could.' The captain laughed. 'But I'm afraid you must handle this matter alone.'

Chapter Eight

Emily's clipped steps carried her across the morning-room rug, crossing back and forth in front of Julia, who stood by the fireplace, tapping her foot in irritation. Every day Emily sounded more and more like Charles and the constant lectures were proving quite tiresome. Cable Grange could not be hers soon enough.

'First you go out riding with the captain, alone,' Emily said.

'We didn't go out riding. He happened upon me at the keep.'

'Then you put yourself in danger by involving yourself with the servants in front of him.'

'You'd rather they fight instead of work?' Julia silently pleaded with her mother, wishing for once she'd intervene, but she did nothing except adjust Charlemagne's collar.

'Come, Emily, don't be so hard on Julia.' Uncle George stepped in, refilling his glass of port from the decanter near the window. 'Girl has responsibilities.'

'Don't you understand the way this behaviour appears? Whether innocent or not, it is compromising.'

'In James's eyes, never.' Uncle George laughed. 'He isn't such an old biddy to get fired up over a ride or an incident with the field hands.'

'I believe you are both failing to see the point.'

'Excuse me, Mrs Howard.' Captain Covington entered the room, respectfully deferential. 'I believe I have some information to put your mind at ease.'

'Information?' Emily asked.

Julia shook her head, but he ignored her, reserving his gracious smile for Emily.

'This afternoon in the forest I asked Miss Howard to marry me and she accepted.'

The room went silent.

'Is it true?' Emily demanded.

Julia wasn't sure how to answer. She hadn't expected him to announce their engagement so soon, but now it was done and she had to play along. 'Of course it's true.'

'But—you hardly know one another.'

'In the short amount of time we've spent together we've discovered a great deal in common. It's as though we've known each other for years.' Captain Covington took Julia's hand and gazed lovingly into her eyes. Her heart fluttered with excitement before she reined in her runaway emotions. Reminding herself it was all a ruse, she returned the loving smile with one of her own, careful not to exaggerate it too much.

Emily twisted her hands in front of her. 'What will Charles say?'

'I have already spoken to Mother and Uncle George,' Julia lied, hoping they would play along, too.

'She did?' Emily asked her mother-in-law, who nodded.

'We discussed it this morning.'

'And you?' Emily turned to Uncle George.

'Jim mentioned it during our ride,' he mumbled, tossing back the last of his port.

Julia let out her breath. Uncle George would demand an explanation, but he could always be counted on to go along.

'Please excuse us, Captain.' Emily grabbed Julia by the arm, pulling her into the hall and closing the morning-room door behind them. 'What's going on?'

'I thought you'd be pleased. You and Charles are always telling me to marry.'

'Yes, but—?'

'But what? Isn't Captain Covington a respectable man?'

'To be sure, but—'

'But what? Uncle George has known him for years, he has a sizeable fortune, and he's amiable and well spoken of. What objection could you possibly have?'

'Marriage isn't something to be entered into lightly.'

'Why shouldn't I be as happy with him as any other gentleman?'

Emily took her by the shoulders, examining her with an older sister's overprotective concern. 'Is there something else to this I should know? You haven't engaged in any compromising behaviour?'

The captain's kiss suddenly came to mind, but her rising anger pushed the memory away. 'Beyond the list you've accused me of?'

'Please, be serious.'

Julia threw up her hands in exasperation. 'Of course not—how could you even make such a suggestion?'

'Because this is all so sudden. Do you love him?'

Julia looked out one of the tall windows flanking the front door where two turtle doves walked in the shade of the portico. Watching them coo to each other, Julia wondered at the question.

Love. How would it feel to truly be in love? The fountain in the garden came to mind. Could she find such passion with the captain? No, he'd only prove as meddlesome as he had with the labourers.

'Well?' Emily demanded, breaking the long silence.

'Of course,' Julia lied. She was pretending to be engaged; why not pretend to be in love, too? 'He's the most interesting, well-travelled man I've ever met and quite handsome. You remarked on those exact qualities yourself the other night at cards.'

'Yes, but you seemed so uninterested.'

'I did not know him well then.'

Emily tapped her fingers on her chin, examining Julia, struggling to comprehend the strange turn of events. 'Do you think you'll be happy with him?'

'Yes. I'll have my own home to run. How could I not be happy?' This certainly wasn't a lie and it helped put Emily's mind at ease.

'Then I am glad for you.' She hugged Julia with all the affection of a sister before her smile tensed at the corners. 'Of course, Captain Covington should have asked Charles's permission first—he is your guardian—but I don't think he'll object. I'll write to him about it at once.'

Julia didn't share Emily's worry. No doubt

she'd already written to him about Julia's behaviour. If so, she knew Charles would jump to
give his consent, if only to see her settled and out
of Knollwood. For once, the idea didn't trouble
her. 'I'll write him, too. I want him to know of
my good fortune.'

They walked back to the morning room, a
slight smile tugging at the edges of her lips.
Cable Grange and freedom were in her grasp.

Inside, Uncle George pumped Captain Covington's hand, the port in his glass sloshing high
along the rim. 'Congratulations, Jim. You don't
know how glad I am to hear it. Julia, you couldn't
have asked for a better man.'

Julia felt a slight twinge of guilt. If he was this
excited by their engagement, how disappointed
would he be when it all came to an end?

'Now I have some news to add to yours,'
Uncle George announced. 'I've secured invita-
tions to the Johnsons' ball Wednesday night. You
two can announce the engagement to everyone.'

'I can't go. I have no dress and I can't have one
made in such a short time.' She hadn't planned
on making a public announcement. If no one
outside the family knew, she could easily break
it off with very few consequences.

'One of your London gowns will do,' her
mother said and Julia blanched. Her mother knew
the engagement wasn't real. Why would she en-

courage the ball? It must only be to convince
Charles of its validity. What other reason could
she have? She was almost afraid to imagine it.
'We'll choose a dress today, in case it needs any
alterations.'

'Yes, of course.' Julia tried to sound excited,
but with no desire to attend the ball it was difficult.

'Do you mind if I have a private word with
your groom-to-be?' Uncle George asked and
Julia had a good idea what he wished to discuss. At least it meant another person on her side
against Charles, one who would speak up for her
far more than her mother.

'Not at all. I must write to Charles and I believe Mother wishes to discuss dresses.'

Once the ladies were gone, George turned a
suspicious eye on James. 'Out with it. What are
you two up to?'

'You don't believe in true love?'

'Until today you've done nothing but tickle
Annette's fancy—now suddenly you and Julia
are engaged? Did something happen out on your
ride?'

'I assure you, it's nothing like that.'

'Then what?'

'Cable Grange.'

George frowned. 'I thought you were over all that.'

'I am—apparently your niece is not. She thinks an engagement might force her brother's hand.'

'It may just force yours. Charles isn't like Paul and Julia. He may make you go through with it.'

James walked to the window, watching the shadow of clouds pass over the gravel drive. 'Perhaps by the end of it I may not mind.'

'You want to marry her?' George stammered.

'I suppose by the auction, we'll see.' He'd taken a chance announcing the engagement and wasn't sure what would happen by the time Cable Grange came up for sale.

'James…' George joined him at the window, dropping his voice, one eye on the morning-room door '…I've known you a long time and we've been through a lot together, but where Julia is concerned I'll side with her if things go badly. I hope it doesn't come to that, but if it does, you'll find me and Charles standing against you.'

James flexed his left hand, keeping his eyes fixed on a tree in the distance. 'I have no intention of allowing things to go badly. I will do the honourable thing where your niece is concerned, but she may not have me in the end.'

'What do you mean?'

James explained her plan to George, who nodded gravely, taking it all in with a large sip of port.

'I see what you mean.' George rubbed his chin with his hand. 'I knew she wanted the place, but I didn't think she'd go this far to get it.'

'I will do all I can to protect her and her reputation. But as you yourself said, she's spirited.'

'Yes, but better you than the fop.' He slapped James on the back, then headed for the port. 'If nothing else, it will be interesting.'

James laughed, joining his friend in a drink. Yes, it would be interesting.

'Well done,' her mother congratulated when Julia entered the sitting room after giving Davies the letter to Charles to post. She'd written it a few days ago in an effort to phrase her case without distraction or emotion, then simply rewritten it, replacing Simon's name with the captain's.

'Emily did not react well.' Emily had yet to join them and Julia knew she was busy writing her own letter. She could only imagine its contents and hoped Charles's business in London kept him from coming home to see the situation for himself. 'I thought she would be pleased.'

'She'll be less pleased if you jilt the captain.'

'When I jilt the captain,' Julia corrected, sitting at the small table across from her. 'You won't tell her, will you?'

'No, though at some point you'll have to tell Charles. That alone may stop you from breaking the engagement.'

'Surely you don't want me to marry the captain?'

Mother offered Charlemagne a titbit from the plate next to her. Julia picked at the lace tablecloth, the silence punctuated by the dog's chewing. It wasn't unusual for Mother not to answer, but this time something about it made Julia uneasy.

'I must also find a way to avoid the ball,' Julia added. 'I can't have the whole countryside knowing of my engagement. It will create a scandal when I break it.'

'You'll have a stronger case if it's public knowledge.'

At least Julia had been correct about her mother's motives. 'Yes, but if everyone knows, I'll be the talk of every country party this winter. I'd rather not subject myself to such gossip.'

'My dear, you must learn not to care so much about what people think.'

If only it were so easy, Julia thought, Emily's entrance ending their private conversation.

What followed was a boring hour of flipping through pattern books and discussing trimmings. They invited Annette to join them, but she de-

clined, stating she had no need to rework a dress
as those she had brought from London were ad-
equate for a country ball. Very soon Emily and
Mrs Howard were debating the merits of their
different dresses and doing their best to engage
Julia.

'See the way they've used the ribbon here.
Wouldn't that be lovely on my white-silk gown?'
Emily asked.

'Yes, lovely.' Julia listlessly flipped through a
pattern book, eager to be free of all this idle chatter and return to plans for Cable Grange. She still
couldn't believe Captain Covington had agreed
to go along with her scheme and wondered why.

Julia touched her lips, the memory of his kiss
searing the flesh. With all the excitement of the
engagement, she hadn't had time to think about
it. Now it came rushing back, followed by an unsettling feeling deep in her stomach. Why had he
kissed her? Could he have feelings for her? Had
she finally turned a man's head? No, of course
not. He had no interest in her beyond their amusing game and she only wanted him in order to
secure Cable Grange. As for the kiss, what did
she expect? She'd acted like a strumpet more
than once, so of course he treated her like one.
She would have to be more careful in the future.

'I think your blue-silk dress will do very well,'
her mother said.

'What blue dress?'

'The one you wore at Almack's.'

Julia shuddered at the memory.

'Oh, yes.' Emily clapped. 'It was so beautiful on you. Fetch it and we'll see if it needs any alterations.'

Julia reluctantly rose and went to her room. Cable Grange couldn't be hers soon enough for she was tired of all this ordering about.

Inside her room, she stood before her wardrobe, wondering which gown Emily meant. She remembered many things about her dreadful night at Almack's, but what she'd worn was not one of them. Too distracted to care, she snatched the first blue dress she saw. Walking back to her mother's room, a ribbon fell off, fluttering to the floor. Julia stooped to pick it up, then stopped at the sound of heated voices from Annette's room.

The door stood slightly ajar and Julia slowly approached, peering through the small crack. It wasn't her habit to stare in keyholes, but the angry tones made her more curious than cautious.

Inside, Annette sat crying on the small padded bench. Simon stood over her, his face red with anger.

'What I do is none of your concern.' For the first time there was emotion in his voice and no hint of his affected dandy lisp.

'Of course it's my concern. You'll ruin us both with your foolery.' Her tears came faster, but they did not soften Simon's hard expression.

'I'm not entirely to blame, dear sister. I've seen your milliner's bill.'

'What choice do I have? I must find a husband before you gamble away my dowry.'

'If you're pursuing Captain Covington, you're wasting your time. I heard him announce to Emily his engagement to Julia. You might as well set your cap at George for all the good it'll do you.'

'I'd rather marry a rich oaf than be sent to the workhouse by you.'

'Don't be so theatrical. You'll always have Mama and Edward to live with.'

'As a spinster if you spend everything. What man wants a penniless woman?'

Julia waited for Simon's response, but all she heard was the muffled sound of Annette's crying.

'If you're finished,' Simon sneered, 'I've hired a coach to take me back to London tomorrow.'

'But Mama and Edward said we must stay until he sorts out your debts with the creditors.'

'I don't care what Edward or Mama say. Stay if you wish, but I'm leaving.'

Simon headed for the door and Julia hurried down the hallway and around a corner. She watched from her hiding place as he emerged stiff-rumped and made his way down the stairs.

In his haste to be rid of his sister, he'd left the door wide open. There was no way to return to her mother's room without walking past Annette's. Releasing her tight hold on the dress, Julia crept down the runner, hoping to sneak by without being seen. Annette still sat on the bench, her face buried in a handkerchief, her shoulders racked with sobs. Despite everything Annette had done and said, Julia felt for the girl. Though she called Charles a great many things in private, he was not quite so hard-hearted as Simon.

Julia took a step and the floor squeaked. Annette's head jerked up in alarm. Caught, Julia hesitated, debating whether or not to comfort the broken-hearted girl. Embarrassment and shame marred Annette's features and Julia knew now was no time for reassuring words. She fled down the hall, hearing the door slam shut behind her.

'What's wrong?' Emily asked when Julia hurried into the room.

'I've just learned the most horrible thing.'

'Is it news from Paul?' Her mother clutched Charlemagne to her chest.

'Heavens, no. It's about Annette and Simon.'

'Oh.' Emily exchanged a knowing look with her mother-in-law. 'So you've found out?'

'Is this what you meant by her situation?'

'Yes, it's the reason they're here.'

'Our brother,' her mother interrupted, for she always referred to her elder brother Edward as 'our brother'. When Edward had married the much younger widow Mrs Taylor, it had sent Uncle George and her mother into fits. 'Thought it wise to remove them from London for a while in the hopes of curbing Simon's expenses.'

'You mean his gambling.'

The older woman nodded.

'Why doesn't his mother stop him? Or Uncle Edward?'

'The inheritance is entailed to Simon. Though he does pay Annette's bills, his debts have taken the vast majority of the money. If he does not stop gambling, he will be bankrupt by year's end.'

'Poor Annette. It certainly explains her peevish behaviour.' Julia sat on the sofa next to her mother.

'She does have a small inheritance of her own, but she regularly spends beyond her income. Our brother hoped you might make friends with her, teach her economy. He failed to take into account her difficult nature.'

'I'd be happy to help if only she weren't so disagreeable.'

She expected Emily to chastise her for the remark, but instead Emily leaned forwards, placing a hand on her arm. 'You must not speak of this to anyone outside the family.'

'Why would I?'

'No, I don't suppose you would, despite how nasty Annette has been to you.'

At least she has a high opinion of me in this regard, Julia thought, but held her tongue.

Chapter Nine

'What a beautiful day for riding, Artemis,' Captain Covington sang out from behind her. At first his nickname had irked her, but the more he used it, the more she liked it.

'I'd ride every day if only the weather would allow it.'

'So you should for that beast should never be cooped up.'

Manfred's ears twitched and Julia laughed, petting his strong neck. 'Ignore him, Manfred. You are no beast.'

Captain Covington laughed. 'Just a poor misunderstood creature.'

'I think we are all misunderstood in our own way, wouldn't you say, Captain?' Julia caught Annette's eyes over the captain's shoulder, but

Annette turned away, fiddling with her gelding's reins.

The good weather had held strong overnight and Julia, Captain Covington and Uncle George decided on a ride after nuncheon. Emily encouraged Annette to join them and, for the first time since arriving at Knollwood, she did. Julia suspected it had something to do with what Julia had discovered yesterday afternoon. Throughout the ride, Annette regarded her with caution, as if waiting for Julia to use her new knowledge in retaliation for everything she'd done. Julia might harmlessly annoy the chit from time to time, but it wasn't in her nature to be deliberately mean or spiteful and she had no intention of taunting Annette about her unfortunate circumstances.

They crested the hill along the boundary between Knollwood and Cable Grange, happening on a bit of excitement in a field on the other side. Two men raced questionable mounts across the field, turning around a moss-covered tree stump at the far end before galloping back to the starting point. The drunken group cheered, their own horses grazing in the grass and waiting for the chance to race. Julia recognised a few riders as the less savoury men of Daringford, more apt to be outside the Sign of the Swan and worse for their experiences inside, than bent over an honest day's labour. The rest of the men were strangers, probably travellers on their way north from London with more hope than brains.

Mr Wilkins sat atop his prize racehorse, Chester, watching the proceedings with a cool eye. Mark stood next to him managing the wagers and collecting a fair amount of blunt at the end of the race. A short distance away, a large barrel balanced on an old stump. Next to it, another of Mr Wilkins's servants dispensed generous tankards of ale to the gathered riff-raff who cheered Wilkins's health with each gulp.

Captain Covington stopped Hector next to Manfred. 'Is this a regular hobby of his?'

'Only when he's lost too much money. How no one has discovered his scam and warned those silly fools, I don't know.'

'Scam?'

'Mr Wilkins doesn't ride Chester into Daringford. Instead he rides Chester's father, Darby, a spry but older horse with markings almost identical to Chester's, but he's not nearly as fast. Inside the tavern, he befriends a few gullible travellers from London then convinces them to race. Once the men agree, Mr Wilkins rides home and exchanges Darby for Chester. These men, sodden with drink, don't realise they're racing one of the finest bits of blood in the county.'

'Don't the country men warn the town men?'

'No, they bet against them and win a few shillings, only to lose them again at the tavern.'

'How do you know so much about it?'

'I heard rumours from the servants after Tom, one of the new ones, lost some money to Wilkins. I wanted to know what he was up to, so I sent Tom back with a few coins and a horse.'

'You spy on your neighbour?'

'Of course. Doesn't everyone? I think it ungentlemanly of Mr Wilkins to wager against unsuspecting travellers. I know they're just as much to blame for trying to win money instead of earning it, but he's sorely mistaken if he thinks he can save Cable Grange off these poor souls.'

'I wouldn't be so sure. A small amount of blunt may be enough to stave off the bailiff.'

'No, he can't.' She watched another set of horses and riders take off across the meadow, noticing the money changing hands with Mark. She'd come too far to let Cable Grange slip from her fingers now. 'We must stop this, if for no other reason than to save those silly men from themselves.'

'For no other reason.' The captain winked. 'What do you propose?'

'It would be wonderful to give Mr Wilkins a taste of his own medicine.'

'So we shall,' Captain Covington replied,

mischief igniting his eyes. 'Manfred against Chester—it's a fitting match.'

'I'd love to race Manfred and reveal Mr Wilkins for the scoundrel he really is.'

'It is unladylike for a woman to race, especially against men.' Annette manoeuvred her horse next to Manfred, the warning in her voice clear. 'Even here in the country.'

Julia wondered at the advice, unsure if it was meant to be friendly or yet another insult. Either way, she couldn't ignore the truth of it. Then the idea came to her.

'Captain Covington, we can change saddles and you can ride Manfred.'

'Won't Mr Wilkins recognise the beast?'

'Tell him he's a different horse. He can't risk challenging you and having his secret revealed. Offer him an appealing amount. I'm sure his greed will overcome any hesitation.'

'You don't fear for my safety?'

'Manfred will take care of you just as he's always taken care of me.'

Uncle George leaned forwards in his saddle to peer around Annette at Captain Covington. 'Has a lot of me in her, wouldn't you say?'

'Yes. Sounds very much like something you would have concocted.'

'Then you'll do it?' Julia asked.

'Of course.' The captain threw his leg over

the saddle and slid off Hector. He walked around
to Manfred and reached up to help Julia down.
'Lean against my right shoulder so I don't drop
you.'

'You won't drop me.'

Julia slid from the saddle into the captain's
waiting arms, careful to place her weight on his
right shoulder. She wound her arm around his
neck, allowing her fingertips to brush the smooth
skin between the collar and his hair. He lowered
her to the ground, the tart smell of his warm skin
filling her senses. Their eyes met and for a moment the sound of the cheering men and snorting horses faded into the distance and there was
nothing but his body so close to hers.

'I knew you wouldn't drop me.'

'Thank you.' He raised her gloved hand to
his lips.

'James, I believe you have a race to attend to.'
Uncle George coughed behind them, clearly enjoying what he saw.

She withdrew her hand, her face warm with
a blush before she recovered herself. 'Uncle
George is right. We must hurry.'

They set to work unbuckling the saddles on
their respective horses. When they were free,
James placed his saddle on Manfred while
George worked to fasten Julia's side-saddle on

Hector. When they were done, James helped her mount, then swung atop Manfred. The horse took a couple of agitated steps at the extra weight, but seemed to recognise him and relaxed and James knew Julia's faith in the beast was well placed.

Out of the corner of his eye, James saw Julia start Hector down the hill and he reached out, taking hold of the stallion's bridle.

'What are you doing?' she protested.

'I'm no stickler for convention, but Miss Taylor is right. It isn't proper for a young lady to be seen in such company. Watch from up here.'

She scowled, but didn't argue. 'If I'm to stay here, then you'd better give me a show worth watching.'

'Don't worry. I'll exact your revenge just as you instructed. Come, George, we have work to do.'

George guided Percy into step beside Manfred and the horses picked their way down the small hill. James kept the reins light, surprised by Manfred's docile turn. The horse, unlike before, didn't fight him, but responded fast and quick to the smallest tap of James's foot or the pressure of his legs, answering to these subtle commands as though the two of them had been riding together for years. James smiled, thinking Julia's acceptance of him had in some way secured Manfred's acceptance, too.

They approached the gathering as a race ended and the men exchanged money while enjoying more ale.

'Good morning, Rowan,' George called out. Rowan nodded coolly at George, his sly eyes fixed on James.

'What do you want?' Rowan sneered.

'To race, of course.'

Rowan's lips curled at the sight of the ladies watching from the top of the hill. 'This is a private race.'

'Nonsense,' George insisted. 'It wouldn't be November if you weren't racing and the captain has a mind to wager some blunt.'

'My poor old Darby is no match for Manfred.' Rowan shrugged apologetically, but James was not about to be put off, especially with everyone now listening intently to their conversation.

'This isn't Manfred—this is Whizzer.' James patted Manfred's flank, trying not to laugh.

'He looks exactly like Manfred.'

'Manfred was a bit lame this morning. Didn't see fit to bring him out. Whizzer here is an older horse and I think a suitable match for Darby.' With a look, James dared Rowan to challenge him and reveal the truth, making it clear he knew Rowan's game.

Rowan hesitated. Julia was right; he would not risk exposing James for fear of exposing himself, but James could tell he was forming another excuse and knew it was time to make his move. 'I'll wager five hundred pounds Whizzer can best Darby.'

Interest replaced the distrust on Rowan's face. 'You seem very confident in Whizzer.'

'He's the fastest old horse in the county. What do you say?'

Greed flickered in Rowan's eyes and James knew he had him.

'I accept your wager,' he answered loudly so the others could hear. 'Five hundred pounds says Darby can beat Whizzer.'

Sharp whistles and drunken shouts went up from the crowd and they rushed at Mark to place their bets.

'Shall we?' Rowan gestured to the starting line and James brought Manfred into place.

A horse whinnied from behind them and Julia turned to see Mrs Wilkins ride up next to her. She wore a tight-fitting habit of deep red. It highlighted her pale skin and emphasised her painted lips. 'Miss Howard, I see you're enjoying the races.'

Julia stuck her chin in the air, determined not to let this strumpet act like her better. 'Any excitement is always welcome in the country.'

Mrs Wilkins squinted at the riders. 'Is James about to race Rowan?'

'Yes, and he will win.'

'How sweet of you to root for him. One would almost think you cared for him.'

'She and the captain are engaged,' Annette volunteered.

Julia went stiff in the saddle, not sure how to react.

'Engaged?' Mrs Wilkins exclaimed in mock amazement, her wicked smile growing wider. 'Oh, you poor dear. I was engaged to Captain Covington once, a long time ago, in Portsmouth. Marry him fast, Miss Howard. He isn't the type of man to follow through on a promise.' She clicked her horse into motion, guiding it down the hill to join the spectators.

Julia watched Mrs Wilkins go, her head spinning, her stomach tight. The captain and Mrs Wilkins? It couldn't be true, could it?

'Why did you tell her?' She turned on Annette. 'I had no intention of sharing such personal information with that woman.'

'Better to tell someone like her yourself than let her hear it from others,' Annette answered, the advice almost friendly. Was she trying to help her? It didn't seem possible.

'You know her?'

Annette shook her head. 'I know of her. She

has a terrible reputation in London. According to the *on dit*, a French count paid her bills when her husband couldn't. No one in good society will have anything to do with her.'

Surely a woman with such a scandalous reputation was capable of lying about the past. The hostile meeting in Daringford came to mind, adding a sickening validity to Mrs Wilkins's revelation. He had said he'd known her a long time ago. Could they have been set to marry? It scared her to think he might not honour the engagement, though she didn't know why since she had no intention of marrying either. She thought of his kiss and the way he'd helped her down from Manfred. Had he held Mrs Wilkins like that once?

No, it doesn't matter, she told herself, stamping down the jealousy. With the race about to begin, there were more important things to think about.

James held Manfred at the starting line, the beast tense and ready to run. He noticed Melinda on her horse making her way down from where Julia and Miss Taylor watched. Anger filled him and he took a deep breath, forcing himself to calm down and focus on winning. He would not lose in front of Melinda.

'I can't wait to give you a beating and knock

down some of that chit's pride,' Rowan spat, his horse pawing at the ground.

James tightened his grip on the reins. 'I hope you have the five hundred pounds to make good on your wager.'

'Gentlemen, are ya ready?' Mark stood between the horses, arms raised.

'Don't fail me, Manfred. Your mistress is counting on us both,' he whispered and the horse's ears twitched in response.

Mark dropped his arms and James dug his heels into Manfred's sides. They shot out over the meadow, James crouched low over Manfred's neck, the wind stinging his eyes. He didn't try to control Manfred, but concentrated on moving with the horse, letting the animal guide them to a win. In a flash of brown, Rowan and Chester raced up beside them, the horses' heavy breaths and pounding hooves drowning out the cheering men. Rowan nearly slammed Chester against Manfred, trying to drive them off course, but Manfred proved the more dominant animal. He bumped Chester's flank, knocking James's legs into Rowan's with a thud.

'Hell,' Rowan cursed as Chester relented, falling behind enough for James to manoeuvre Manfred around the stump first and place a bit of distance between the racers. Under the crook of his arm, James watched Rowan slap Chester's flanks with his crop, urging him faster and faster, but the gap was too wide and Manfred dashed across the finish line.

'Well done!' Julia shouted, her kidskin gloves muffling her exuberant claps.

The captain rose up in his saddle, saluting her before the men crowded around, cheering as money changed hands.

'That'll show the Wilkinses,' Julia laughed, her excitement fading at the sight of Mrs Wilkins riding up next to the captain. They exchanged a few words, then James pulled Manfred's reins to the right, trotting over to where Uncle George and Percy stood.

Watching them, Mrs Wilkins's revelation sat like a dark shadow over Julia, dampening her enthusiasm. How could he have ever been involved with such a woman or had she once been respectable?

'Do you know anything about Mrs Wilkins's past?' Julia asked and Annette shook her head.

'No. I only know the rumours.'

Had Mrs Wilkins fallen from good society because of her involvement with the captain? Did the same fate await her?

'We shouldn't be here. It isn't proper.' Julia ignored the way Annette's eyebrows rose in disbelief. Without waiting for an answer, Julia turned

Hector around and galloped back to Knollwood. She wanted to be alone, to think and settle the trouble gripping her heart. Surely there was another explanation. The captain didn't seem like the sort of man who ruined women and Uncle George would never have such a friend. Whatever the truth, she must make certain they played at nothing more than the pretend engagement. Her reputation would suffer enough when she jilted him. She did not need the additional scandal of being a fallen woman.

James walked with George back from the stables, a sense of unease nagging at him. Melinda's sudden appearance combined with her happy salutations for their engagement made him suspicious. He knew from her malicious smile she'd told Julia of their engagement, probably portraying their relationship in the worst possible light. Who knew what lies she'd attached to it? He had to find Julia and undo any damage the vile woman had done.

Davies met them at the back door with a letter. 'This arrived for you, Captain Covington.'

James took the note, not recognising the hand until he broke the seal and scanned the contents. Crumpling the letter, he stuffed it inside his coat pocket.

'What's wrong?' George asked.

'She wants to see me.'

'Julia?'

'Melinda. She wishes to discuss Rowan's debt and the sale of Cable Grange.'

'So you do still want it. Julia won't take kindly to you purchasing it out from under her.'

James laced his fingers behind his back. 'With Rowan in my debt, perhaps I can convince him to sell it to her. It's more reliable than an auction. Please tell everyone I had business to attend to in Daringford. I'll return as soon as I can.'

'Let me come with you. I don't trust Melinda or you with her.'

'You think I'm so weak?'

'I think you're too angry. I thought you'd let go of the past, but I can see by your reaction to that letter that you haven't. My guess is, neither has she.'

The past still stung, but it no longer dominated his mind. Nor did the future seem so vague or purposeless thanks to Julia. Her spirited laugh, hopeful eyes and honest manner helped him imagine a life filled with travel, family and friends, all of it with her by his side. He loved her and he wanted to capture her heart, make it burn for him as powerfully as it did for her beloved Knollwood. He could no longer deny it was the real reason he'd agreed to the engagement.

Fear tinged the revelation. He'd been deceived

by a woman once before, but he couldn't imagine Julia ever betraying him. She loved as strongly as she lived and would give herself completely to the man who captured her heart. He hoped by the end of next week he could make her his. If securing Cable Grange meant winning her, then he would buy it. 'The past is done. It's time to see to my future.'

James knocked on the heavy oak door of Cable Grange and waited, drawing his coat tight around his face to ward off the frosty night air. The sun had slipped below the horizon and although light still filled the western sky, the night's first stars sparkled overhead. The scrape of wood across stone and the squeak of rusty hinges split the silence as Mark pulled open the door. The single candle in his brass holder flickered in the draught, shadowing his bloodshot eyes.

'She's waiting for you upstairs,' he snarled.

James stepped inside, the dingy entrance hall no warmer than outside. Larger and more spacious than Knollwood's, it echoed like an old cavern, the chandelier overhead thick with cobwebs. 'Then lead the way.'

Without ceremony, Mark started up the staircase, the smoking tallow candle not doing much more than threatening to burn out. James peered down through the wavering shadows, trying to get a sense of the place. Dust covers sagged over the few scattered pieces of furniture and glaring clean spots on the dirty walls betrayed the paintings long since sold to pay bills.

At the top Mark turned, leading James down the dank hallway. The carpets were missing here, too, along with the furniture.

'She's in here.' Mark stopped at the last door at the end of the hall. 'You can find your own way out when she's through with ya.'

'I trust I can.'

Mark walked off, taking the light with him.

Without knocking, James pushed open the door, blinking against the sudden light. The house might be decaying around them, but no expense was spared to make Melinda comfortable. The room resembled a Cyprian's palace with gilded chandeliers filled with candles. A grand four-poster bed hung with sumptuous draperies sat in the far corner of the room. At the other end a large fireplace blazed with a well-laid fire. Melinda reclined on a chaise before its heat, dressed in a mantua of red silk. A bottle of wine sat on the table in front of her, along with a small box of sweets. James could see half the contents of both had already been consumed.

'I didn't think you'd come.' She ran her fingers across the back of a velvet pillow.

'I almost didn't. What do you want?'

'Please sit down.' She motioned to the sofa across from her. In the low light there was something of the woman he'd once loved, the faint echo of her girlish beauty, the tempting smile and inviting eyes that had captivated him in his youth. Back then he hadn't recognised the worldliness in their shallow gleam, but it stood out now, repulsing him.

'You said you had news.' He sat on the edge of the cushion, eyeing the minx with caution. The elaborate scene felt like a gilded wire waiting to ensnare him.

'I do. Wine?'

He shook his head. 'Let's have it out. I can't stay here all night.'

'Why?' She leaned over the table to refill her glass, her mantua gaping open to reveal her breasts almost to the nipples. 'You have no wife to go home to.'

'But you have a husband.'

Disgust crossed her face before she hid it behind the wine glass, taking a long sip. 'He's in town trying to win enough money from your friend Mr Taylor to ward off the bailiff and you. I suspect Mr Taylor is as destitute as we are.' She chuckled callously, lying back on the *chaise* like an Egyptian queen. 'So you're to be married to the Howard girl? She's not woman enough for a man like you.'

'What do you know of me?' he demanded and she rose, sauntering forwards, the firelight silhouetting her round hips and curving body.

She sat down next to him, her eyes heavy, the sickeningly sweet smell of her perfume mixing with wine in the air between them. 'You loved me once.'

'I was too young to know the difference between love and lust.' He leaned back against the arm of the sofa. 'And if I remember correctly, I didn't have enough money to suit your tastes.'

She shrugged off the accusation. 'But you're here now.'

'Only to discuss the sale of Cable Grange.'

She smiled out of the corner of her hard eyes. 'You plan to give it to your fiancée.'

'How do you know?'

'Everyone knows she wants it. Her father offered to buy it before he died. He hoped to leave it to her. I convinced Rowan not to do it. As much as I hate this tomb, I'd rather see the bailiff sell it than let that bitch have it.'

He was on his feet in an instant, staring down at her with a rage he fought hard to control. 'We have nothing further to discuss.' He stormed to the door, determined to leave her in the past once and for all.

'I have an offer to make,' Melinda called after him.

He stopped, his hand on the doorknob, but didn't turn around. 'I'm listening.'

She slid up to him, wrapping her hands around his shoulders and laying her head on his back. Her fingers played with the skin of his neck, working their way under his collar and down to his chest. He resisted the urge to flinch. 'I'll talk Rowan into selling you this crumbling pile of bricks if you spend the night with me.'

He whirled around, grabbing her wrists and pulling them from around his neck. 'You overvalue any feelings I ever had for you.'

Her wine-heavy eyes flared and she snatched her arms from his grasp. 'When did you ever care for me? You indulged your whim, then abandoned me?'

The accusation struck his sense of honour, increasing his anger. 'You gave yourself with wild enthusiasm, then trampled over me to get to Rowan and his money.'

'If you'd truly loved me, you'd have won me back, not left me to that drunkard. My life is a shambles, ruined, and it's your fault.'

'You have no one to blame but yourself.' He reached for the doorknob, but she threw herself between him and the door.

'If you go, I'll tell the trollop you were here tonight.'

He leaned in close, waving a menacing finger

inches from her nose. 'You say anything and I'll tell your husband you tried to seduce me.'

Fear flashed in her eyes. 'He wouldn't believe you.'

'I have your letter. If he finds out I was here, he'll toss you in the gutter where you belong.'

'You wouldn't dare,' she whimpered like a spoiled child.

'Not as long as you keep your mouth shut.'

He pushed her aside and strode into the hallway, his eyes struggling to adjust to the darkness. At the top of the stairs, his hand found the banister and followed the dusty wood down into the empty hall. He pulled open the front door, wincing at the sharp scrape of wood on stone.

Not until he was free of the house and galloping back to Knollwood did he dare reflect on what had happened. Why had he answered her letter? He should have known it was all a ruse, but once again he'd allowed himself to be fooled by her. Now there was a new fear. She might twist tonight's events to her own advantage and throw them in Julia's face. What would Julia think of him then? Only the worst and all hope with her would be lost. No, there was little chance she and Melinda would meet and even if they did, Melinda had no proof of their meeting.

James brought Hector to a stop at the turn to Knollwood. If he continued straight, he'd reach the road to London and it was little over two hours' steady riding to town. Melinda might hate Cable Grange, but Rowan had proved obstinate about selling it. Now, with his debt to James hanging over him, Rowan might be more desperate and willing to part with the estate. James could instruct his solicitor to make enquiries and to keep his identity secret since he doubted the Wilkinses would sell to him, no matter what their circumstances. It might all come to nothing. For all he knew, Rowan's luck had changed and he'd won enough to halt the auctions. However, if the deed to Cable Grange meant securing Miss Howard's affection, he was willing to try.

Julia lay in bed, turning over on her back for what seemed like the hundredth time since she'd blown out the candle. Captain Covington hadn't come to dinner. Uncle George said he'd gone to town, but by nine o'clock he still hadn't returned. She'd waited up for him in the study, hoping to discuss Mrs Wilkins and put some of her fears to rest, but by eleven o'clock she could no longer endure the silent waiting so she went to bed.

She rolled on her side, pulling her cool pillow close. The moon had set at least an hour ago, casting the room into darkness. Closing her eyes, she tried to sleep, but the memory of his lips, warm and tender, parting hers, kept her awake.

She bit her lip, trying to banish the strange yearning coursing through her. Tracing a crease in the sheets, she remembered the feel of his neck beneath her fingers when he'd helped her off Manfred, his hands around her waist, his eyes riveted on hers. She imagined him laying her down in the soft grass, his body covering hers, his mouth doing things to her she could almost feel.

Julia sat up, smacking her pillow in frustration. She's never given a fig for any gentleman, yet the captain filled her with all sorts of sinful thoughts. They brought to mind another curiosity: Paul's book, the secret one she'd discovered hidden in the back of his wardrobe a few years ago. She wondered if it was still there and if she could get it without being seen. Everyone else was in bed and she had not heard anything to indicate the captain was back from Daringford. She could sneak in and out of his room without anyone ever knowing.

Rising, she threw on her wrapper, then cracked open the door and peered down the hallway. Small candles flickered in the sconces and a sliver of light showed under the door of Emily's room, but her mother's room was dark. Thankfully, she was a sound sleeper and Julia didn't expect her to rise. She listened for evidence of servants walking about, but only baby Thomas's muffled cries broke the sleeping silence. She sighed with relief, knowing his wails would cover any sound and keep Emily from leaving her room.

The hardwood floors alternating with the soft plush of the rugs teased her bare feet as she stole down the hallway. Stopping at the captain's room, she peeked through the keyhole to make sure he hadn't returned unnoticed. Orange coals glowed in the grate, throwing some light on the flat bed with its unwrinkled coverlet. Twisting the doorknob, she froze when it squeaked, her heart pounding against her chest while she listened for any evidence of discovery. The only sound was the continued cry of baby Thomas.

She pushed open the door and slipped inside, swiftly closing it behind her. The faint light from the fireplace barely illuminated the room, but Julia knew it well. It was just as Paul had left it with a large wardrobe on the right, a four-poster bed between the two windows and a washstand and chair against the far wall.

Julia hurried to the wardrobe, pulled open the double doors and began feeling for the book. Her hands ran over the scratchy wool of Paul's old uniforms, slid under the folded trousers and bumped a pair of worn Hessians. She caught them before they hit the floor and, with a relieved breath, put them back. Reaching in deeper, she thought maybe he'd moved the book but then her fingers brushed against the leather tome.

She eased it out, careful not to disturb the folded garments or boots. Once it was free, she stood, clutching it to her breast. She traced the gold-edged pages, eager to open them and explore the forbidden content. The possibility of being discovered in a single gentleman's room added a certain thrill to the anticipation, but having no wish to be discovered in such a compromising situation, she moved to close the wardrobe doors. Only then did she hear the heavy fall of a man's boots in the hallway. She froze, her heart almost drowning out the sound. The footsteps drew closer, followed by the flickering light of a candle visible beneath the door. Julia searched for an escape, but there was no way out. As the doorknob turned, splitting the silence with its metallic squeak, she stepped inside the wardrobe and pulled the door closed behind her.

The wardrobe door hadn't fully closed, allowing Julia to see through the slight opening. Crouching low, her knees on the scratchy wool uniform, she watched the captain enter and place his candle on the washstand before closing the door. He removed his blue-wool coat and she clutched the book tight, afraid he might hang it in the wardrobe. She let out a long, silent breath when he threw it over the chair next to the bed. He poured some water from the pitcher into the basin, then splashed it on his face. Large drops dripped from his chin while he examined his face in the mirror, a dark scowl marring his features. Whatever he'd done that evening must not have been pleasant.

He walked around the bed, sitting down hard, facing the wardrobe. Julia rocked back away from the crack, her legs crying out from the impossible position. She hoped he went to bed quickly for she had no desire to stay in such a cramped situation all night. He removed his boots, tossing them off to the side, then reached over his head and pulled off his shirt. Julia's breath caught, but this time it was for quite a different reason. Through the crack, she examined his solid chest, the tight muscles of his stomach and his slim waist. In the candlelight his smooth skin glowed, soft and strong at the same time. She noticed at the base of his left collarbone the puckered skin of a scar. He stood and turned away from her, revealing a similar scar on his back. If only she could slip up behind him, run her fingers over his wide shoulders, trace the line of his spine to where it tapered down to his trousers and explore what lay covered by the fabric. He walked back to the washstand and she gripped the book, leaning further forwards to take him in. As he examined his scar in the mirror, his hands flew to his neck and he jerked up straight.

'Damn.' He tore through the fabric of his discarded shirt and jacket, then tossed them back on the chair in frustration. He dropped to his hands and knees, feeling under the bed. Whatever he searched for remained missing for he sat back on his heels, balling his fists on the edge of the bed, his anger changing to sad resignation.

He must have lost his medal. He said he always wore it, but she hadn't seen it when he'd taken off his shirt. She felt for him, knowing it must hurt to lose something so personal.

Her sympathy vanished when he stood, his fingers working the buttons of his trousers. She moved closer to the crack, a delicious sort of anticipation filling her. He hooked his thumbs in the waistband of his trousers and she leaned forwards, placing her hands on the wardrobe door, waiting, eager, hungry to see all he was about to reveal. Suddenly the door swung open and she tumbled out, her knee hitting the floor hard, the book landing with a thud in front of her.

'Artemis?' The captain buttoned his trousers with one hand while the other took her by the arm and pulled her to her feet. 'What are you doing in the wardrobe?'

What she wouldn't give for a good answer, but she had none. Instead she continued to stare at him, too embarrassed, shocked and bruised to answer.

'Well?' he demanded, his face inches from hers, his voice low and gruff.

'You weren't here and I wanted one of my brother's books.'

'From the wardrobe?'

'It's special.' Her eyes darted to where the book had fallen, relieved to see it lay closed. Then the captain reached for it.

'No, I'll get it.' She lunged for it, but he was faster, snatching it up and away from her.

'I know this book.' He turned it over in his hands, then to her horror flipped it open. He thumbed through the pages, his eyes widening, then his mouth settled into an amused grin. 'Special indeed.'

She wished the floor would open up and swallow her. It was bad enough to be caught in his room, but worse with him half-naked and with that kind of book. She followed the small line of dark hair leading down from his bare stomach into his trousers. His chest rose and fell much quicker than before while he examined the illustrations.

'May I have my book back?' She put out her hand, determined to reclaim as much of her dignity as possible.

He closed the book, then held it out, struggling to remain serious.

She took it, clutching it to her chest like a plate

of armour. Her mind kept telling her to turn and leave before she compromised herself even further, but she found her feet rooted to the floor, her eyes riveted to his.

'I should be going,' she whispered.

He nodded, stepping closer. 'Yes, you should.'

She didn't move, but continued to stare until he bent his face down to hers. She closed her eyes, feeling his soft lips envelop hers. The heat of it spread through her body and her mouth responded, parting to accept his tongue. It caressed the line of her lips, sending a shiver through her body.

The book fell, landing with a thud on the carpet as he pulled her close, pressing every inch of him against her, his deep kisses making her forget about the noise and consequences. Only the captain mattered. As she leaned into his chest, her shift and wrapper did little to separate their bodies or hide his hard anticipation pressing against her stomach.

She slid her arms around his waist and ran her hands up his back, her fingers brushing his scar before curling over the roll of his shoulders. She'd imagined being this close to him, but never realised how delicious it would feel or the way it made her whole being come alive. Suddenly, she understood something about those pictures in Paul's book, but none of them captured the desire she felt in the captain's arms.

She inhaled the faint scent of smoke and wine in his hair as he traced the line of her jaw with his lips. Where had he been? She didn't know or care as his teeth grazed her earlobe, his breath hot on her neck. Julia closed her eyes, his touch increasing the need coiling within her.

'Captain?' she whispered, unable to tell him what she wanted, but eager to follow him wherever his caresses led.

'Artemis.' His husky voice tickled her ear before his lips found hers again.

He guided her to the bed and pressed her down on the thick coverlet. His body covered hers, firm and strong, as his hands caressed her arms, then trailed the side of her stomach. A shock went through her when he cupped her breast and his thumb stroked the nipple, bringing it to a tender point. Closing her eyes, she realised now how a man could make a woman forget herself.

He slipped the shift from her shoulder, exposing her breast, and the cool air tickled her heated skin. She gasped, her fingers digging into his arm when he took her nipple in his mouth, flicking it with his tongue. Pleasure curled deep in her body and she moaned, wanting everything the captain offered. His deft hand traced the line of her leg, skimming the smooth flesh of her hip and sliding the shift up around her waist. While his tongue circled her breast his fingers brushed the top of her thigh until they found her aching centre.

Clinging to him, she thought she would die when he caressed the delicate skin. No pictures in any book could have prepared her for this. She moved against him, her body tightening, craving, hungry, and soon she was without reason, her breath fast, her body bending towards something she couldn't name, but it was there, in his fingers, his mouth, the smell of him. She arched her back, his mouth covering hers to muffle the cries as waves of pleasure tore through her body.

He withdrew his fingers and she lay against the pillows, weak and trembling like a newborn foal, but at the same time eager and anxious.

'Again,' she whispered, kissing his neck, his need evident against her leg. She ran her hand over the firm muscles of his chest, following the ripples of his stomach down to his breeches, knowing there was more and wanting to experience it all.

He took her hand and she opened her eyes, studying his face in the dim light. It burned with passion and wanting and something very much like guilt.

'We can't do this.' He pulled her shift down over her legs, then stood.

She sat up, confused and in some way wounded. 'Why?'

'Because it's not right. And there might be consequences.'

What she wouldn't risk to feel such pleasure again, but his sober face drained away her passion, replacing it with shame. 'You don't want me?'

'I want you very much.' He traced her jaw with his finger, brushing the hair back off her shoulder. 'But I can't dishonour you like this.'

'No, of course not.' He didn't want her. No man did and the hurt cut deep. She pulled her shift tighter, her embarrassment more powerful than her sense of caution as she fled the room, struggling to hold back tears.

In her haste, Julia failed to notice Emily standing in her darkened room, her door ajar. Baby Thomas had finally settled to sleep and she'd heard a loud thump. She never expected to see her sister-in-law emerging from Captain Covington's room.

Chapter Ten

Julia pulled back the bow, aiming for the centre of the target. Opening her fingers, the arrow flew, hitting the large white area outside the target. She nocked her next arrow with a huff, convinced nothing was meant to go her way this week. Even riding Manfred this morning hadn't cleared her mind. Luckily the captain had accompanied Uncle George to Creedon to help make some decisions concerning the repairs, sparing her the embarrassment of sitting across from him at breakfast.

Memories of last night tortured her. She let another arrow fly, watching it sail over the target to land in the grassy field. He was right—what they'd done was wrong—but the lingering sensation in the deepest parts of her and the delicious way he'd brought her to pleasure replaced the shame and increased her yearning. Only the thought of his quick dismissal made her blush with embarrassment.

She pulled back the bowstring, struggling against her shaking hands to aim. How did one face a gentleman after such an encounter? How would he react to her? He would be discreet and she'd never tell anyone, but she feared when they were together with other people, the pleasure of their brief encounter would be written all over her face for everyone to see.

She released the arrow and this time it hit closer to the centre.

'Excellent shot, Artemis,' Captain Covington congratulated from behind her.

She whirled to face him, her chest tight with fear. A meeting was inevitable, but she hadn't expected it so soon.

A smile graced his features, but it fell when Julia pinned him with a hard glare. He stood near the equipment table arranging the arrows, his tousled hair falling over his forehead. She longed to run her fingers through the dark strands, then caress the smooth skin of his face. Plucking the bowstring, she willed the urge away and forced herself to remain calm. This constant craving for him made her feel like a runaway carriage no one could stop and she hated it.

'There is a slight wind, otherwise I would

have hit the mark.' She tried to sound nonchalant, but it came out more irritable than intended.

'I see.' He held up the fletched end of the arrow, but not one feather moved. 'I think the wind has died down. Perhaps you should try again.'

She snatched it from his outstretched hand, then stormed back to her mark. Knocking the bow, she aimed and fired. The arrow missed the bullseye again but stuck in one of the centre rings.

'Yes, I see the wind has increased,' the captain observed dryly, his meaning all too clear. She realised this probably wasn't his first awkward morning encounter with a lady. If only she were as well schooled in after-pleasure etiquette.

Julia stepped aside, sweeping her arm in the direction of the range. 'Please, take a shot. Being a sailor, you must know a great deal about how the wind blows.'

'I do, though I'm not always correct.' He nocked his arrow, pulled back the bow and let it fly. The arrow stuck in the outer ring of the target. Lowering the bow, he grimaced in pain before recovering himself. Despite her anger, she moved to comfort him before catching herself, feeling a little guilty at goading him once again into straining his wounded shoulder.

'It appears you judged wrong this time.' Julia

clapped, the sound hollow in the quiet between them. Selecting an arrow, she stepped forwards, aimed and hit the target dead centre.

'You seem to have a much better grasp of how it blows—perhaps you can advise me?'

'A gentleman of your experience hardly needs my advice.'

'My experience is not quite as developed as you believe.'

Julia moved to choose another arrow but Captain Covington stepped in front of her, his eyes pointed. She smiled up at him, refusing to betray the fluttering in the pit of her stomach at his commanding presence. Despite her anger and embarrassment, having him so close only made her think of his hands on her bare skin, the strength and weight of his chest, the hot feel of his lips and tongue playing with hers. She turned away, laying the bow on the table and fingering the leather strap of her armguard. She did not want to have feelings for a man who only feigned interest in her or who might abandon her as he had another.

'Let us be frank with one another. I apologise for my inappropriate behaviour. It will not happen again. Can you forgive me?'

Something in the sincerity colouring his blue eyes while he searched her face for a response made her want to forgive him, to throw herself in his arms and reveal—reveal what? How could she express feelings she barely understood herself? If she told him, he would laugh and she couldn't face more humiliation.

'Perhaps we should end our sham engagement now.' She worked the leather knot of her arm-guard, refusing to meet his face. If they ended the game, they wouldn't be forced into each other's presence and she could collect her thoughts and return everything back to normal. There was still time to find another way to get Cable Grange.

'If that's what you wish.' He took her elbow and untied the leather strap. His eyes told her the truth but the way he held her arm said more and it scared her. If she asked him to end this, he would. She only needed to speak, but she didn't possess the words or strength to end the pleading in his eyes.

'Please know this is no longer a game for me. I am quite serious and I believe you are, too.' He moved nearer and she closed her eyes, his breath warm on her cheek before he kissed her. In his lips she felt a need and hope echoed in her own heart. She added her silent questions to his, unsure of the answers. No, this was no longer a game. It was something much deeper.

Someone cleared his throat and they jumped apart. Davies stood a short distance away, his calm demeanour betraying nothing. 'Miss Howard, your presence and the captain's is requested in the study.'

'Requested? By who?'

'Captain Russell.'

Julia almost reprimanded Davies for interrupting them, then realised she should thank him. Once again she'd been weak in the captain's presence. Davies might be the most discreet of servants, but what if someone less reliable had seen them?

'Shall we?' Captain Covington offered Julia his arm and she took it.

The tangle of emotions continued to plague her until she wanted to scream with frustration. What did he mean it was no longer a game? She knew, though she refused to admit it. Why couldn't people leave her alone so she could think? Instead here was yet another demand and from Uncle George of all people. Usually, he was the one person at Knollwood who didn't order her about. Perhaps there was news from London or of Paul? A new fear filled her and her hand tightened on the captain's arm.

'Is something wrong?' the captain asked, squeezing her hand.

She shook her head. 'Davies, is it news of Paul?'

'No, Miss Howard.'

Her grip relaxed and they followed Davies

up the stone steps and through the back sitting room. The instant they entered the study, everything became clear.

'What are you doing here?' Julia demanded.

Charles turned around, his grey eyes growing darker at the sight of her hand on the captain's arm. Her mother sat quietly in the window seat, her lips drawn tight, and Julia knew she'd been forced to endure another of his long-winded tirades.

'I received Emily's letter.' He held up the wrinkled paper as though Julia needed reminding. How typical of Charles to be so dramatic.

'I was told Uncle George wanted to see me,' Julia answered.

'I'm the one who summoned you. I knew you wouldn't come if Davies said it was me.'

'I thought as much.' Julia crossed her arms, already tired of Charles. 'Did you bring my inheritance?'

He stepped closer, but she did not step back. Try as he might, he didn't scare her for she knew he was more bluster than any real threat. To his credit and her relief, the captain remained by her side. 'I'm here to find out what you're up to and save you from who knows what scandal.'

'What scandal?' *If only he knew.* Julia dug her nails into her palm to keep from laughing. For once Charles was correct, but she'd deny it to the grave before she let him know.

'Riding alone with a gentleman, confronting a mob of angry men...' Charles ticked off on his fingers '...visiting a gentleman in the middle of the night.'

He knows! Someone must have seen her leaving the captain's room. It didn't matter for she had no intention of admitting anything. 'I don't know what you're talking about.'

'Don't dare deny it. Emily saw you last night.'

Over Charles's shoulder, Emily sat, shamefaced, the tips of her pale ears red. Julia's heart pounded in her chest and she tried to think of some explanation or way to redeem herself. No, despite his proof, she would give him nothing. If she let him bully her now, she'd never be free of his heavy hand. She drew herself up to face him, but the captain spoke first.

'Mr Howard, I assure you nothing inappropriate took place. She was retrieving one of your brother's books while I was gone. Unfortunately, I came back early.'

'Thank you, sir, for your explanation, but you have a great deal to answer to in regards to my sister's honour.'

'Charles,' her mother chided, 'you of all people should not give such lectures.'

Charles's face went red and his mouth fell

open, his stunned expression matched by Emily's. Julia threw her mother a silent question, but received no response before Charles recovered himself.

'Captain Covington, please excuse us for a moment. I wish to have a private word with my sister before you and I speak.'

'Of course.'

James closed the door behind him, taking a deep breath in the cool dark of the hallway. Through the heavy oak he heard Julia and Charles arguing at the top of their voices.

'I don't know what you're up to with this rash engagement, but after last night you will marry him,' Charles insisted.

'I will do no such thing.'

'Be reasonable.'

'Reasonable, from the man who is the most unreasonable.'

'It's only a matter of time before the story is known.'

'Why? Do you and Emily intend to spread it?'

James had not confessed his feelings to her. He'd been on the verge when they were interrupted. Now everything stood in the balance. Charles knew about their encounter last night, but Julia's stubborn nature worried him more than Charles's. Despite her true feelings, of which he had a good sense, she would never marry him if her brother insisted.

The door opened and Mrs Howard marched up to him.

'Captain Covington, if you have any interest in my daughter, now is the time to make it known, especially to her.' She walked off down the hall, her spaniel trotting behind her.

Inside the study, the sibling argument rose three octaves.

'If you had no intention of marrying him, why did you become engaged?' Charles demanded.

'You wouldn't understand.'

'Then Emily's suspicions were right.'

'You'd like nothing better than for all your suspicions to be right. Perhaps if you suspected good in me, you'd be less disappointed.'

'Please lower your voice.'

'Stop ordering me about.'

'Julia, be reasonable.'

If he didn't intervene now, he might lose all chance with her. The more her brother insisted, the more she'd resist, no matter what was in her heart. And what was in her heart? He'd seen it in her eyes outside: passion, longing and the faint traces of love. But there was trepidation there, too, of loving without return, broken trust and betrayal. He knew the power of those emotions, but, striding into the study, he refused to succumb to either her fears or his own.

Charles sat at the desk, his head in his hands. Julia stood on the other side, her back to James, her palms flat on the smooth wood surface. Did she know how formidable she was? He doubted it, for with men like Charles always underestimating her, she greatly underestimated herself.

'Excuse me.' James cleared his throat.

Brother and sister looked at him.

'Tell him nothing happened for he obviously doesn't trust me,' Julia insisted, her eyes pleading with him to help.

'If I may,' James addressed Charles. 'I believe I have a solution to the current dilemma. But I must speak to Miss Howard, alone.'

Charles studied the two of them, his frustration reflected in his nervous, wide-eyed wife, who sat by the window. 'As you like. But I only wish to entertain one resolution.'

'On this we are both in agreement.'

Charles nodded. 'Come, Emily. Let's leave them alone.'

Emily took Charles's hand and together they left, closing the door behind them. Once they were alone, Julia turned fiery eyes on James.

'There is nothing you can say to solve the situation. I suggest you return to London at once so we may avoid any more of these awkward situations.'

'I have another, more practical solution.'

'Which is?'

'For us to marry.'

'Marry?' Her eyes widened with surprise and, unless he was mistaken, flattered hope, before narrowing in suspicion. 'Whatever for?'

'Mutual enjoyment and benefit.' At this moment with her temper high, he doubted she'd believe him if he told her the truth behind his very sincere proposal. Once he had her, there would be time to reveal his heart. 'I know you don't relish the idea of marriage, but do you really wish to stay here at Knollwood with your brother, for the rest of your life?'

'Of course not. I want Cable Grange.'

'What if I offered you more than Cable Grange?'

'More?'

He cocked one suggestive eyebrow. 'Much more.'

She crossed her arms over her chest. 'And when the thrill of much more fades?'

'There is a great deal more than that.' He drew her to the atlas, the delicious scent of rosewater filling his senses. He longed to touch her face, caress her cheek with his hand, but he had to proceed slowly or she would spook and all would be lost. 'The Caribbean, perhaps, or Venice, even India.'

His fingers traced the illustrated countries and seas and her eyes followed the routes with interest. 'But what about Cable Grange?'

'You may still have it, and this—' he tapped the gilded pages '—but unmarried, you'll have neither.'

She shook her head. 'And when there is a parcel of children dragging at my heels, will I really have this?'

He leaned in with a wicked smile. 'I'm a Navy man. I know a great deal about a great many things, including avoiding a parcel of children.'

'You didn't last night.'

'I was unprepared by your sudden appearance. In the future I'll be more ready for such situations.'

Her eyes widened in shock. 'Really?'

'Yes, my little Artemis. Though I may insist on one or two children.'

'Well, that's not unreasonable.' She turned back to the atlas, eyebrows knitted while she pondered his suggestion. 'Why me? Why not Annette or some other woman?'

'Because you have a courageous nature well suited to adventure.'

'And the rest?' The word lingered between them.

'In time, it will come.' He brushed her lips with his own, feeling her excitement and anticipation.

Gently, his mind cautioned. He stepped back, her sultry eyes stealing the wind from his chest, yet he found the breath to whisper, 'Marry me?'

Chapter Eleven

With a single word, Julia found herself at the centre of a frenzy of activity. For two days she was tugged in a hundred directions while Emily and her mother rushed to plan the wedding. The captain was spared the madness. Shortly after his proposal, he received word from his solicitor in London and departed to take care of business. He also planned to buy their wedding rings and make arrangements for a short honeymoon while in town. He was set to return this evening, in time for the ball, and there they would make their engagement public.

She shivered at the thought.

'Are you all right, miss?' The seamstress looked up at Julia from where she knelt, pinning the hem of the London dress they'd chosen for the wedding.

'Yes, thank you.'

'You'll need a proper shift, perhaps more than one,' Emily said from the sofa, reviewing the ever-growing trousseau list.

'Whatever you think is best,' Julia agreed, her mind still whirling. What had she done?

'I don't believe you'll need linens,' Emily mused and her mother nodded.

'She can have my mother's set.'

Julia did her best not to roll her eyes in frustration at this inane conversation. Here she was, prepared to lash herself to a man she barely knew, and all Emily could think about was linens and lace. Though the captain's long friendship with Uncle George gave her some measure of confidence in her current and what would very soon be her future situation, she still worried. A gentleman was apt to act differently with other gentlemen than he was with ladies, especially a wife.

The seamstress motioned for her to turn and she complied, her mind lingering on the memory of the captain when he'd asked—no, bargained with her to marry him. His eyes had held a pleasant mix of hope and—dare she believe it—love? No, it wasn't possible. But if it wasn't, then why would he insist she marry him? He had nothing to gain by the union. And what had he meant at the archery range by the game meaning more?

'My man of affairs secured the special licence

and I spoke to the vicar. The ceremony is set for tomorrow at three,' Charles announced, stepping into the room. A wave of dread hit Julia, but she couldn't move for fear of being stuck by one of the many pins in her dress. Besides, she wasn't about to let Charles know she harboured any doubts about her decision.

'I can't possibly arrange everything by then,' Emily complained, tapping her list. 'And what about Captain Covington's family? He isn't expected back from London until this evening and with his mother and sister in Wiltshire, how can he possibly arrange for them to be here by tomorrow?'

'I'm sorry they'll miss it, but if Julia wants her inheritance and Cable Grange, she will marry tomorrow.'

'Or, instead of being so high handed, you could simply allow me to purchase the estate. Then the captain and I can marry at our leisure,' Julia suggested, her brother more irritating than the pins in her dress.

'No, I don't want any reason for you to decline. I've sent instructions for my solicitor to arrange the money for Saturday's auction. Once you and Captain Covington are married, I will bid for Cable Grange on your behalf, then establish it in trust for you.'

Baby Thomas let out a small cry. Charles

picked him up from where he lay in the rocker at the nurse's feet. He held the baby in his arms, his hard expression softening as he carried the infant to the window, laying a kiss on his little head. Emily rose and joined them, moving aside the blanket so they could see more of the baby's smiling face. For the first time in her life, Julia envied Charles and Emily. They both annoyed her, but they loved each other and always did what they thought best for everyone in the family.

Julia's stomach tightened. What if she never found such love and happiness with the captain?

'Enough wool-gathering,' her mother interrupted, picking up Emily's list and examining it. 'There is still much to do.'

Julia slipped out into the garden, eager to escape all the talk of both her wedding and the ball and be alone so she could think. She pulled the neck of her pelisse close, trying to warm her cheeks in the high collar. The fine weather had turned and, though the sky was clear, the air was sharp and cold. As she ambled over the gravel, the confidence she'd felt a few days ago while sitting here with her mother felt like a distant memory. Her future at Cable Grange had seemed so secure then; now she could see nothing but the unknown dotted with the chance of adventure and travel. What would life hold for Mrs James Covington? Would it really be like he promised or did she run the risk of becoming Mrs Wilkins? Wandering into the hedged garden, she sat down in front of the fountain, listening to the gentle plunk of water dripping into the pool from the clinging bodies.

Captain Covington offered many things in his proposal, but not love. He said it would come in time, but there was no guarantee. If he never grew to love her did it matter? Cable Grange would be hers and she could live the way she'd always dreamed of, but with the freedom of a married woman. The thought should have comforted her, but it didn't. Instead it only added to her loneliness and confusion. Turning back to the fountain, she felt her heart catch. Love was not part of their deal. It never had been.

The sound of someone walking on the gravel caught her attention and a moment later, Annette came around the corner, her heavy dress and pelisse more appropriate for the chilly day.

'Good afternoon, Julia,' she greeted with a light voice.

'Good afternoon,' Julia mumbled, in no mood for her stepcousin.

To Julia's surprise, Annette sat down next to her, drawing her pelisse tight. Julia watched her with caution, wondering what she wanted.

It wasn't like her to be so cordial and her sudden nearness felt awkward. In no mood to entertain the chit and knowing she did not possess the patience to be polite, Julia moved to make her excuses and leave, but Annette stood first. 'Would you please take a turn with me around the garden?'

Julia almost declined, but something in Annette's manner, less arrogant than before, made her curious. She didn't like the idea of spending time alone with Annette, but with nervous fretting over the wedding being the only thing waiting for her inside, walking seemed very appealing. 'Of course.'

She rose and led Annette away from the hedges and down the main garden path. Small birds, searching the stones for food, hopped out of their way, then flew up into the surrounding bushes, chirping in protest at being disturbed.

Annette further surprised Julia by taking her arm in a casual, sociable manner. Julia didn't pull away but braced herself for an insult, knowing all this friendliness had something to do with Julia discovering the girl's secret.

'You are aware of the situation concerning my brother and myself?' Annette asked, confirming Julia's suspicion.

'I inadvertently learned of it.' There was no

reason to lie since they both knew what Julia had seen.

'I realise our relationship has not been the best these past few weeks.'

It has never been good, Julia thought, but remained silent, wondering where all this was leading.

'I know I have no right to ask for your confidences or your discretion, but I implore you to keep what you know a secret.'

'I have no intention or reason to tell anyone.' And she didn't. Besides, Julia guessed from previous comments by both the captain and Emily that everyone already knew their situation.

'Why wouldn't you tell?' Annette demanded. 'It would be perfect revenge for my less-than-courteous behaviour.'

'Yes, but I'm not interested in revenge.' Julia sympathised with Annette, knowing she lived in a world where people tore each other to pieces without hesitation or remorse. The same pity she'd felt for her a few days ago came back along with Uncle Edward's hope that Julia could advise Annette on her finances. Helping Annette would prove a welcome distraction from Cable Grange, Charles, Emily, Captain Covington and everything else determined to plague her this week. 'I might be able to help you, if you wish.'

She snatched her hand from Julia's arm. 'I don't need your charity.'

'I don't mean charity,' Julia continued in an even tone, 'but advice on how to arrange your finances. Emily told me about your small inheritance. Perhaps we can devise a budget to relieve some of your debts and your worries.'

Annette's eyes softened, then narrowed as if contemplating many things at once, all of which seemed somewhat incomprehensible. 'I didn't think, especially after how mean I've been, that you'd be so generous. Why?'

'Because I know what it's like to have one's future influenced by a less-than-understanding brother.'

'At least Charles genuinely cares for your happiness.'

'Does he?'

'He's gone to a great deal of trouble to maintain your reputation and assure himself of the captain's suitability. Simon would never do the same for me.'

Julia resumed her languid pace, Annette staying by her side. She didn't want to admit it, but Charles did have her best interest at heart. If he wasn't so domineering, she might appreciate it more.

'I'll have to examine your finances to decide the best course of action,' Julia hazarded, the opportunity to review figures irresistible. 'You'll need to make a list of everything you owe, your expenses and your income.'

Annette fingered the lace of her pelisse, contemplating Julia's offer. 'Why do you want to help me?'

'Because it's the proper thing to do.'

'You're right—London is ridiculous,' Annette admitted with a laugh. They'd spent the last two hours reviewing her debts and income. She owed a great deal to a milliner and other London merchants, but her situation was not beyond hope.

'I never thought I'd hear you say it.' *Or be so friendly*, Julia thought, enjoying the new warmth between them.

'I don't think I'd admit it to anyone else. The silly things I have to do to try to secure my future.' She waved her hand over the scraps of paper littered with figures. 'And still nothing is settled.'

'Since you live with Uncle Edward and your mother, you can save a great deal, but you'll have to economise. No more lace and no more dresses.'

Annette sat back with a sigh. 'It won't be easy, but I suppose I must.'

'Just until you find a rich husband,' Julia teased, putting the finishing touches on Annette's plan to pay her debts and invest her inheritance, then passing it to her for inspection. 'I think this will do very well.'

'Yes, it will.' She laid the paper aside. 'I'm truly sorry for being nasty to you, only I've been so worried lately, what with Simon's gambling and Mama no help. I thought Captain Covington might be an answer. I never thought of taking matters into my own hands. You're lucky to have a man like the captain. He'll make a good husband and you two will be quite the talk of the ball tonight.'

Julia twisted the pencil in her hands, apprehension replacing her former calm. 'I don't particularly care for balls.'

'Why? You can dance, can't you?'

'Yes, it's one of the few social graces I mastered while in London.' Charles had hired a dancing instructor for that purpose and Julia had proven a quick study. If only everything else about London society had come so easily.

'And you can converse with people.'

'Of course.'

'Then why are you afraid?'

'Because everyone sneers at me for running Knollwood instead of painting screens. They seem to have nothing else to occupy their simple minds except how I choose to spend my time.'

'Well, I can't stop them from thinking that

running an estate is strange, but I can teach you not to care.'

Julia shook her head. 'It's not possible?'

'Of course it is. All London women do it. Do you know how many girls would cry in the halls of Almack's if they didn't pretend not to care?'

'No, I've seen the women in London. They possess more confidence in society than I could ever master.'

Annette stared her straight in the eye. 'Come now, Julia. I've seen you stand up to Mrs Wilkins and your brother. I know you aren't lacking in courage. You helped me—now allow me to help you.'

'How?'

Annette stood, taking Julia's hand and pulling her to her feet. She spun Julia around, studying her with a practised eye. 'First, to play the part, you must dress the part.'

An hour later, Julia stood before the mirror, admiring her transformation into a diamond of the first water. She wore her finest London gown of white silk with thin, shimmering gold stripes running through the fabric and a gold ribbon around the waist. At the gentle swell of her bosom, Annette fixed one of Emily's diamond brooches and loaned her a pair of teardrop-pearl earrings. Annette then instructed Mary on how to style Julia's hair in the Roman fashion with a gold ribbon threaded through the *coiffure*.

'Anyone who saw you would instantly think you're a member of the *ton*.' Annette stepped back, inspecting her handiwork.

Julia gazed at her reflection, turning from one side to the other to view her dress and hair. For the first time in a long while, she felt beautiful, but there was more to commanding a ballroom than a pretty gown. 'I may dress the part, but I don't feel it.'

'It's an easy one to play. Come, I'll show you.' Annette led Julia to the far side of the room. 'When you walk, keep your head up, your shoulders back. Meet everyone with confidence and don't forget to smile.'

Annette demonstrated the walk, then motioned for Julia to try it. Julia felt silly, but she'd come too far to stop now. Pulling back her shoulders, she put her chin in the air and crossed the room.

'Very good, but this time smile, acknowledge everyone and remember to hold their gaze a moment before moving on.'

Julia repeated the walk with more purpose, smiling and nodding to the imaginary guests.

Annette clapped at the performance. 'If the captain wasn't already in love with you, then he'd lose his heart tonight.'

Julia stopped, stunned by Annette's announcement. 'The captain doesn't love me.'

'Of course he does. It is as plain as the sun.'

Julia opened and closed the ivory fan dangling from her wrist. 'Now you're teasing me.'

'Do not think so little of yourself, Julia. He loves you as much as you love him.'

Julia opened the fan, studying the painted roses twining together along a vine. Yes, she loved him. She'd spent days denying it, but hearing Annette state it so plainly she could no longer pretend it wasn't true.

But did he love her?

She examined herself in the mirror and for the first time saw not Julia, the awkward girl of Knollwood, but a sophisticated lady engaged to the handsome captain. It seemed too unbelievable to be real. Deep down, she feared everything would come crashing down and she'd wake tomorrow to find it was all just a dream. Unless, as Annette thought, he really loved her. If not, the humiliation would be more than she could bear. It seemed there was only one thing to do. Tonight she would have to find out.

Chapter Twelve

Julia stepped out of the carriage, the biting night air cutting through the delicate material of her gown. Young people, accompanied by matrons and older men, wound through the crush of carriages to the Johnsons' wide front door. Julia followed her mother and Annette, admiring the tall, white columns lining the façade, thinking similar details would make Cable Grange stately. She tried to take in more of the house's architecture, but the crowd pressing into the entrance hall made it difficult. They were supposed to arrive earlier, but baby Thomas had taken ill, causing a delay when Emily and Charles decided to stay behind. She'd noticed Uncle George's carriage outside and knew he and the captain were already here. The captain had returned from London in the early evening, but Annette refused to let him see her and insisted he and Uncle George ride on ahead to the ball. She wanted Julia to make an entrance and surprise the captain.

Once inside, Julia looked for him, eager for him to see her. However, nothing except the tall ostrich feather in the hair of the lady in front of her was visible in the crush.

They stepped into the receiving line, moving forwards to where Mr and Mrs Johnson and the eldest Miss Johnson stood and Julia's stomach tightened. Despite Annette's lessons, she didn't relish the idea of facing the scrutiny of the other country families. Picking up the short train of her dress, she knew she had no choice but to carry on.

'Mrs Howard, how lovely to see you,' Mrs Johnson addressed Julia's mother, who curtsied with her usual grace. She turned to Julia, her beady eyes wide with astonishment. 'And, Miss Howard, your gown is beautiful.'

'The colour makes you glow,' the eldest Miss Johnson offered. Taller and less buxom than her younger sisters, she'd always been kinder than either they or their mama.

'Thank you.' Julia curtsied, enjoying Miss Johnson's compliment and taking pride in showing Mrs Johnson she could dress as fine as any other lady.

Her mother led her off to the left and through

the hall leading to the ballroom. Numerous gentlemen and ladies filled the space, chatting and enjoying aperitifs and ices. Julia paused at the threshold, taking in the crowd before Annette linked her arm in hers.

'Remember what I told you. Everyone will be watching us for I am new and you are unexpected. There'll be lots of stares and whispers, but walk like you know, but don't care.'

They stepped together into the thick of the revellers and a hundred glances and whispers were thrown their way. The mothers and young ladies who'd always ignored Julia now stared, taking in the fine style of Julia's dress and the graceful figure she cut. She did her best to emulate Annette, smiling at Miss Diana Johnson, who sat surrounded by her usual set of admirers. Miss Diana spied Julia, her jaw dropping before she fell to whispers with the young bucks, but Julia never let her smile falter. For once Julia enjoyed being the subject of so many conversations.

The soft strains of Handel greeted them at the entrance to the ballroom. Sweeping the room, her eyes immediately set upon the captain. His blue uniform highlighted by a crisp white shirt, brass buttons and gold epaulettes made him stand out in the sea of men in sober black evening attire. The unmarried young ladies and their mothers covetously examined the captain while Miss Caroline Johnson claimed the envious position of chatting with him. Her fan fluttered in front of her face while they spoke, but Julia could tell he wasn't listening for his eyes roamed everywhere but over the silly goose's round, exuberant face.

He's looking for me. Her heart jumped with excitement and she started forwards, eager to join him, but Annette held her elbow tight.

'Wait. Make him come to you.'

She could barely stand still, waiting for him to notice her. As if sensing her presence, he turned, starting at the sight of her. His blue eyes swept her before an impressed smile spread over his face. Making his excuses to Miss Johnson, he started across the room. Many ladies dipped behind their fans to comment on the handsome stranger striding towards Julia. She didn't care what they said or thought—only the captain mattered. She hadn't seen him since the proposal and until this moment didn't realise how much she'd missed him.

'You're gorgeous, Artemis,' he breathed, standing over her and taking in the transformation.

Julia arched one saucy eyebrow, enjoying the confidence created by his admiration. 'Are you trying to flatter me?'

'No flattery of mine could do you justice.' The

musicians began an allemande and the captain offered her his elbow. 'May I have this dance?'

She hesitated. It had been a long time since she'd danced and, with her confidence soaring, she didn't want to trip over her feet and bring herself crashing back down to the ground.

'Come now. A woman who faces fighting men isn't afraid of a dance?' he teased.

Julia laid her hand on his arm. 'I'm not afraid.'

'Good. I'm glad to hear it.'

The captain swept her through the steps of the dance, the heat of his body radiating between them during the turns and acting like wine on her senses. The image of him shirtless above her filled her mind and she nearly stumbled, but his strong presence kept her steady and with even steps they moved in time with the others over the polished floor.

Whispers swirled around them from all those who knew her and her family and for the first time Julia didn't care. Instead of wanting to escape, to run back to Knollwood and the comfort of the study, she grasped the captain's hand tighter and raised her head higher. She enjoyed exceeding these people's expectations, for most of them believed spinsterhood to be her fate. It felt wonderful to prove them wrong and be more than they, and perhaps even Charles, ever thought she'd be.

All too soon the dance ended and the captain escorted her to where Annette stood.

'Well done, Julia,' she congratulated. 'You've set the room ablaze and are to be commended.'

'Do you really think so?'

'Most definitely.' Annette strolled off to rejoin Mrs Howard as Miss Diana Johnson hurried up to them, her eyes raking over the captain.

'Miss Howard, we did not expect to see you here tonight. I didn't think you liked balls,' Diana said, her voice innocuous, but the cutting remark clear.

'Whatever gave you such an idea?' Julia asked.

Diana's smile faltered, leaving her at a loss for an answer. Not wishing to prolong the awkward moment, Julia turned to the captain. 'Allow me to introduce my fiancé, Captain James Covington.'

'Fiancé?' Diana dipped a wobbly curtsy, her small eyes wide with surprise.

'Yes, I asked Miss Howard to be my wife and she accepted me.' The captain patted Julia's hand proudly.

'Best wishes to you both. If you'll excuse me.' She hurried off across the room to rejoin a group of young ladies Julia recognised, but didn't know well. They bowed together in a furious mingling of waving fans and gasps while Diana conveyed the news.

'The whole room will know in a matter of minutes,' Julia remarked.

'Good.' Behind them the musicians started the next dance. 'Shall we?'

'Of course.'

The hour slipped by in a blur of music and the captain's touch. She revelled in the feel of him next to her while they moved through two more dances, oblivious to everything but each other. She could dance with him for ever if only one fear didn't continue to plague her. She was no closer to knowing the truth of his heart, but she was reluctant to break the ball's beautiful spell with an awkward discussion or some horrible revelation. Tomorrow she'd discover the truth. Tonight she'd enjoy herself.

At the end of the Scottish reel, he led her to the edge of the room. She waved her fan, the heat of the crowd and the rousing dance making her flush.

'Would you like some punch?' the captain asked, his hair damp at the temples from the exhilaration of the reel.

'Yes, thank you.'

He made his way to the refreshment room, leaving Julia near a large painting of some Johnson ancestor. She wrinkled her nose at the round face staring out from the canvas, thinking it very unfortunate such a feature should be so dominant in the family.

'Good evening, Miss Howard.'

Startled, she turned to see Mrs Wilkins standing behind her. She wore a deep-green dress of velvet cut too low, her modesty saved only by a wide gold necklace.

'Mrs Wilkins,' Julia greeted icily, making it clear she had no wish to speak to the woman, but Mrs Wilkins seemed indifferent to the rebuke.

'Had I not seen it for myself, I never would have believed it. You strike me as too dour for a man like James.'

'The captain likes his women refined.' Julia's heart pounded in her ears. She'd never been confronted like this and she wasn't about to let the woman get the better of her.

'You needn't be so high and mighty with me, Miss Howard,' Mrs Wilkins snapped. 'Do you really think he'll marry you?'

'I believe you're bitter because he didn't marry you.'

'I could have had him if I'd wanted him, but I'm not one to pine for the past. Perhaps this time he'll actually go through with the marriage.'

'Come to the church tomorrow at three o'clock and you'll see for yourself.'

'I think not. Please give him this. He left it

in my room when he came to see me the other night.'

Mrs Wilkins held out James's dented medal and it dangled between them, glittering tauntingly in the candlelight. Julia held out her hand, struggling to control the shaking while Mrs Wilkins coiled the gold chain in her upturned palm. 'Oh, and please tell him we sold Cable Grange yesterday.'

'You sold it,' Julia choked.

'Yes. A solicitor in London purchased it for his employer. Rowan and I just returned from London this afternoon to see to our things as the new owner wishes to take possession at once. Frankly, I'm glad to be rid of the place. I never did enjoy the country. I always found the society a bit too small.' Mrs Wilkins sauntered off across the room.

Anger, hurt, betrayal, disappointment and sorrow all slammed together, making it impossible to think or make any sense of the emotions crushing her. Julia gripped the medal tight, her heart shattering along with her dreams. After everything she'd done, Cable Grange was gone and with it Captain Covington. She forced herself to remain composed, refusing to fall apart in front of everyone who'd seen her so happy only a moment before. She needed somewhere to go, a place to hide, but the crowded room offered no sanctuary.

Before Julia had a chance to think or clear her mind, the captain appeared at her side. 'What did she want?'

'To offer her congratulations,' Julia replied through clenched teeth.

'What's wrong?'

She laid open her palm, revealing the medallion. He turned to where Mrs Wilkins disappeared in the crowd, his eyes narrow with seething hate. 'That miserable woman. Whatever she told you, it is a lie.'

'Were you with her the other night?'

'Yes, but allow me to explain.'

She shook her head, the room around her threatening to whirl. If Mrs Wilkins had the audacity to confront her tonight, it wouldn't be long before she told everyone the story of James's indiscretion. Moments ago she'd been the belle of the ball; now she'd end the evening the subject of vicious gossip. They'd laugh and say she wasn't ladylike enough to keep her intended. They'd watch her with a mixture of pity and condescension all because she'd trusted him and allowed herself to believe he loved her. How could she have been so foolish? He'd dallied with Annette in jest, then turned to her when it suited his lust only she'd been too blind to see the truth.

'Please, let's go outside and discuss this?' the captain said, taking her elbow.

'Why?' she retorted. 'So you may tarnish my reputation further?'

Before he could answer, a loud gong reverberated through the room. Everyone turned to watch Mr Johnson, accompanied by a servant carrying the gong, step up on the dais in front of the musicians.

'Everyone, please may I have your attention?' The music trailed off, bringing the dancers to a halt. Whispers swept the room, everyone speculating on what announcement was important enough to interrupt a ball. 'News has just reached us from London. The British Navy met Napoleon's fleet at Trafalgar and won a stunning victory.'

The room erupted in cheers, applause and whistles, but Mr Johnson rang the gong three more times, cutting the excitement short. 'Britain has also suffered a great loss. Though we won the battle, Admiral Nelson was killed.'

Men gasped and women burst into tears, the hero's death touching everyone.

Uncle George appeared next to Julia. 'There is other news from London.'

Fear turned her cold. 'Paul?'

'Yes, we must return to Knollwood at once.

Your mother and Annette have already left. We'll take my carriage.'

Uncle George led them through the sober crowd and out of the large front doors to the waiting carriage. Inside, James sat next to her as Uncle George climbed into the seat across from them. He rapped on the roof, setting the carriage in motion.

'Do you know anything?' Julia asked, barely able to get the words out, her throat dry with dread.

'Only that Charles received a letter concerning Paul. I don't know the contents. Jim, did you hear anything in town about the battle?'

He shook his head. 'No, I was too busy this morning and I didn't see any of the papers before I left London.'

They fell into worried silence, the jangling equipage grating on her strained nerves. Anticipating the awful news waiting for her at Knollwood made her body shake. Was Paul dead or just badly wounded? What would she do without him, especially now?

The captain slipped his hand in hers and squeezed it, but she snatched it away, in no mood for his sympathy. She felt him watching her, the weight of his concern adding unwanted tension to her already tormented mind. She scanned the darkness outside the carriage for any landmark indicating their distance from home, but only the vague silhouettes of trees stood out in the dim light of the rising moon. The carriage drove for what felt like an eternity before the bright windows of Knollwood came into view. The moment the carriage stopped, she threw open the door and rushed inside, James and Uncle George close on her heels.

She hurried into the morning room, taking in Mother, who sat next to Emily, her face a white mask of controlled pain. Annette stood behind them, sombre.

'Is Paul all right?' Julia asked.

Mother held out her arms and Julia rushed into them, doing her best to hold back tears of worry.

'He's alive, but wounded and missing,' Mother answered and Julia sat back.

'What do you mean?'

'Lieutenant Lapenotiere, his commander, sent us a letter. *HMS Pickle* arrived in Falmouth on Monday. They came home because Lieutenant Lapenotiere was charged with telling the Admiralty about the battle and Admiral Nelson. Paul, because of his wound, rode with Lieutenant Lapenotiere to London to see Dr Childers.'

'Excellent fellow,' Charles muttered.

Mother scowled at Charles, then continued her story. 'They arrived very early this morning and Lieutenant Lapenotiere, after finishing his duties at the Admiralty, paid a call to Dr Childers to make sure Paul was all right. According to Dr Childers, Paul never arrived and now no one knows where he is.'

'Perhaps the wound is worse than he realised and Paul's in some hospital, alone,' Julia said worriedly.

'Lieutenant. Lapenotiere doesn't know and, because of his official duties, he can't search for Paul. It's why he sent us an urgent letter suggesting someone from the family come to London at once to find Paul.'

Julia turned to Charles. 'When are you leaving?'

Charles looked aghast. 'I'm not leaving. I've written a few letters and will send them tomorrow.'

'Letters? You're sending letters?'

'What else would you have me do?'

'Go to London and search every hospital until you find him.'

'Search the hells and coffee houses, you mean,' Charles scoffed from his place by the fire, tapping the mantel. 'No doubt instead of going straight to Dr Childers, Paul decided to visit his mistress, or some hell to run up more debts.'

'How can you say such a thing?' Julia demanded, her voice high and tight. Only the firm squeeze of her mother's hand prevented her from hurling more words at Charles.

'I can say it because I've spent more time than I care to admit dealing with our brother's creditors. Now, through his foolishness, he's gone and got himself in another mess.'

'He's wounded. He may be ill and in need of our help. Now is no time to preach about his responsibilities.'

'Why not? He's a grown man and it's time he took them seriously.' Charles snatched up the poker and jabbed at the logs. 'Besides, Paul has a talent for surviving and for trouble. He's sure to turn up soon.'

Julia stood, balling her fists at her sides to keep from pounding them against Charles's unfeeling chest. 'London and all your airs have made you hard.'

'You don't understand the ways of the world,' he replied with marked condescension, returning the poker to the stand.

'I quite agree with Julia.' Her mother rose, pinning Charles with angry eyes. 'You have become too hard for my liking.'

'Mother, please, you misunderstood my meaning,' Charles began, but his mother raised a silencing hand, then swept out of the room.

Charles chased after her, his weak protests trailing them both down the hall.

Julia dropped into a chair, biting her thumb. Across the room, Uncle George and Captain Covington stood by the fireplace, each contemplating the evening's news. Her eyes briefly met the captain's, their blue depths filled with a need she would not answer.

Paul wasn't dead, but wounded, and Charles had no intention of helping him. She knew the condition of hospitals and how a healthy man could easily succumb to illness while a wounded one stood almost no chance of recovering. Paul must be found and brought back to Knollwood to be cared for properly, not left to die in who knew what squalor.

'Charles will find him. Everything will be all right—you'll see,' Emily offered, patting Julia's shoulder. Reaching into her dressing-gown pocket, she produced a letter and handed it to Julia.

'What's this?' She recognised Paul's large handwriting.

'It arrived after you left for the ball. He must have sent it some time ago.'

Julia sat on the edge of her seat, fingering the letter, afraid to open it for fear it might be the last she ever received from him.

Emily made her way out of the room, followed by Annette, who offered a comforting smile.

Julia tore open the letter.

Dear Julia,

    Forgive my brevity. We are in port taking on supplies for the fleet and I wanted to send word since it may be my last opportunity to write for some time. I hope everyone at Knollwood is doing well. Uncle George wrote to inform me of his plan to bring Captain Covington to stay at Creedon Abbey in November, and to meet you all. I was shocked by his announcement, given our history, of which Uncle George has surely informed you. Perhaps it means the captain has finally forgiven me and will rescind his poor recommendation and I shall have my ship after all. If he hasn't forgiven me, I depend upon you to do nothing but speak of my great character and change his mind for you can be quite persuasive when you want something.

    I must go now, but I'll write more when I can. Give my love to Mother.

    Your devoted brother,
    Paul

Without thinking, she marched up to the captain, the paper fluttering in her shaking hands. 'It was all about revenge, wasn't it?'

He stared at her, stunned. 'I don't understand.'

'You wrote Paul's poor recommendation. You stopped him from getting his own ship.'

'I did.'

'Why?'

The captain ran his hand through his hair. 'Your brother served with me many years ago in Portsmouth. During that time he failed to demonstrate qualities necessary to command a ship. There were questions about whether or not he could be trusted to follow orders or do the honourable thing.'

'It was more complicated than that,' Uncle George added.

'You knew about this and didn't tell me?' She gaped at Uncle George, who tugged on the sleeves of his jacket. She felt lied to and betrayed by both of them and, combined with her worry for Paul, it was more than she could bear.

'Julia, please.' Captain Covington moved forwards, but she stepped away.

'How dare you speak of honour when you have none. For years you've had a grudge against Paul and when you couldn't strike at him you decided to take advantage of me.'

'That's not it at all. Please allow me to explain.' He took her by the arms, but she shook off his grasp.

'Explain what? How instead of receiving his own ship and perhaps being hundreds of miles from danger, he's now missing? How you went to Mrs Wilkins, exposing me to the humiliation of the entire countryside because you made me think you cared?'

'I do care. Don't you see?'

'No, I won't have any more of your lies.' She ran from the room and up the stairs, not daring to breathe until she crumpled to her knees in the privacy of her room, large tears rolling down her face.

'I was a fool to go or at the least I should have taken you along,' James lamented, remembering his brief time in Melinda's room. He should have known she'd strike at him like this. Once again he'd underestimated her. He thought of her letter in the drawer upstairs. He could make good on his promise and send it to Rowan, but what difference would it make now?

'What I don't understand is how she got your medal.' George paced back and forth across the room with slow, heavy steps.

'I remember Melinda putting her arms around my neck. She must have taken it then.'

'Sounds more like a cutpurse than a lady.'

'From everything I heard of her while in London, I wouldn't be surprised if she's turned to thievery to keep herself from ruin.'

George paused near the card table, fingering

the deck, his face long. 'I should have been honest with Julia, told her about you and Paul. I hate to think I've hurt her.'

'She loves you too much not to forgive you and once everything is settled, she'll understand why you did it. She might even thank you for it,' James offered, trying to bolster his friend's spirits. He'd only seen George this upset once before when a young officer they both admired was killed in a skirmish off Martinique. Despite winning the skirmish and taking a grand prize, the entire crew had been affected by the officer's death, much like tonight's news had touched everyone at Knollwood.

'I hope you're right. She means the world to me.' George took a deep breath, flipping over a card and laying it face up on the table. 'I only kept it a secret because I wanted her to give you a chance.'

'Then why did you write Paul about it?'

'Because I didn't think he'd write to her about it. Apparently, I was wrong.' He flipped over another card and laid it beside the other. 'But enough about my troubles. What'll you do?'

James shook his head. 'Tonight, nothing. In the morning I'll make her listen to me—whatever it takes to get her to the altar.'

Julia leaned against her bedroom wall, wrung out and tired. The evening had started out so glorious, and now it was gone, all of it: the captain, Cable Grange, her future. Fresh tears rolled down her face at the thought of enduring the wagging tongues of the countryside and Charles's endless sermons. She scowled, hating her brother very much at this moment.

Across the room, she noticed her books and agricultural tracts stacked in a neat pile on a table next to the window. On top sat the book Paul had given her on India. Where was he? Why wouldn't Charles search for him? She would if she could.

She sat up, drying her cheeks with the back of her hand as the plan began to form in her mind. Paul. She could find him, nurse him back to health if need be and live with him, away from Charles, Knollwood and the captain.

It was dangerous and if she went through with it, there would be no going back, not that it mattered now. Even if Julia told Charles the truth about Captain Covington, he would still insist on a wedding. No, she wouldn't be bound to a man who didn't love her or who wouldn't be faithful. Life with Paul was the only option, if she could find him, if he was still alive.

Rising, Julia cracked open the door and peered into the empty hallway, listening to the muffled voices of the captain and Uncle George from downstairs. Hurrying along the hall, she slipped inside Paul's room, careful to lock the door behind her. Pulling open the wardrobe, she grabbed one of Paul's old uniform jackets, a shirt, a pair of breeches, the Hessians, a hat and haversack. Stuffing the clothes in the haversack, she felt around, hoping to find a pistol or even a sword, but there was nothing else except a few old blankets. Closing the wardrobe, she carefully opened the bedroom door. Charles's whining tone carried from their mother's room, his pleas fading down the empty hallway.

A few candles flickered in their holders, the flames dancing as Julia stole by. At the bottom of the stairs she stopped, listening for the captain and Uncle George. The clink of a crystal stopper followed by a slight cough punctuated the low cadence of their voices. The bottom stair creaked and she froze. The men's muffled conversation didn't falter and she slipped unnoticed past the door and to the study.

Inside, she didn't dare light a candle. Pulling the key from its hiding place in the ink blotter's handle, she unlocked the top desk drawer and drew out the money pouch. It jingled loudly and she clutched it tight, silencing the coins. Slipping it into the haversack, she locked the drawer, returned the key to its hiding place, then fled the room, making her way out of the house through the back.

Her feet flew over the gravel walkway as she

ran down the hill to the stables, gripping the haversack with one hand while her other one held up the hem of her dress. The frosty night air bit at her exposed skin while the satin slippers failed to protect her feet from every stone embedded in the path.

Pushing open the stable door, the horses whinnied, then shifted back and forth in their stalls. They watched her run to the small room at the back where she stripped off the white-and-gold dress and hung it on a peg. It sagged there like an old skin, taunting her with what might have been. Why had she tried to be anything other than who she was? And who was she? Not Mrs James Covington, nor a polished London lady, only the fallen, spinster sister of a lieutenant in his Majesty's Navy. She forced the bitter sadness from her mind, knowing she'd never accomplish anything tonight with such heartache weighing on her. Paul needed her and he was all that mattered.

She slipped on the jacket, the rough wool scratching through the simple linen shirt, but giving welcome relief from the cold stable. She pulled on the trousers and then the Hessians, which fit surprisingly well for being two sizes too large. Walking in a tight circle, she admired the easy way the outfit allowed her to move. Removing the pins and ribbon from her hair, she arranged her locks into a ponytail, securing it with the ribbon and tucking it up under the hat. It was a poor disguise, but with luck it would be enough to keep anyone with a mind for trouble from picking her out. Tossing the haversack over her shoulder, she pulled open the door, letting out a yelp when she came face to face with John.

'Miss Howard,' he gasped, holding a pitchfork tight. 'I thought you were a thief. What are you doing here at this time of night and dressed like that?'

She pushed past him, grabbing Manfred's saddle. 'I'm going to London, to find Paul. He's been wounded and he's missing.'

'You can't.' John took hold of the heavy saddle, but she didn't let go. 'Not without Mr Howard or Captain Russell. If anyone found out, you'd be ruined.'

'I have to find him.'

'But think of your mother and brother.'

'Charles doesn't care about anything but his propriety.' Julia tugged on the saddle, but John held it tight.

'Miss Howard, I can't let you do this.'

The concern in his face touched her. He'd kept so many secrets for her in the past. Now she needed him to keep one more.

'Please, I must. Paul needs me. He's wounded and might die if I don't find him.' She hated sounding so desperate, but she couldn't keep the fear out of her words.

John shook his head, relaxing his grip on the leather. 'You know I can't refuse you.' He took the saddle into Manfred's stall and threw it over the horse's back.

Julia joined him, helping with the buckles. 'Thank you, John.'

When they were done, John led Manfred out to the paddock, then helped her up.

'Please be careful. Your family needs you. Knollwood needs you.'

Regret hit her with surprising strength and for a moment she considered returning to the house and finding some other way to help Paul. No, there was no other way and no life except the one she could create with him in some distant port. For all his silly faults, at least he would understand and not judge her. He was her future now, not Knollwood, Cable Grange or Captain Covington.

'I'll be careful.' She kicked Manfred and horse and rider cantered out into the night.

James leaned against the mantel, watching a smouldering log collapse. Admiral Nelson was dead. He'd been wounded so many times, survived so many battles and now, on the brink of perhaps his greatest victory, he'd been killed. A shiver ran through James—he might have shared the same fate a year ago, or perhaps even today if he hadn't resigned his commission. He'd wasted so much time lamenting the past, mourning everything he'd lost instead of living. And what had he lost? He wouldn't know until morning when he could speak to Julia, explain what had happened at Cable Grange and confess his love. He berated himself for not telling her sooner.

'Excuse me, sir.' John stood in the doorway, his hair dishevelled and his lined face stricken.

'What's wrong?' George asked.

'Miss Howard—she's taken Manfred and left for London.'

'What?' James couldn't believe it.

'She's gone to find Mr Paul Howard. Found one of his old uniforms and rode off dressed like a sailor.'

'Why did you let her go? Don't you know how dangerous it is for a woman to travel the roads alone at night?'

The groom shrunk back. 'I couldn't stop her.'

It seemed too far-fetched to be real, but knowing Julia's impetuous nature it sounded exactly like something she would do. 'Saddle up Hector. I'm going after her.'

'Thank you, sir.' John left to prepare the horse.

'I'll go with you,' George said.

'No, I need you to stay and tell Julia's mother

what's happened, but not until morning and not unless we haven't returned.'

'What about Charles?'

'Wait as long as you can to tell him. I don't want him following us. He'll only make things worse. I'm sure I can catch up to her and convince her to come back.'

'And if you can't?'

James opened and closed his left hand. 'Then on to London to find Paul. I'll send word when I can.'

George clapped him on the back. 'I hate to miss this adventure. Good luck, Jim.'

James ran upstairs to change into his older uniform, buckling his sabre to his waist before he left the room. Outside, he hurried down the hill to the stable where John waited in the paddock with Hector. The lanterns from the stable shone off the stallion's dark coat but did little to pierce the darkness beyond the building.

'When did she leave?' he asked, pulling himself into the saddle, ignoring the sting to his shoulder.

'Right before I came to get you. She's sure to take the main road, but if you go through the woods, there's a path that leads west. It's not hard to find and comes out further down the road. If you hurry, you can cut her off. She's not likely to run Manfred in the dark and risk injuring him.'

'Thank you.' James turned the horse for the woods, riding as fast as he could without risking Hector. Despite the high half-moon, heavy clouds kept passing in front of it, plunging the countryside into periods of darkness.

He rode a good distance without finding a break in the trees or anywhere where the bald path diverged. He thought of doubling back, fearing he'd missed the fork when the trail split, veering off into the dense copse. He slowed the stallion, nudging him to the right and the trees closed in around them, blocking out all but the faintest slivers of moonlight. James's eyes strained against the darkness to see the hard-packed earth in the dim light.

A low, sharp branch caught his neck and he reached up, feeling warm blood. Wiping it away, he laughed, remembering the last time he'd ridden hell-bent towards a town in the middle of the night. It was in Bermuda and he never thought he'd be doing it in England or chasing after a headstrong girl to aid a man he disliked. Life would never be this exciting without her and, if helping her find Paul meant winning her, he'd ride the length and breadth of the country.

An owl screeched, dipping down over the road in front of Julia and Manfred before flying off over the trees. Julia sat up straight, startled, her skin crawling with goose bumps. She might be dressed like a man, but any thieves in search of easy prey would discover the truth the moment they pounced. Then what would she do? She didn't have so much as a riding crop to defend herself with.

Somewhere in the distance a dog barked and Julia hunched over in the saddle, pulling the coat closer around her face. The ball, Mrs Wilkins and the captain's betrayal all mingled with the night to press down on her and dampen her spirit and resolve. What seemed a rational idea in the midst of a disappointing evening now felt like a mistake. Even if she made it to London, she had not the first idea where to begin her search. She should go home. It would be easy to slip into the house without anyone being the wiser, but then what would she do? Charles was too stubborn to help and even Uncle George had sided with the captain against Paul. If only the captain hadn't been such a scoundrel. He would have helped her.

Fresh tears threatened to fall and she bit her lip to keep from crying. She'd been so forward with her silly engagement scheme. No wonder he took advantage of her and thought nothing of exposing her to the censure and ridicule of the entire countryside. Though if he only sought to amuse himself with her innocence, why had he stopped the night he found her in his room and why had he suggested they marry? She smacked the saddle as she remembered the momentary weakness and the easy way he'd cast her aside. It must have all been a cruel joke because he obviously preferred the charms of a Cyprian like Mrs Wilkins to a silly girl like her. Wiping her eyes, she wondered if she'd ever be able to love again and her heart tightened with loss.

Rustling in the bushes up ahead put her on edge. Manfred's dark ears, tipped with moonlight, turned towards the noise and he raised his head higher, sensing something in the trees lining the road. She squinted, trying to see the source of the sound, but a heavy cloud passed over the moon and everything darkened. Branches cracked and her body tensed, her feet ready to kick Manfred into a gallop.

She heard the unmistakable thud of hooves on packed earth before the horse and rider sprang from the trees. The strange rider positioned himself in the middle of the road in an attempt to block her, but she moved fast, digging her heels into Manfred's side.

'Yah!' Manfred bolted past the rider, his hooves pounding the road. The stranger launched into pursuit, his horse matching Manfred's steady gait, but not his speed. Fear gripped Julia. She couldn't take Manfred into the forest without risking a broken leg. All she could do was rely on him to outrun the danger.

'Come on, Manfred,' she urged before the faint strain of a familiar voice reached her ears.

'Julia, wait.'

The stranger called out twice more before she recognised the captain's voice. Pulling Manfred to a halt, she watched the captain bring Hector to a stop a few feet away.

'What are you doing here?' she demanded, hoping the horses' heavy breathing covered the sound of her thundering heart.

'I've come to stop you from making a mistake.'

'I've already made many mistakes.' The sky briefly cleared and the moon's soft light caressed his face. Sadness hit her more powerfully than the fear she'd experienced only a moment before. They'd never be together with the same love and desire as before. She turned Manfred around and started him down the road and Captain Covington brought his stallion alongside hers.

'Why are you doing this?'

Julia didn't answer, unwilling to tell him the truth and be vulnerable to him again.

'Julia, please?' He manoeuvred Hector in front of Manfred, bringing them both to a stop. 'Tell me what's wrong and how I can help.'

'Why? You don't care. Go back to Knollwood and Mrs Wilkins. Leave me be.'

'Whatever she told you was a lie.'

'She said you were at Cable Grange. Is that a lie?'

He drew in a ragged breath. 'I was. But not for the reasons you think. I received a note from her regarding Rowan's debt. I'd hoped to use the money he owed me from the race as leverage to purchase Cable Grange. When I arrived she was alone and threw herself at me. I refused her, which is why she did what she did at the ball.'

'You wanted to buy Cable Grange? Why?'

'For you.'

Hope flared in Julia's heart, but she stamped it down. 'I don't believe you.'

'Would I be here on a lonely road in the middle of the night following a woman dressed as a naval officer if I was lying?'

Was it possible? Did he really want her with all of her silly habits and unconventional traits? Her heart wanted to believe him, but her mind couldn't. The image of Mrs Wilkins smiling in victory crushed her hope. No, she could not trust the captain in matters of love.

'Go back to Knollwood.' She manoeuvred Manfred around him, but he refused to be put off.

'I'm coming with you to London.'

'You needn't bother. I don't need your help.'

'I'm still coming.'

'Why?'

'Because you must have an accomplice in this adventure, especially someone who knows his way around town and can help you.'

'Adventure?' Until this moment she hadn't thought of it in such terms, but now the idea, despite her hurt and anger, appealed to her.

'What else would you call it?'

He was right, though she didn't want him to be right. She didn't want him to be anything but a distant memory. However, now that he was here and determined to stay, he could prove useful.

'Do as you like. But as soon as we find Paul, I never want to see you again.'

'Let's get to London first. We'll worry about the rest later.'

He started Hector down the road and Julia followed, the darkness not as frightening or lonely as before. Despite her decision to remain wary and angry with him, she felt a genuine thrill to be on an adventure like all the ones Paul and Uncle George had described. Her excitement was tempered by the heartache spurring her on. Despite his betrayal, deep down she knew he was honourable enough to protect her if they met any unsavoury characters. This offered some measure of comfort and she settled into the saddle for the long journey.

* * *

The time passed slowly, the moon falling towards the horizon before disappearing behind dark clouds. Early on he tried to talk to her, but she cut him short, unwilling to hear any more of his lies or to speak for fear her voice would reveal too much of her true emotions. Eventually, he gave up and they rode for miles in silence. Fatigue crept into her muscles and soon the gentle bob of Manfred's gait made her sleepy. She nodded off before a sturdy hand roused her.

'Don't fall asleep.'

Her head jerked up. 'I wasn't sleeping.'

A distant flash of lightning streaked across the horizon. 'The storm will be upon us soon. Is there an inn near here or a house, anywhere we can take shelter until it passes?'

Julia examined their surroundings, trying to get her bearings. Another distant lightning flash silhouetted a large, twisted oak tree near a bend in the road, a familiar marker she knew well.

'There's a coaching inn not far from here, but it isn't the most reputable establishment.'

The captain laughed. 'Two lone travellers, one a single woman dressed like a man. Sounds like a perfect place for us.'

The first heavy drops started to fall when they reached the inn and the quiet stable next to it.

'Stay here while I see to the horses,' James ordered. Julia didn't argue, but waited near the stable entrance while James spoke to the groom. The weather kept the rest of the patrons indoors, leaving only the groom and one stable boy who ignored them while he mucked out a stall. James paid the groom well to see to the horses then, taking Julia by the arm, led her across the muddy yard to the inn's front door.

'What are you doing?' she demanded, stepping through a large puddle.

'Shhh.' He pulled her under the eaves where two large drops slipped off the wood overhang and dripped down his neck. 'Once inside, say nothing. Your voice will give you away.'

'Do not order me about.'

He held up a warning finger. 'You have no experience in these matters. As we are both dressed in our uniforms...' he shook his head at the absurdity of the situation '...take direction from me as any junior officer would.'

'But—'

'No disobedience. Follow me or I'll throw you over Manfred and drag you back to Knollwood.'

'Yes, sir.' Julia saluted.

'That's more like it.' He pulled open the door. 'Come along, Julius.'

'Julius?'

'A suitable name for a boy of your temperament.'

They stepped inside, the overpowering stench of dirty travellers, tobacco and meat assaulting them. He expected Julia to blanch, but she stared through the smoky room, fascinated by the men hiding in dark corners and the barmaids plying their trade.

'What do you think?' he asked, enjoying her reaction.

'It's exactly like Paul described.' Her eyes followed a voluptuous blonde who walked by with two tankards and a surprising amount of uncovered flesh. 'Is she a—?'

'Yes. Come along, Columbus. Let's get something to eat.' He took her arm and pulled her through the benches of drinking, carousing men to a small, isolated table near the stairs. From a shadowed corner across the room, a man leaned against the wall, chewing on the end of a pipe. James noticed the way he watched them from under a dirty tricorn hat pulled low over his face. Something about him seemed familiar, but the stranger tilted down his head, obscuring his features.

'Wait here. I'll see to our room.' He pushed her into a chair with her back to the wall and a good view of the patrons.

'Shouldn't we stay here, in public?' she whispered with unmistakable worry.

Being alone with him seemed to frighten her more than a lonely road or a common room full of thieves, drunks and whores. He cursed himself for allowing the distance between them to widen, determined by the end of today to fill her eyes with wanting and love, not suspicion and worry.

'Privacy is safer in a place like this.' He was about to walk away when a woman with wild red hair and large breasts teetering precariously along the top edge of her dirty dress perched herself on the table.

'Fancy something special, Captain?'

'No, nothing, thank you.' James smiled, eager to send the woman on her way without any trouble.

The trollop's hooded eyes swept Julia. 'Then perhaps something for the lad?'

'He's fine, I assure you.'

'Seems kind of green to me. Perhaps he needs just a taste.' She leaned across the table and slid her hand between Julia's legs. The woman's eyes met hers in stunned shock, but before either of them could say anything James took the harlot's hand, slipping two sovereigns into her palm and placing it against his chest.

'I know you can understand such a delicate

situation and as a true lady will maintain your discretion.'

Her fingers closed on the coins, a sly smile spreading over her pocked features. 'Whatever you like, love, makes no difference to me.'

'I knew you'd understand. And I know you'll do anything to help us.' He held up two more sovereigns in front of her face. 'We need a room, the best you have, and your continued discretion regarding the lad.'

'Anything you say, Captain.' She took the coins, then walked off, her large hips swaying.

He sat down next to Julia, noticing the wary mistrust in her eyes. 'You seem quite practised in the art of charming women.'

'Better a woman is your friend than your enemy.'

'What am I?'

'Much more than a friend.' He reached for her hand under the table, but she pulled it away.

'Don't.' She leaned back in the chair, watching the room from under her hat. James missed her easy trust and wondered how he could regain it. He wanted to reveal his true feelings, but this was no place for such an intimate conversation.

Very soon the harlot hustled back to them. 'Your room is ready, milord.' She dangled a key in one dirty hand while the other held a candle in a pewter holder.

'Not milord, just Captain.'

'Is that what she calls you?' She threw back her large head of red hair and laughed, the gravelly sound barely carrying over the din. James nodded for Julia to rise and they followed the wench up the stairs and down a pokey hallway to the back of the inn. The stench of unwashed bodies and stale beer increased, as did the heat, laughter and other assorted sounds from all the people packed into the small space under the eaves.

'Here ya are. The best we have.' The harlot threw open the door and James held up another coin.

'Your help is very much appreciated.'

'My pleasure,' she purred, taking the coin from his hand and sliding it over the flesh of her breasts and down the front of her dress. 'Ya wouldn't be needin' me to help you and the lad, would ya?'

From beside the harlot, James saw Julia's jaw fall open. 'Thank you, but we couldn't possibly intrude on your hospitality any longer.'

'Well, ya know where to find me if you change your mind.' She handed James the candle, then sauntered off down the hall.

'Did she just ask if...?' Julia gasped.

'Yes, she did.' James nudged her into the room, not wanting to linger in the hallway or explain any more about the proposal than Julia had already grasped.

He closed the door, placing the candle and key next to the chipped china bowl on the battered washstand near the door. Julia approached the narrow bed situated against the wall and pulled back the thin blanket with her thumb and forefinger to inspect the sheets.

'Does it meet with your approval?'

She jumped back, almost knocking over the rickety chair under the window. The room was tight, with little space for two people to walk around. He stood over her, keenly aware of her warm body so close to his.

'Yes, I suppose it will do.'

'What do you think of your adventure now?' The tightness in his voice caught him off guard and he realised he'd only been alone with her like this once before. The memory of it made his body ache with need and he busied himself removing his gloves.

'It keeps getting stranger.' She took in the small, dingy space, her hat shadowing her nervous eyes. 'Where are you going to sleep?'

'The floor.'

'The floor?'

'It's only appropriate.' Disappointment flashed across her face before she sat down to pull off her boots. 'Leave your clothes on and keep your coat and boots nearby in case we need to make a hasty retreat.'

Her eyes lit up. 'Really?'

'Yes, now get some sleep.' James slid the coat off his shoulders and a bolt of pain shot through him. He sucked in a quick breath, waiting for it to pass.

'What's wrong?'

'Nothing. I overworked the arm perhaps.' He grimaced, working to slide off the coat without making the pain worse.

'Let me help you.' She reached up to assist him, but he pulled away.

'I can manage.'

'Please, I insist.' She took the coat by the collar and gently pulled it down his arms. Once it was off, she draped it over the back of the chair. The tender move touched him and he knew, despite everything that had happened tonight, she still cared for him.

'Thank you.' He started to rub his sore shoulder, but she pushed his hand away, massaging his aching flesh with her slender fingers. The nearness of her teased his senses and clouded his mind.

'If it bothers you too much, I can sleep on the floor and you can have the bed,' she offered.

'I'm not weak enough to kick a lady out of her bed.' He laughed, but it came out choked.

He stood, removing her hands from his shoulder to keep from losing all self-control. Did she know how she affected him? He wasn't sure, but he couldn't take advantage of her innocence, no matter how much hesitant yearning filled her eyes. He'd never win her back if he gave in to the desire raging through him. 'I can leave if you prefer and try to find another room.'

Her hand clasped his tighter. 'No, I don't want to stay here without you.'

He glanced at her chest, the linen shirt barely hiding the gentle curve of her full breasts rising and falling with each fast breath. He stepped closer, a desire deeper than lust driving him forwards. He wanted to smash all the obstacles between them and feel her in his soul. Did she want the same thing? 'Are you sure?'

'Yes.'

Pulling her to him, he covered her lips with his.

Julia slipped her hands around the captain's neck, heady with the heat of his body so close to hers. She knew she should stop, but she couldn't. She'd already abandoned good society tonight. Now she wanted to give in to her desire and curiosity and experience everything she'd been denied the night he'd first touched her in Paul's room. In the morning she could regret again.

His free hand slid up under the shirt, cupping her breast and she moaned softly as his thumb made her nipple hard. With his other hand, he pushed the linen from her shoulders and she pressed against him, dizzy with need. He kissed her neck, then lowered to take one pert nipple in his mouth. Her legs went weak when his tongue traced wet circles around the tender point, his breath on her damp skin making her sigh. Scooping her up, he laid her on the bed, then stood over her, removing his breeches and revealing his desire. A twinge of fear filled her for she knew something of what came next, but wanting drove all other thoughts from her mind.

He pulled his shirt off over his head, dropping it on the floor before settling down next to her in bed. Perched on one elbow, he admired her body, the hot desire in his eyes making her shiver. She reached for the sheet to cover her nakedness, but he stopped her.

'Don't.' His hand traced the curve of her stomach, heightening the need coiling within her. She grasped his arm when his fingers slid into her moist depths, his gentle caress bringing her closer and closer to her passion. Then he stopped, withdrawing his touch.

'No,' she pleaded, wanting him to fill the emptiness and lead her to the same ecstasy she'd experienced the other night.

'We shouldn't,' he whispered, but she was beyond reason or caring about anything except being close to him.

'Yes. Please.'

His knees nudged open her legs and he settled his hips between them. The heat of his manhood touched her thigh and she trembled in anticipation. He covered her mouth with his, his member probing her depths, sliding, stretching her until she opened to take him in. She gasped at the pain, but it quickly disappeared, replaced by a sensation of fullness as he rocked within her.

His thrusts were slow at first, caressing, teasing, but grew more frenzied as she tightened around him. Clinging to his back, she moved her hips to match his pace, thrilling at the sound of his heavy breath in her ear while he continued to push into her, deeper, harder until the spasms of her pleasure exploded through her. Inside she felt his body quiver before he collapsed on top of her, panting with his own release.

Julia stroked his back, their heavy breathing subsiding as they clung to one another. The thump of someone stumbling down the hallway accompanied by a wench's throaty laugh reminded Julia of where she was and why.

'James?' she ventured, wanting to know what this all meant to him and them. Did he love her?

Did he care for her or did he think her no better than the harlot who'd showed them to their room?

He withdrew, kissing her forehead, then cradling her against him. 'Tomorrow, everything will be clear,' he whispered as if sensing her questions. 'Tonight we need sleep.'

Julia closed her eyes, his damp skin on her cheek, his beating heart soothing her worried mind. Yes, tomorrow they'd deal with everything and one way or another it would seem right. Or would it? She didn't know. Snuggling into the crook of his arm, she closed her eyes, fatigue pulling her into a deep sleep.

Julia awoke with a start, struggling through thick sleep to recognise her surroundings. The dirty walls and rough sheets on her bare body brought the events of the night before rushing back. Emotions collided: betrayal, love, pleasure, heartache—all plagued her as powerfully as the exhaustion pulling at her muscles. Wrapping the sheet tighter around her neck, she sank back into the bed, snuggling close to James, eager for more sleep, but it eluded her. His steady breathing reminded her just how far she was from Knollwood and good society, and she had no idea what would happen when he awoke. For a brief moment he'd made her forget his unfaithfulness and the reason she'd first set out for London. Paul.

Her eyes flew open. Outside the window, the orange glow of the inn's lantern mixed with the grey morning light. Muffled snoring punctuated the silence, the other patrons deep in either their travel-weary or ale-laden sleep. She gazed at James and the way the dim light outlined his features. Reaching up to stroke his cheek, she stopped, afraid to wake him. She'd trusted him with her body, savouring the pleasure and hope in his touch, but she couldn't trust him with her heart. Under different circumstances, perhaps they could be happy together, but not with his infidelity hanging over them. There was no use continuing the journey with him or torturing her mind with what could never be. If she left now, she'd have the beautiful memory of their lovemaking instead of the awkward scene of facing him and listening to his lies and explanations. He'd surely follow her, but with a head start, he'd never be able to find her in the crowds of London.

She slid from the bed, careful not to disturb him. Gathering up her clothes from the pile on the floor, she dressed, anxious he might awake, but his breathing remained steady. Tying back her hair, she tucked it up under her hat. She grabbed the boots, unlocked the door and slipped into the hallway, closing it behind her. She didn't pull on her boots until she reached the top of the stairs, then she descended into the common room, noting the few people asleep at the tables or stretched out on the wooden benches. One man remained awake. He sat in the corner, a tricorn hat pulled down low over his eyes. She sensed something familiar in the cut of his jaw, but she could not see his features clearly through the heavy shadow covering his face. Having no desire to be recognised dressed as a man in a coaching inn during the early hours of dawn, she didn't linger, but hurried across the room and out of the door.

A few stars still twinkled in the grey sky, but the horizon glowed lighter with the approaching sunrise. The stable was empty except for the horses and, walking along the stalls, she found Manfred, who greeted her with a nervous toss of his head.

'Steady, boy. It's only me.' She reached up to caress his nose, but he pulled back, his dark eyes wide. Only then did she hear the sound of boots crunching the hay on the floor behind her. Turning around, she expected to see the groom or James and let out a scream when the man with the tricorn hat flew at her.

He grabbed her by the throat, pinning her up against the wall, his hands cutting off her scream. His hat toppled off and she recognised

Wilkins's man, the one who'd challenged her about the fight.

'I thought it 'twas you. How lucky for us to meet when I'm on me way back from London,' he sneered, pressing his body against hers. 'Not so high and mighty now, are ya?'

'Get away from me,' she choked, scratching at his hand, but his grip on her neck remained tight.

'Oh, no, me minx, now you've shown yer true colours, old Mark's going to have a reward. I sees you and I thinks to myself, what would a proper lady like yourself pay to keep me from spreading this around the whole county?'

'You'll get nothing from me,' she spat, her throat burning with the effort to breathe.

'Oh, I think I shall have something.' He leaned closer, his ale-laden breath stinging her face.

A large shadow rose up behind him, pulling him back. The fingers around her throat released and she dropped to the ground, gasping for air. James slammed Mark against the opposite wall, his sword pointed at the scoundrel's throat.

'Please, governor, I meant no harm,' he pleaded, his eyes wide with terror. 'I only wanted to help the lady, her being a good neighbour and all.'

'You have a strange way of helping,' James growled.

'Please, sir, I was helping. I can prove it. I know about her brother, the one in London.'

Julia was next to James in an instant. 'What do you know?'

'I know where he is.'

'How? Where?' Julia's heart leapt with hope.

Mark hesitated and James brought the edge of his sword up against Mark's neck.

'Answer her.'

The servant started to shake. 'Giltspur Street Compter.'

'Debtors' prison?' Julia cried.

'You're lying.' James pressed the sword deeper against Mark's flesh. A small drop of blood slipped out from beneath the blade and Mark's eyes widened, his fingers clawing at James's hand.

'No, I helped put him there. Mrs Wilkins told me to do it. She saw him when we was in London. Mrs Wilkins knows one of his creditors, so she sent me to fetch the man and he had me fetch the bailiff. It's why I'm back from London so late.'

'Why would she have Paul arrested?' Julia asked, trying to make sense of it all.

'To spite you both for wanting Cable Grange and for putting Mr Wilkins in debt to Captain Covington at the race.'

'But Paul had nothing to do with it.'

'The loathsome woman doesn't care. If she can strike a blow, she'll do it, no matter who it hurts.' James released Mark, who slumped to the ground, clutching his bruised neck. 'Mrs Wilkins paid you well for this?'

'Yes, sir.'

'I'll pay you better for your silence.' James tossed a few sovereigns at Mark's feet. Forgetting his sore throat, Mark snatched up the coins. He stretched to reach the last one, but James stopped him with his sword, resting the shiny blade against his cheek. 'I hear one whisper of either Paul's story or Miss Howard's and you'll regret it. I know a press-gang boss who'd gladly take a man like you for a ship. Do I make myself clear?'

'Yes, sir.' He cowered back, clutching the money to his chest.

James hauled Mark to his feet, shoving him at the stable door. 'Now get out of my sight.'

The servant stumbled before running off into the morning.

James sheathed his sword, fixing Julia with hard eyes. 'Why did you run off?'

She turned away from him, her shaking hands fumbling with Manfred's saddle. 'I don't owe you any explanations.'

He stepped up behind her, his body vibrating with anger. 'Do you know what could have happened if I hadn't found you?'

She knew exactly what she'd have suffered if

he hadn't followed her. Having come so close to danger, she wanted to cry from fear, throw herself into his arms and let him comfort her, but she didn't have the courage to face him.

'Don't ever scare me like that again.' He walked to his own horse, throwing the saddle over its back in a noisy clank of stirrups and buckles. Tears burned at the corners of her eyes, but she refused to let them fall, determined not to cry in front of him.

Chapter Thirteen

The sun crested the horizon, glinting off the tightly packed roofs and wet streets of London. Smoke rose from the thousands of chimneys, joining the voices of ballad singers, fishwives and hawkers beginning their day. Despite the growing tightness in her stomach, Julia followed James into the sprawl of farmers, dyers and the like crouched outside the city proper and spreading into the surrounding countryside. The stench of rot and filth grew stronger the closer they got to town, the smell instantly taking her back to her Season in London and conjuring up the feelings of loneliness and inadequacy she'd suffered then. She wondered at the odd circumstances bringing her back here today. Was this her future, the rank air of London instead of the clean air of Cable Grange?

James sat rigid atop his horse. They'd barely spoken since leaving the inn and if he didn't want her before, she felt sure he couldn't wait to be rid of her now. How tired he must be of chasing after a hoyden with a knack for getting in trouble. He'd probably leave her the moment they found Paul.

She buried her nose in the wool sleeve of her jacket, noting how James seemed impervious to the odours. 'How can you stand the smell?' she asked, unnerved by his continued silence and eager to reclaim the easy familiarity between them.

'Compared to a few months at sea with filthy men, bilge water and dead rats, this smells positively charming.' He sounded almost jovial and her shoulders relaxed, glad to see he'd lost some of his irritation. The feeling disappeared when his eyes went stern. 'Here, just as in the inn, do as I say.'

Julia nodded, rubbing her sore throat.

They manoeuvred their horses down the wide streets, dodging carriages, carts and various workers going about their morning business.

'How do you know where it is?' she asked.

'This isn't the first time I've had to bail a fellow officer out of debtors' prison. Though I never thought I'd be doing it for Paul Howard.'

'I find it hard to believe you dislike one another. You're so much alike.'

'No need to insult me,' James laughed.

'I meant it as a compliment,' she teased, happy to see the light return to his eyes.

They approached the old stone prison, the morning sun just beginning to rise over the tops of buildings. Giltspur Street Compter seemed strangely situated next to shops, its uninspiring façade dotted with rows of windows. A parade of women and children wandered in and out of the iron gates. The more fashionable ladies buried their faces in white handkerchieves, crying over the loss of a dowry or their only source of income while the common women carried large baskets of food or dragged crying children into the prison.

James signalled for them to dismount, then handed her his reins. 'Stay here while I speak with the guards.'

'I want to come with you.'

'No. We can't leave the horses unattended or some desperate person might steal them. Don't worry. It isn't as bad as you think.' He cuffed her under the chin, then hurried across the street to talk to the guards lounging on either side of the main door. She watched them perk up when he slipped them a few coins before they ushered him inside.

She stood with the horses, cautious of the people walking the streets. Shady characters eyed the horses with appraising interest and she wondered how many of them would gladly slit her throat to steal the animals. Clutching the reins, she worried as she waited, imagining Paul lying in some dank cell, his wounds uncared for and at risk of infection. Once James had freed him, she'd take him straight to the London town house and call for Dr Childers. Hopefully, she was not too late. She didn't know what she would do if she lost him to gaol fever or gangrene.

Finally, James emerged from the jail and if it weren't for the horses, she'd have rushed across the street to meet him. Instead she waited, her fears receding some when he came to stand next to her.

'I spoke with the warden. He'll summon your brother's creditors, then I'll settle the debt.'

'I brought money.'

He held up his hand to silence her. 'Allow me, please. I've dealt with these matters before and will not be cheated.'

She nodded, embarrassed once again at how unprepared she was for London. At Knollwood she was master of her realm; here she found herself at the mercy of others. 'Can I see Paul? I want to make sure he's all right.'

'Yes, I've made arrangements.'

He paid a guard to attend to the horses, then

escorted Julia inside. The stench of unwashed bodies and damp stone rivalled the smell outside and Julia covered her nose with her hand.

He led her into a small office off the main entrance. Inside a large man wearing a dirty wig sat behind an old desk, poring over paperwork. Julia took a deep breath, the dusty smell of the office preferable to the noxious odours outside.

The gruff man ignored Julia in favour of James and what he knew to be a large and generous purse. 'You want to see him?'

'The lad wishes to see him, older brother and all. Mother wants to make sure he's being treated right.'

'A visitation will cost ya,' the warden finally acknowledged her, his wig slipping off to one side of his bald head.

'Cost?' Julia's voice came out high and she covered it with a cough. 'Cost?' she repeated, trying to deepen her voice.

'You'll have to excuse him—he's young.' James fixed her with a reprimanding glare, then slid two coins across the desk. 'He doesn't understand things the way we do.'

'Young officer needs to learn this is a business. A man has to make a living.' The warden stuck two fat fingers on the coins and drew them to him. He dropped them in his dirty pocket, then nodded to the man standing behind Julia. 'Har-

vey there will take you back. Captain stays here
to discuss the financial arrangements.'

'But—' Julia started, but James waved her off.

'Not to worry, Julius. The warden here is a
sensible man. He knows the value in making
sure no harm comes to you.'

The warden raised a greedy eyebrow, grasping James's meaning. 'Of course. Harvey will
see nothing happens to the lad.'

'Yes, sir.' Harvey opened the door, hustling
Julia into the hallway. 'This way.'

Julia followed him deeper into the prison,
worry helping her ignore the eye-watering smell.
At every cell they passed, a man's hand jutted
out between the bars, his hoarse voice begging
for money to buy food, his own cell or freedom.
They reached the day rooms where children of
various ages ran circles around men and their
wives, who sat nursing babies.

'There are families here?' she asked, aston-
ished.

Harvey grunted at her ignorance. 'Them that
can afford it lives in the Rules of the Compter.'

'Rules?'

'Three miles 'round the Compter. Them that
can't stay here.'

Taking in the wretched conditions, Julia
fell silent, afraid of what she'd find when they
reached Paul. He might already be sick, lying

in squalor at death's door with no one to even bring him water.

Finally they reached a small row of cells near the back of the jail. The accommodations here weren't nearly so dirty, but Julia wouldn't call them 'clean'. A rat scurried across their path and she jumped back with a high squeal.

Harvey laughed, the key ring in his hand jingling. 'You wouldn't make it long on a ship.'

'How is my brother?' Julia adjusted her coat, following him to the last wood-and-iron door.

'Doing as well as ya can imagine. Here ya are.' He slid a large, black-iron key into the lock. The grating sound of metal against metal filled the hall before he threw open the door. ''ave a visitor for ya, Lieutenant.'

Julia stepped forwards, steeling herself for the worst and caught off guard by what she saw inside. The room, by no means palatial, was tidy and better appointed than the one she'd slept in last night. A wooden bed with white linens took up one wall while a well-built writing desk occupied the other. In the centre of the room, in a cushioned chair, Paul sat with a book in his lap, reminding her very much of a pirate captain surrounded in a cave by his sumptuous loot. Only the angry red cut on his forehead kept her from laughing.

He started at the strange sight in front of

him, then rose, taking in the uniform with a lopsided grin.

'Well, fancy this. I didn't expect you of all people to rescue me, especially not like this.'

'Rescue you—' Julia balked, looking around at the cell '—I should have known you'd arrange the best accommodations, even in gaol.'

'Right crafty, this one,' Harvey mumbled. 'Wouldn't mind if we had more like him.'

Despite the humour, the emotions of the last day combined with the exhaustion of the night and her relief to find Paul overcame her. She threw herself into his arms, hugging him tight, quite forgetting herself and her disguise.

'Now then, lad, I know the ship has missed me, but really.' Paul patted her back, attempting to maintain the charade.

A deep, raspy laugh rolled out of Harvey. 'No point pretending. She ain't the first to come here dressed like that.'

'She's my sister,' Paul protested and Harvey laughed harder.

'Ain't the first to say that, too.'

Paul hugged Julia close while she cried into his dirty coat. It smelled of smoke and gunpowder and the scratchy wool reminded her of James. 'Now then, what's all this? You've never been this excited to see me.'

'I was so worried. They said you were injured.' She reached up to touch his head and he caught her hand. 'What happened?'

Julia and Paul sat down on the bed and Harvey stepped out of the cell and closed the door, giving them a little privacy.

'After the battle, we were rescuing French seamen. We should have left the scoundrels to drown. They were so thankful, they tried to take over *HMS Pickle*. We beat them back, but not before one of the French dogs got hold of a sword and rushed at Lieutenant Lapenotiere. I stepped between them, running him through just as he brought down his sword. He caught me here.' He touched his wound and winced. 'I was out for a while and bled like a stuck pig. Lieutenant Lapenotiere thought I might die, but the surgeon patched me up. Said all I needed was rest and I'd be back to fighting form in no time, though I'll have a scar to show for it. Lieutenant Lapenotiere was so grateful, he invited me to accompany him back to London.'

'Thank heavens.' She hugged him again, but he leaned back.

'Now, what are you doing here and dressed like that?'

'You have no idea what's happened this last week.'

'Then tell me all about it.'

She described at length the events of the last

week, telling him everything except her very intimate encounter with the captain last night. Paul might listen without judgement, but she knew even he had limits where her honour was concerned. A few moments after she finished her story, Harvey pulled open the door.

'Come on. It's time for you two to go.'

They followed Harvey out of the cell and back down the halls.

'Paul, Dr Childers said you never arrived at his office. What happened?'

Paul rubbed his neck, a shamefaced smile spreading across his face. 'I'm afraid I didn't go straight to Dr Childers, though I wish I had.'

'Yes, it would have saved us all a great deal of trouble and worry,' Julia chided. 'Where did you go?'

'I was on my way to Dr Childers when I ran into an old friend and he invited me to a card party.'

'Paul, how could you?' She wasn't sure who she was more angry with: Paul for being so silly or Charles for being right. 'You were supposed to rest.'

'I spent the last two weeks of our voyage back to England resting. I needed a little fun. I saw the Wilkinses there. Mr Wilkins was bragging about selling Cable Grange for more than it's worth.

I'm sorry you weren't able to get it. You'd have really made something out of it.'

She offered him a half-hearted smile, not wanting to think about it.

Harvey stopped at a small sitting room across from the main office. 'You can wait here while the captain finishes settlin' your accounts. It's the warden's private room.'

'Thank you, good man. We'll have cake with our tea,' Paul ribbed.

'I've changed my mind. I'm glad to be done with ya,' Harvey grumbled, closing the door.

Paul walked leisurely about the shabby room, fingering the chipped porcelain knick-knacks probably left behind by some long-ago tenant. 'Now that Cable Grange is gone, what will you do?'

'I'll stay with you.'

He leaned against the thick windowsill, crossing his arms over his chest. 'You can't stay with me.'

'What other options do I have? I can't go back to Knollwood, not under these circumstances.'

'You could marry Captain Covington.'

'Haven't you heard anything I've told you?' Julia threw up her hands, for the first time in her life frustrated with Paul.

'I heard it all, which is why I think you should

simply admit you're in love with him and put all this business behind you.'

'I don't love him.' Julia threw herself into a nearby chair, a puff of dust escaping from the threadbare fabric. New tears fell down her cheeks, leaving small watermarks on the dingy chintz. 'I did love him, but not any more.'

Paul sat on the chair's matching ottoman, taking Julia's hands in his. 'I think you still love him very much. Do you know how I know?'

She shook her head, wiping her eyes with the back of her hand.

'Because I've never seen you cry.'

'Of course I cry.'

'Not like this.' He pulled a stained handkerchief from his pocket and handed it to her.

'Well, what do you expect? I'm not a statue.' She wondered if she shouldn't have taken Charles's advice and left Paul in London.

'Come now. Why the tears?'

'Because he doesn't love me.'

'What makes you think he doesn't love you?'

'Mrs Wilkins.'

'He explained why he was there.'

'He was lying, like all Navy men.'

'Captain Covington may be a Navy man, but he's no liar. He's also not a man of whims. If he didn't love you, he wouldn't have come to London to help you, especially not to help me. I think he loves you just as much as you love him. He just needs to get around to telling you so you'll finally believe him.'

Julia twisted the handkerchief, unable to deny his logic. The captain had followed her to London, saved her from Wilkins's servant and helped her find Paul, but she'd continued to doubt him because of her own fears and because he hadn't said the words. Could the answer be so simple? Her head ached from trying to figure it all out. 'What about your recommendation?'

'I understand why he wrote it. At the end of my first year, we were in Portsmouth waiting for our orders. It was rather dull there and I got into some trouble with a parson's daughter.'

'Paul, you didn't.'

'Unlike your captain, I am a typical Navy man. But I wasn't the first officer she'd taken long walks with in the woods. I just had more money than the last bloke. The next thing I know she tells her father I ruined her and the parson complains to my superior officer.'

'Captain Covington.'

'Of course. Well, it's his first ship so he's a real stickler for rules and orders me to marry her.'

'But you refused.'

'I wasn't about to introduce a girl like her to Mother, or Charles for that matter. Luckily, before Captain Covington could bring me up on charges, her fiancé comes in to port. His ship took a frigate off the coast of Africa, so now he has money and they run off to Gretna Green.'

Julia clapped her hand over her mouth to cover a laugh. This was just the kind of trouble and escape Paul always managed to find. 'Once the truth came out didn't Captain Covington understand?'

'He did, but I'd still disobeyed a direct order. Caused him quite a bit of embarrassment.'

'So now, all these years later, he writes a poor recommendation. Seems rather petty.'

'I don't blame him. Besides, he's more than made up for it now.'

He patted her hands, then the door opened and James entered the room.

James took in brother and sister. She clutched an old handkerchief, watching him with large, red eyes glistening with tears. He could only imagine what she'd told her brother and wondered how his old crewmate would react. He didn't relish the idea of a duel.

To his amazement, Paul crossed the room, holding out his hand in greeting. 'Captain Covington, thank you for getting me out of this pinch.'

'You have Miss Howard to thank.' James

hesitantly took his outstretched hand and Paul pumped it heartily.

'Don't be so modest. I know you played a part in it. My sister told me all about your exciting journey last night.'

'Did she?' James tightened his grip and Paul matched the hold with a smile. *The man is as arrogant as ever*, James thought, determined to make Paul relent first, despite the numbness in his fingers.

'Come now, Jim.' Paul leaned forwards, dropping his voice. 'We both love the little lady, so why not put the past behind us?'

James released Paul's hand, flexing his fingers to bring the blood back. What had she told him?

'Now, if you'll both excuse me.' Paul moved towards the door. 'I have some private business with the warden and you two have a great deal to discuss.'

'Paul, wait.' Julia jumped to her feet, but Paul didn't stop, winking at her before slipping out of the door.

A small porcelain clock on the mantel ticked off the long seconds of silence. James stood unmoving, his eyes watching her with honest longing. Could Paul be right? Did he really love her? She searched for the words to ask, the right phrase to confirm everything in her heart and cross the chasm of uncertainty dividing them, but words were unnecessary. He marched across the room, swept her into his arms and kissed her.

All the worry about her actions and future disappeared. Pressing close, she surrendered more now than she had in the late hours of the night, giving him her heart, soul and life, knowing he would guard them as faithfully as he'd guarded her through this entire journey, binding their hearts together so nothing could ever separate them again.

Their lips finally parted and she felt the rough stubble of his cheek against hers. 'I love you,' he whispered.

'I love you, too.' She buried her face in his jacket, revelling in the peace and comfort of his beating heart. She'd never felt this happy or content and it filled her with a new energy and the eager anticipation to begin their life together.

'There's plenty of time to make it to Gretna Green,' she suggested, tracing a brass button with her finger.

'Nonsense. If I know George, he's convinced your brother not to cancel the wedding.'

'I'm surprised Charles hasn't hurried after us with a vicar already.'

'Then I know the wedding will still take place. We just have to get there on time.'

The clock chimed eight o'clock.

'Then we'd better hurry or we'll never make it.'

Outside the jail, Paul waited with the horses, winking at a young woman sauntering past.

'I'm glad to see you've resolved your differences.' He laughed as Julia and James approached.

'I suppose it's my turn to thank you,' James said.

'You'll have plenty of time to thank me once you're married. But first, we need to eat. I know a place not far from here where we can get some food and a horse.'

'You mean I'll have to hire a horse for you since you have no blunt,' Julia corrected.

'How kind of you to offer, sister, though I have plenty of blunt, just not here in London—'

'If you don't mind,' James interrupted, 'I have a much better suggestion.'

Chapter Fourteen

◯◯◯◯◯◯◯

'I thought you said your suggestion was better?' Julia hissed, taking in the dark-wood entrance hall of the well-appointed town house, her stomach tight with worry.

The captain put his arm around her shoulders and offered an encouraging squeeze. 'Have faith, Artemis.'

Her worried eyes met Paul's, not sure what to expect. The butler had left them to fetch the mistress of the house, which belonged to none other than James's mother.

'Perhaps we should go to Charles's town house,' Julia pleaded, stepping back towards the door.

'No, I want to introduce you to my mother.'

'Like this?' She waved her hand over the uniform, not wanting to meet her future mother-in-law in such scandalous attire.

'She'll understand.'

A stout woman in her early fifties appeared at the top of the stairs, her plump frame draped in a silk morning wrapper. A linen cap covered her dark hair and she had the pinched groggy expression of someone who'd just been roused from bed. 'What are you doing here?'

'Good morning, Mother.' He met her at the bottom of the stairs with a respectful hug. 'I see you're safely returned from Charlotte's.'

'And very, very late last night thanks to the miserable roads, which is why you'd better have a good reason for disturbing me so early this morning.'

'Who's in a spot of trouble now?' Paul chuckled in Julia's ear and she elbowed him silent.

Mrs Covington stepped back from her son, taking in the motley, unwashed group dressed in dirty uniforms, her forehead wrinkled in confusion. 'I thought you were in the country?'

'I was but I had business in town, some of which might interest you.'

'I doubt it, but get on with it so I can return to bed.'

He took Julia's hand and pulled her forwards. 'I want to introduce you to my fiancée.'

'What kind of joke is this?' she sputtered,

grasping her robe tight around her neck. 'I will not stand for this kind of tomfoolery so early in the day.'

'I assure you, this is no joke. I'd like you to meet Miss Julia Howard.'

He pulled off her hat and Julia's long braid tumbled down her back. She squared her shoulders, put her chin in the air and stepped forwards with as much grace as she could muster in a pair of men's Hessians.

'Mrs Covington, I'm delighted to meet you.' Julia curtsied, using everything Annette had taught her about behaving in society to stay poised, but Mrs Covington's eyes remained stony.

'And the gentleman?' she asked, nodding at Paul.

'My brother, Lieutenant Paul Howard.'

'A pleasure, madam.' He swept into a low bow, more to cover his smile than to show his respect.

'Am I to assume the three of you have stopped here on your way to Gretna Green?'

'Of course not,' James said. 'We have an appointment at the church near Miss Howard's estate today at three. Miss Howard is George Russell's niece.'

Mrs Covington's stony eyes warmed. 'The one who runs the estate?'

'The very young lady.'

'Well, why didn't you say so sooner?' She rushed at Julia with arms outstretched, enveloping her in a big hug. 'My dear, I'm so pleased to have you here.'

'Thank you.' The sudden change in emotion caught her off guard, but she preferred it to the rebuke she'd imagined.

Mrs Covington stepped back, clasping her hands together in excitement, the lace at her sleeves fluttering. 'Your uncle told me a great deal about you, but of course my son doesn't write to tell me he's getting married and to George's niece of all people.'

'It all happened very fast and you were travelling. The letter wouldn't have reached you.'

'That's no excuse for showing up like a vagabond and announcing it.' She wagged a reprimanding finger at Paul. 'I hope you have more respect for your mother.'

'Of course.' Paul nodded solemnly but Julia noticed the laughter in his eyes.

'Mother, we must borrow the chaise if we're to make it back to Knollwood in time,' James informed her, attempting to regain control of the situation, but Julia could tell Mrs Covington had no intention of relinquishing it.

'Borrow—oh, no, I'm going with you. But

first, we must get Miss Howard some suitable travelling attire.'

'There isn't time.'

'Then we'll be quick because if you think I'm going to have my future daughter-in-law traipsing about the countryside dressed like a man, you're quite mistaken.' She examined Julia's dust-covered uniform, tutting under her breath. 'You're about Charlotte's size. My daughter always leaves a couple of dresses here. One is sure to fit. Come along and we'll find one. And, James, arrange to have breakfast sent up to your sister's room. You probably haven't even fed the poor girl. You two can have breakfast in the morning room.' Mrs Covington took Julia's arm and escorted her up the stairs.

Julia wasn't sure which moved faster, their chaise or Mrs Covington's conversation. The woman talked without breathing or pausing, jumping from one topic to the next as they sped past the mile posts. Paul had left town shortly after breakfast, riding ahead on James's London stallion to inform Knollwood of their impending arrival and to arrange their meeting at the church. Manfred and Hector were stabled in James's mews, enjoying a well-deserved rest.

James, Julia and his mother had not started for Knollwood until nearly eleven. Business had delayed them in London, something to do with the Admiralty, though James never said what. Now, if they hoped to make it to Knollwood by three, they had to hurry. Mrs Covington's post-boy was an excellent driver and they made good time, despite one stop to change the horses.

They'd maintained a sensible pace until the turn to Daringford, then Mrs Covington insisted on speed. Despite the post-boy's skill, Julia found the fast pace unsettling. She might have developed her brother's taste for adventure, but an overturned carriage did not figure into any of her plans.

'Perhaps we should slow down? If the vicar was convinced to hold the ceremony today, he'll be just as easily persuaded to hold it tomorrow,' Julia suggested while Mrs Covington paused to take a breath. The woman shook her head, grasping the windowsill when the carriage took a sharp corner, forcing James to hold the strap to keep from leaning into Julia.

'Heavens, no, my dear. You two have a date at the altar and I intend for you to keep it. Do you know how many years I've waited for James to marry? I have no intention of putting it off any longer. Besides…' she leaned forwards, patting Julia's hand and smiling '…I like you and I have no intention of letting you get away from him.'

'Or perhaps you have no intention of letting George get away from you,' James suggested.

'I have no idea what you mean.' Mrs Covington flapped her handkerchief in front of her face.

The captain offered Julia a conspiratorial wink. 'Perhaps we can make it a double wedding.'

'Oh heavens, who said anything about marriage?' Mrs Covington hid a wicked smile behind the coloured silk.

Julia's mouth fell open. 'You mean she and Uncle George?'

'Exactly.'

'How long have you known?' Julia asked, still trying to take it in.

'I've suspected it for a while, but she only just confirmed it.'

'Oh, you think you are so clever,' Mrs Covington huffed.

'I don't know if I approve of my mother conducting herself in such a fashion,' James playfully chastised and Mrs Covington pointed one stern finger at her son.

'In your present circumstances, you have no right to criticise.'

Julia didn't know what to say after the stunning revelation, but then Daringford appeared in the distance, ending the discussion.

Hesitant anticipation filled her at the sight of

the familiar rolling hills and river-etched valley. Though very eager to reach the altar, she had no idea what waited for them at the church. Mother and Uncle George would take the events of the last day with their usual detached demeanour. It was what Charles might say which worried her. Would he object to the marriage, afraid to entrust his sister and her inheritance to a man he might now view as a scoundrel? Or would he drag her up the aisle as fast as possible in an attempt to keep her and the family's reputation intact? Either way, he was sure to cause a scene she had no stomach for.

'What's wrong?' James asked. 'Not having second thoughts, are you?'

'I'm dreading another of Charles's lectures.'

'He has no cause to lecture anyone.'

'What do you mean?'

'Haven't you guessed about your nephew?'

The truth she'd somehow missed before hit her like a ton of stones. 'Thomas wasn't early. Charles and Emily, they—I mean, well, you know, it must have happened before they were married.'

'According to George it did,' James confirmed.

'It explains why they were so quick to marry last February. I can't believe I never realised it before.' Julia sat back, shaking her head in indignant disbelief. 'All this time Charles chastised me for my behaviour when he'd done so much more.'

'The fallen ones are always the most puritanical.' Mrs Covington sniffed. 'You must stand up to him, my dear, for you will have to stand up to James. He can be very stubborn at times.'

'Good, for if he weren't I might not be so happy.'

'We might not be so happy,' he corrected, kissing the back of her hand. The gentle tickle of his lips raised a shiver of delight along her spine. She saw the wanting in his eyes, felt their heat spreading through her and lowered her head so Mrs Covington wouldn't notice the burning exchange.

The carriage entered Daringford, slowing its mad pace and clattering through the narrow streets to the church situated on the other side. Her heart leapt with the excitement of being so close to home, but it was tempered by a new feeling. Though the familiar stone buildings were comforting, everything now seemed old and small. This place would never be far from her heart, but she couldn't wait to leave it and embark with the captain on the next journey and adventure.

The carriage jostled to a stop in front of the church, the long shadow of the steeple falling over the churchyard. James stepped out, then handed her down. She was not two steps from the carriage when the church's large oak doors flew open and her family rushed to greet them.

'You made it.' Emily threw her arms around Julia. 'We were so worried about you. I brought your dress. You can change in the vestibule.'

'Where are Charles and Paul?'

'Inside, speaking with the vicar.'

'Jim, I brought your other uniform, thought you might need it,' George said before running his hand over the chaise's high mudguard. 'I recognise this coach.'

'I thought perhaps you might.' Julia laughed.

'Hello, Captain Russell.' Mrs Covington sat forwards at the door, meeting Uncle George with teasing eyes.

'I see you've finally learned her name,' he whispered to Julia.

'You never could keep a secret.'

'Hello, Mrs Covington.' Uncle George held out a steadying hand and she took it, descending from the carriage, her eyes never leaving his. He tucked her hand in the crook of his arm, then led her to Julia's mother, Emily and Annette. 'Everyone, may I introduce Jim's mother, Mrs Covington.'

Emily and Annette stood dumbfounded at the announcement. Only Julia's mother maintained her usual grace and confidence, moving around the others to welcome her.

'It is a pleasure to meet you. We are so delighted you could be here.'

'I wouldn't have missed it. I've waited a long time for this day.'

'We all have.' Her mother winked at George, who tugged on his cravat.

'You made it.' Paul bounded out of the church, washed and cleaned and wearing a fresh uniform. 'The vicar is ready. And who is this?'

He bowed to Annette, who stood away from the group, doing her best not to be seen. A slight blush spread over her cheeks at Paul's sudden attentiveness and Julia stepped forwards to rescue her. 'This is Miss Annette Taylor, Uncle Edward's stepdaughter.'

'I've heard a great deal about you.' Paul motioned for Annette's hand, which she offered with her usual measure of grace.

'Hopefully not too much.'

Julia noticed Annette's lack of affected London airs, thinking the natural reaction suited her very well. Obviously Paul thought so, too, for he lingered over her hand.

Emily chuckled, breaking the spell. 'Come along, Julia. The vicar will not wait for ever.'

Julia followed Emily and Mother into the church and up the dim side aisle to the vicar's small room behind the nave. The musty smell of cold stone and smoke hung heavy in the air. Charles paced in front of the door, stopping at the sight of her. She cautiously approached, expecting anger but his eyes were soft, almost sheepish.

'I'm glad to see you returned unharmed. We were worried about you.'

'Were you?' Julia ventured, noticing the tender concern in his eyes. She'd only seen it once before, when he'd comforted her after Father's death.

'Of course. I know you believe I think little of you, but I don't. I'm only trying to help and protect you. Perhaps I've been going about it the wrong way. Mother told me about your bargain with the captain. I also spoke to Emily, who gave me quite a tongue-lashing for being so unsympathetic about Paul. I think some of your nature has rubbed off on her for she was quite forceful.'

'She'll need a strong hand to run Knollwood.'

He took her hands. 'You don't have to marry him if you don't want to.'

'I do.'

'Do you?'

Julia nodded.

'Will you be happy with him?'

'I love him and he loves me. Besides, I have a fondness for Navy men.'

He pulled her into a hug. 'Then I'm very happy for you. You couldn't have chosen a better, more deserving man.'

'Thank you.' She rose up and kissed him on the cheek, then slipped into the vicar's room. Her mother helped her exchange the borrowed gown for the London one altered for the wedding. Emily instructed Mary on how to arrange Julia's hair, then they stepped back to admire their work.

'You're beautiful.' Emily smiled and Julia's mother nodded.

'I think the captain will be very pleased.'

Minutes later, Julia stood at the back of the church on Paul's arm. The organist began a hymn, the church doors opened and the guests stood. Some faces she knew well, others were less familiar and she imagined a number of villagers and country folk had come to see for themselves the maid of Knollwood finally married.

Of all the eyes watching, she sought only James's. He stood near the altar with Uncle George, his smile taking her breath away.

'Are you ready?' Paul whispered.

'Yes.'

He escorted her down the aisle, offering her hand to James at the vicar's instruction. The rest of the ceremony passed in a blur and she was conscious of nothing but the vicar's even voice and James standing beside her. She thought of the fountain at Knollwood and her old longings. Standing beside a man who loved her and who she loved with all her heart, those days seemed liked a lifetime ago.

'You may now kiss the bride,' the vicar announced and James leaned over, placing his warm lips on hers. She met his kiss with all the passion in her heart, forgetting the guests and even where they stood.

'Patience,' Uncle George whispered, interrupting them and they broke into happy laughter, hurrying back up the aisle and into the soft evening light.

Outside the church, they received everyone's congratulations, enjoying the festive atmosphere.

Paul approached, twirling her in a large hug. 'I'm so happy for you, Sister. And you, too, Captain Covington. Congratulations.' He held out his hand to the captain, who took it without hesitation.

'Congratulations to you as well.'

'Pardon?'

'I paid a quick visit to Admiral Stuart while we were in London.' The captain reached into his coat pocket and presented Paul with a letter sealed with red wax. 'I rescinded my previous recommendation. Congratulations on your new posting, Lieutenant-Commander Howard.'

For the first time ever, Paul stood at a loss for words. He took the letter and opened it, a wide smile spreading across his face as he devoured the contents.

'My own ship. I can't believe it.'

'It's a sad vessel, barely fit for duty, but if you make something of her, you'll earn a name for yourself.'

'I will. Thank you. You won't regret this.'

'No, I don't believe I will.'

Paul hurried off to show his mother his new orders and Julia threw herself into James's arms.

'Thank you. Though you didn't have to do it.'

'Of course I did. If it hadn't been for Paul, you may never have come to your senses.'

More congratulation accompanied them to the Howard family carriage. Stepping up into it, she noticed, over the heads of the revellers, Uncle George escorting Mrs Covington to his carriage. It seemed she wasn't the only one destined to find love this November.

The carriage set off and with a sigh of relief, Julia settled against the captain's chest, enjoying the feel of his arms around her.

'I have a present for you.' He reached into his coat pocket.

She ran her hand up his thigh, eager for all the wedding events to be over so they could be alone. 'I think you shall have much more before the night is out.'

'Saucy wench.' He pinched her cheek, then held out a slim leather wallet. 'This is for you.'

She took the worn leather and untied the straps. Her heart leapt when she unfolded it and read the old paper. 'The deed for Cable Grange!'

'It is.'

'But how did you manage it? Mrs Wilkins said it was sold to a London gentleman.'

'I told you not to believe her. I had my London solicitor arrange the purchase anonymously. It seems Mr Wilkins owed more to creditors than even his wife knew. He was very eager to part with the estate for the sum I offered. I've since learned their debts were so crushing they fled to France right after the ball. Not even the amount I paid for Cable Grange was enough to save them from ruin.'

'Thank you. Thank you.' She gave him an enthusiastic kiss, teasing his tongue with hers before sitting back. 'But what about Venice and India? You promised to show me the world.'

'So I shall, but we need somewhere to live between travels,' the captain whispered, nibbling at her neck, his breath heavy. 'Do you still have that book of your brother's, my sweet Artemis?'

'I think I can remember enough of it,' she breathed, pushing his jacket off his shoulders.

He kissed the exposed skin above the bodice of her dress, his tongue making sweet circles on her sensitive breasts. 'Don't you wish to wait?'

'No.' He was hers now without shame or censure and she wanted to feel him deep inside her again.

His jacket fell to the carriage floor and she pulled his shirt from his breeches, then slipped her hands beneath the linen to trace the taut muscles of his stomach. Answering her invitation, he settled her on his lap, his hands firm on her waist, anchoring her body to his. In his strong grip, she felt the security of their future while his tender lips filled her with the excitement of today.

She wrapped her arm around his shoulders, revelling in the feel of him so close to her. With her tongue, she imitated the wet circles on his neck, breathing on the moist skin and smiling when he groaned.

She had little time to delight in her newfound wickedness before his other hand slid beneath her dress, teasing the skin along the line of her calf and thigh. She gasped when he found her centre, unable to think of anything except the pleasure building inside her.

'No,' she protested when he withdrew his hand.

'Yes,' he answered, heavy desire igniting his eyes and making her shiver.

He helped her shift astride him, holding her hips to keep her steady as she worked open the buttons of his breeches. She pulled the material down about his thighs and, taking his desire in her hands, stroked the firm shaft.

'You do remember the book,' he rasped.

'I can't wait to try the positions.'

'First let's begin with just one.'

Pushing up her skirts, he settled her on to the heat of his manhood. She gripped the squabs behind him as he filled her, biting back a cry of delight.

She drew in deep breaths as he moved within her, his fingers digging into the flesh of her thighs. She closed her eyes, bringing her cheek next to his as the rocking carriage made each thrust more fierce. His breath in her ear matched by her own quickened as she tightened around him until they cried out together, clasping each other in quivering excitement.

She laid her head on his shoulder as everything around them came back to her.

'I think we shall have quite an adventure, my

beautiful Venus,' he breathed and she looked up, her face close to his.

With one finger, she traced the curve of his smile, feeling his joy deep in her own heart. 'Yes, I think we shall.'

* * * * *

A sneaky peek at next month…

HISTORICAL

IGNITE YOUR IMAGINATION, STEP INTO THE PAST...

My wish list for next month's titles…

In stores from 1st November 2013:

- ☐ Rumours that Ruined a Lady — Marguerite Kaye
- ☐ The Major's Guarded Heart — Isabelle Goddard
- ☐ Highland Heiress — Margaret Moore
- ☐ Paying the Viking's Price — Michelle Styles
- ☐ The Highlander's Dangerous Temptation — Terri Brisbin
- ☐ Rebel with a Heart — Carol Arens

Available at WHSmith, Tesco, Asda, Eason, Amazon and Apple

Just can't wait?

Special Offers

Every month we put together collections and longer reads written by your favourite authors.

Here are some of next month's highlights— and don't miss our fabulous discount online!

On sale 1st November   On sale 1st November   On sale 18th October

Save 20%
on all Special Releases

Find out more at
www.millsandboon.co.uk/specialreleases

*Visit us
Online*